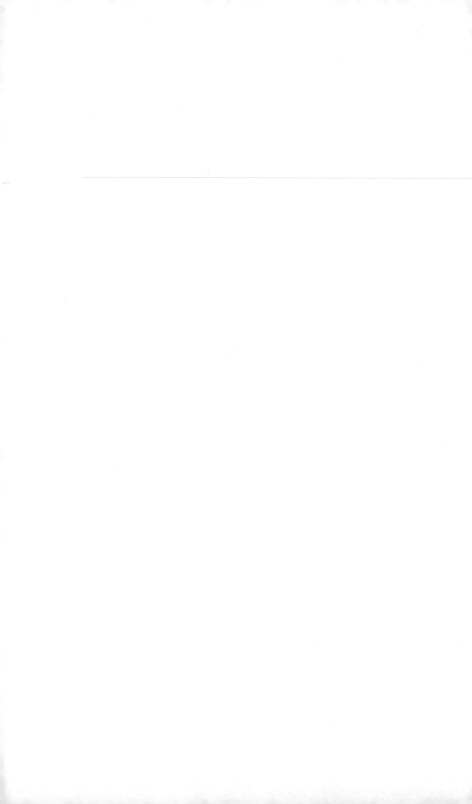

Louder Than
Than
Words

Louder
Than
Words

LAURIE PLISSNER

𝓜eritPress

F+W Media, Inc.

Published by Merit Press
an imprint of F+W Media, Inc.
10151 Carver Road, Suite 200
Blue Ash, Ohio 45242
www.meritpressbooks.com

ISBN 10: 1-4405-5665-2
ISBN 13: 978-1-4405-5665-4
eISBN 10: 1-4405-5666-0
eISBN 13: 978-1-4405-5666-1

Printed in the United States of America.

10   9   8   7   6   5   4   3   2   1

This book is available at quantity discounts for bulk purchases.
For information, please call 1-800-289-0963.

Chapter 1

Every night it's the same thing. Screeching brakes. Crunching steel. A rush of cold, wet air as the glass crumbles, letting in the snowy night. The chorus of screams, and then nothing—just the slow drip of fluids from the mangled wreck and the hiss of steam escaping the crushed radiator. And the stench—scorched rubber, gasoline, the metallic smell of blood, burning electrical wiring—all mingled with a sweet, flowery smell I couldn't identify. Was I dead? Did God work behind the perfume counter at Bloomingdale's?

Why couldn't I dream about something else? The accident was four years ago, and the dream never faded, never changed. If only I could remember more, then maybe I could figure out what really happened. Waking up exhausted every morning, my sheets in a tangle, my nightgown drenched in sweat, I was stuck. More than once I'd wished that I wasn't the one who had "miraculously escaped death," as the newspapers put it, "pulled dazed and bleeding from the wreckage." Reliving my family's last moments night after night was not my idea of living, and if I had the guts, I probably would have figured out a way to join them, wherever they were, instead of staying here in a sort of no-man's-land. But that wasn't going to happen anytime soon. I was a coward and a big talker. Well, actually, I wasn't a talker at all anymore.

When I woke up in the hospital on that Christmas Eve, three days after the accident, my Aunt Charlotte was sitting next to my bed, wringing her hands as I rubbed my eyes, a fluffy mountain of her crumpled tissues on the bedside table.

"Sasha, you're awake. Oh darling, are you okay? Are you in pain?"

I opened my mouth to answer her, to tell her that I felt fine, a little sore, but none the worse for wear. And I wanted to ask her what had happened, why I was in a hospital, judging by the mechanical bed, the IV in my arm, and that horrible antiseptic smell. But nothing came out. Like a fish out of water, gasping for air, my mouth opened and closed, but there was no sound. It was as if someone had pressed my mute button.

Desperately needing to communicate, I mimed a pencil and paper, and when Charlotte handed me a pad and pen, I wrote furiously. **What happened? Why can't I talk? Where are Mom and Dad and Liz? Why am I in the hospital?**

At that point I hadn't yet started having the dream and had no recollection of the accident. My mind was a jumble, and my lost voice and the panicked expression on Charlotte's face terrified me more than I thought possible.

"You can't talk? I don't know what's wrong." Jumping up, knocking over the plastic water pitcher on the table next to the bed, Charlotte ran to find a nurse while I tried to rouse my vocal cords.

Hours later, after what seemed like a dozen doctors had looked down my throat with exotic instruments that looked more suited to medieval torture than medical diagnostics, a young man, who barely looked old enough to drive let alone practice medicine, appeared in the doorway. Before he could produce a flashlight or a tongue depressor I was shaking my head and covering my mouth with my hand. No more doctors. Whatever was wrong with me, this wasn't helping.

"Sasha, Mrs. Thompson, I'm Dr. Klein. Don't worry, I'm a different kind of doctor. I won't be putting anything down your throat."

He smiled reassuringly at us both and took my aunt out into the hallway, leaving me to visualize the worst that a kid could imagine. A doctor only left the room when there was bad news. By the time they returned I had decided that I was dying. Tears gushed down my cheeks, my shoulders shook, but even then, not so much as a whimper.

"Sasha, it's okay. You're going to be fine. I promise."

Charlotte didn't look as convincing as she sounded, but my parents were nowhere to be seen, and I needed to believe in someone. I bit my lip, blinked back my tears, and tried to suck it up. If she could be brave, then so could I. We both looked at Dr. Klein, who just stood with his arms folded, a sympathetic thin-lipped smile on his face.

"Sasha, your aunt's right. You will be just fine. Miraculously, you suffered virtually no injuries in the accident—no physical injuries, that is. Your inability to speak is a phenomenon called hysterical mutism, a rare manifestation of posttraumatic stress. As an adolescent—how old are you?"

What accident? I wanted to scream. What was this weirdo talking about?

"She's thirteen today," my aunt said softly.

I hadn't known what day it was myself. So this was what it felt like to be a teenager. Not at all what I'd expected.

"Oh, dear. Wishing you a happy birthday doesn't seem particularly appropriate. Anyway, as I was saying, the adolescent brain is in a state of flux and is especially vulnerable to psychic trauma. But the good thing is that the pubescent brain is also very elastic, capable of healing itself in ways that an adult brain cannot." He paused to let this sink in, but when he noticed my bewildered expression, he seemed to realize that he wasn't talking only to adults, and that I hadn't understood a word he'd said, other than the part about my birthday. "I'm sorry, sweetheart. What I'm trying to say, and not doing a very good job, is that although your body was not seriously injured in the accident, your mind was. In response to this terrible thing that has happened to you, your brain has reacted by taking away your ability to speak. Your vocal cords are perfectly fine. While you may remember very little of what happened the night of the accident in your conscious mind, the deepest part of your brain remembers everything and is very upset by it."

Dr. Klein, overcompensating for his initial, convoluted explanation, was speaking incredibly slowly, enunciating every syllable, as if my inability to speak had somehow affected my ability to understand English. Unbelievable. Who knew my brain was that powerful, and that stupid? How could it shut down my voice box like that? What for? I couldn't even remember what happened that night, or much of the rest of my life, for that matter. I nodded at Dr. Klein. What else was there to do? Why couldn't I have a broken leg or a ruptured spleen, something run-of-the-mill that could be healed with a cast or some stitches?

"I'm a general psychiatrist, but I think Sasha would benefit most if she worked with someone who specializes in the area of posttraumatic stress. Dr. Colleen O'Rourke, who is at the forefront of this field, recently moved here from Boston. She works primarily at New York General, but she does see a few patients locally. She's eager to take your case." Dr. Klein patted my feet through the blankets and handed

Charlotte a business card. "I wish you a speedy recovery, Sasha, and I'm so sorry for your loss."

Charlotte glared up at him, shaking her head violently from side to side. "I hadn't . . ." She didn't finish the sentence.

"I'm so sorry. I didn't realize." Dr. Klein reddened, realizing that he had let the cat, the dead cat, out of the bag. But it didn't matter—I already knew.

There was a knock at the door, and a woman peeked in. Unable to face another doctor, I yanked the sheet over my head.

"I hope I'm not interrupting."

"Perfect timing," said Dr. Klein. "Mrs. Thompson, Sasha, this is Dr. O'Rourke."

"Hello. Please accept my condolences for your terrible loss."

Charlotte gently pulled the sheet from my face. "So nice to meet you, Dr. O'Rourke. Thank you for taking us on."

The two women shook hands, and Dr. O'Rourke nodded at me.

"I very much look forward to helping Sasha cope with what has happened. You are a brave little girl."

Brave was the last thing I was, but she didn't know me yet.

"She is," Charlotte sniffed.

"I actually knew your father many, many years ago. We went to high school together in Boston. He was the captain of the football team, the quarterback."

Three pairs of eyes stared at my mouth, as if waiting for me to have a breakthrough right there, as if a famous doctor standing at the foot of my hospital bed would be enough to jog my memory and cure my voice. I didn't remember that my father had grown up in Boston or played football in high school. It was like they were talking about a complete stranger. Not knowing what else to do, I nodded. Maybe if I agreed with this person, she would leave.

"That should make things easier, shouldn't it?" Charlotte said, sounding desperate for something positive to grab onto.

"Absolutely," said Dr. Klein, and Dr. O'Rourke nodded. "The fact that Dr. O'Rourke knew Sasha's father, even so long ago, gives her insight into the entire dynamic."

Since when did my dead family become a dynamic? What did that even mean? I closed my eyes. I couldn't make them stop talking, but at least I didn't have to look at them.

Dr. O'Rourke whispered, "You need to rest, Sasha. I will see you very soon. Mrs. Thompson, call me in a few days and we'll set something up. Goodbye."

"I'm going to go, too," Dr. Klein said.

The door clicked shut and I opened my eyes. For a few minutes, Charlotte and I just looked at each other. Then I tapped the pad of paper where I had earlier scrawled my questions. My parents and my sister were gone forever. There was no denying it. At the moment it didn't really matter how it had happened, but I might as well get it over with.

Haltingly, Charlotte began telling me her version of events, still dancing around the fact that my entire family was dead. My mother and Charlotte were sisters, only a year apart, and had been as close as twins.

"You were driving with Liz and your folks to the church for the holiday concert when the accident happened. It was snowing, but the roads looked okay, and your dad had just put the snow tires on the car. I spoke to your mom right before you left, at about seven o'clock. She wanted to know if Stuart and I wanted to join you, but we both had court in the morning and had work to do. Do you remember any of this?"

Charlotte seemed more comfortable now that she could be helpful, using her lawyerly skills to remind the witness of what had happened. The color was slowly returning to her cheeks.

I shook my head. Church? Christmas concert? I remembered I had two parents, a sister named Liz, and Aunt Charlotte, but not much else before waking up in a hospital bed. My brain was wrapped in thick fog, and no matter how hard I concentrated, the haze wasn't lifting.

"Do you remember the car ride?" she coaxed.

Charlotte leaned forward, her hands clutching the thin, white cotton blanket, as if she were physically trying to pull the memories from wherever they were trapped inside of me. I squeezed my eyes shut tight, trying to picture what had happened in the car, during what had been my family's last few minutes alive. What was I wearing? How hard was it snowing? What was playing on the car radio?

Nothing, just a thudding pain behind my eyes and sudden, unbearable fatigue. Turning my head away from Charlotte, I slipped into blackness.

◆

Two days later I was released from the hospital and moved into Charlotte's house. Although I knew I had lived elsewhere before the accident, I had no conscious memory of that place and no desire to remember. If I could have made time stop, made myself disappear, I would have. Like a robot, I sat where I was told to sit, ate what I was told to eat, and settled into a new life with my aunt and uncle, which unfortunately started with my family's funeral. When I woke up that morning, for a glorious second I thought I had dreamed it all, that my dad was going to march past my bedroom humming Beethoven's Ninth Symphony to himself, just as he did every morning at exactly 7:03, and a few minutes later, the smell of coffee brewing would float up the stairs and under my bedroom door. But then, like a lens coming into focus, my real life emerged from the shadows inside my head.

I don't want to go, I wrote. A yellow legal pad and a pile of Ticonderoga pencils were my only link to the outside world. I was still in my pajamas, and we were due at the cemetery in less than an hour. **You can't make me.** I stomped my foot on the wood floor, but my socks muffled the sound, undermining the fury that I was so desperate to express.

Charlotte said, "Darling, I know it's hard, but I think—and Dr. O'Rourke agrees—that it's important for you to go."

I had met the storied Dr. O'Rourke exactly once, and here she was, making decisions for me, giving unwanted advice, issuing orders.

But I know they're all dead . . . I get it. My pencil dug into the paper as I wrote the word *dead*. **Why do I have to see it? Why can't everybody just leave me alone?**

I closed my eyes, imagining three coffins lined up next to three perfectly rectangular holes in the ground. Why wasn't there a fourth for me? It would be so much easier. In the days after the accident I spent much of my time fantasizing about an accident that took four lives instead of three. Charlotte blathered on about my life being spared because I must have some special purpose. Total bullshit. At this point I was just taking up space. Opening my swollen and bloodshot eyes, I stared out the window at the snow-covered trees. By now I should have run out of tears, but I seemed to have an endless supply.

"It's closure. You need to say goodbye to them." She could barely get the words out, turning her back to me so I wouldn't see her cry.

I knew she must be as devastated as I was, but I had no room in my heart for empathy. Feeling sorry for myself was taking up all my energy.

What's the point of saying goodbye to three wooden boxes? Like that's going to help me get over it? They're already gone. The tip of my pencil snapped with the force of my words.

Charlotte gave Stuart a pleading look. Standing at the island in the kitchen, he stirred his tea and looked on helplessly. I felt bad for him. This wasn't supposed to be his life either. Putting down his spoon, he came and sat down next to me on the sofa.

"Sash, funerals suck, and going to your family's funeral is an unthinkable task, but it's just something you have to do. It's not right, but it's what everybody's expecting. If you don't show up, they'll never leave you alone. So let's get this over with, and then you can come home and I won't let anyone bother you. I promise." He held up three fingers in a Boy Scout salute.

That made sense. If I knew my public misery was limited to an hour or two, I could manage. I nodded. No wonder Stuart was so good at his job: he knew how to get things done. As horrible as I felt, I wasn't immune to logic, and Stuart's plan was reasonable and finite.

"But Stu, what about the reception afterward?"

Charlotte stood in front of us, filing her fingernails furiously. She was like a taut guitar string, ready to snap at the slightest touch, but Stuart maintained his cool.

"Sasha and I are coming straight home after the funeral. No reception. You can go, and you should, to represent the family, but I don't think any good is going to come of standing around talking about the good old days. It's too soon." Stuart kissed me on the forehead and patted my knee. "She's just a baby," he whispered into my hair. "She needs time."

Charlotte sighed and wiped her eyes, inspecting her hands for mascara. "I suppose you're right. Of course that makes sense. I was so busy thinking about what we were supposed to do that I wasn't thinking about what was the right thing for Sasha. I'm so sorry, kiddo. This is all new for me. We'll figure this out. It's just going to take time to get used to everything."

My tears dripped on the yellow paper, smudging my words. **It's okay. I love you guys. Thank you for taking me in. I know you didn't want to have a baby, and now you have me. It must be hard.**

"Don't *ever* say thank you for this. It's a privilege to have you in this house. No more discussing it—let's get this over with. Go get dressed, Sasha," Stuart ordered. Everything about Stuart made me feel safe.

◆

It was a graveside ceremony, and all three coffins were lined up, just as I had pictured. Shiny dark wood, they looked like giant cigar boxes. Two of the caskets were blanketed with pink roses—my mother, sister, and I had all loved pale pink roses. Not anymore. Although it was bitterly cold, there must have been close to a hundred people huddled around the trio of holes in the ground. I didn't recognize most of them—amnesia or shock, I didn't know which—so I sat between my aunt and uncle, surrounded by a crowd of strangers, staring at my muddy shoes, trying not to think about my parents and sister being dropped into those pits and covered with dirt.

The worms crawl in . . . I remembered that Liz hated bugs. When there was a spider in the bathroom, she would holler until someone came in to kill it for her. And although she didn't like to admit it, she was a little afraid of the dark. I used to make fun of her, because even though she was two years older, she was the scaredy cat in the family. Now she was alone in the dark, with the bugs, and I couldn't help her. Jamming my fists into my eyes, wishing I could scream out loud, I tried to erase the image of three dead bodies, maggots crawling in and out of their ears.

The minister rambled on about lives cut short, some heavenly grand plan, and the duty of the living to carry on the memories of those no longer here. It sounded like a load of crap to me, but I couldn't speak and I don't think the words I wanted to say would have been very well received. What kind of fucking higher power would let this happen? And if He/She/It were going to let this happen, then the least He/She/It could do would be to wipe out the whole family at once. I didn't even have any grandparents: two cancers, one heart attack, and a stroke had decimated my family tree long before the crash. Leaving one person behind, a child no less, smacked of poor judgment and bad planning. Where was the mercy in that? Somehow I knew I wouldn't be finding comfort in religion.

Twenty minutes later, it was all over. Three hunchbacked men in black raincoats and rubber boots lowered the caskets into the holes with some cranking device. Charlotte, Stuart, and I stood like a tiny receiving line at a vampire wedding, while people said horrible, well-meaning things. "We're so sorry." "If there's anything we can do . . ." "Are you all right?" "How do you feel?" Stupid, obvious, unanswerable questions. And then, as they walked away, I could still hear them, talking about me instead of to me. "How will she survive?" "Did you hear that she may never be able to speak again?" "She looks terrible."

"Come on, sweetie, let's get you home," Stuart said, wrapping his arm protectively around my shoulders. "You're frozen solid."

I nodded and leaned against him, comforted by the feel of his rough wool coat against my face. His other arm was around Charlotte. If not for Stuart, we would probably both keel over.

"Honey, are you all right? You don't have to go to the reception, either."

Charlotte sniffled. "I have to go."

"There is no such thing as 'have to' in this situation."

"No, I want to go. I won't stay long." We stopped in front of the black Lincoln Town Car that had brought us to the cemetery. "I'll see you at home." The three of us stood with our arms around each other for a long minute.

My life was at the bottom of three holes in the Riverside Cemetery, but I had to keep on living. How was I supposed to do that?

Chapter 2

Dr. O'Rourke specialized in the treatment of posttraumatic stress. But after four years, I was still mute, and my memory was still murky—mild retrograde amnesia she called it. Maybe my tragedy was too mainstream for her. Girls my age who had been raped and beaten, or soldiers who had seen their entire units blown up before their eyes—these were the tough cases, the seriously damaged psyches that the doctor was accustomed to cobbling back together. My family was dead, but it was nobody's fault. No one had purposefully hurt me. There was no evil in my life. I was just the victim of bad luck and black ice, in the wrong place at the wrong time.

In the beginning, once a week, and then later twice a month, I visited Dr. O'Rourke. I listened to her talk, did the homework assignments she gave me, unsuccessfully tried hypnosis, swallowed all kinds of colorful pills, meditated, kept a dream journal. But nothing helped. The books on her shelf spoke to her expertise. *Lost and Found: Rediscovering Yourself after Experiencing Tragedy; Why Not Me?—Navigating Survivor Guilt; Now What?—Reconnecting with Life after a Near-Death Experience;* and my personal favorite title, *Climax: Healing Your Psyche with Sex.* Reading her books, except the last one, had been part of my homework over the last few years, and as educational as they were, they did nothing for my voice, or for my dreams, for that matter. She was a very nice lady, and she had helped plenty of other people, but I think I could have saved Charlotte and Stuart thousands of dollars and been in exactly the same place: plagued by a really bad nightmare and dependent on a computer or pad of paper to communicate.

Approaching the four-year anniversary of the accident, Dr. O'Rourke had scheduled an extra session. She did that every year, probably in the hopes that some major psychological breakthrough would coincide with the date my family died. So far it hadn't, and the idea sounded a little bit too much like a Lifetime TV movie, but after four years of silence, I was willing to try anything, no matter how hokey it sounded or how miserably it had failed in the past. Maybe this would be the year when all my stars would be in alignment, and I would emerge from my silence like a songbird from its shell, fully formed, with a sweet, clear voice. Who was I kidding?

"For the thousandth time, there is nothing wrong with you physically. It's called somatoform conversion disorder." Her voice betrayed her growing frustration. A doctor's failure to cure a patient was like Charlotte or Stuart losing a lawsuit, and I knew my aunt and uncle took such defeats very personally. "There is no physiological reason you cannot speak. Your mind is controlling your body." Dr. O'Rourke flipped through my chart, which had grown thick in the last four years.

For the umpteenth time I nodded my head. This speech was a regular part of Dr. O'Rourke's repertoire. She hauled it out when she was feeling discouraged by my lack of progress, which usually happened around this time of year—as predictable as Christmas carols and fruitcake. But if she truly understood my disorder, then why was she acting as if I had some conscious control over this? Didn't she believe me when I told her that more than anything on this earth I wanted to be able to talk again? Didn't she realize how hard, and lonely, my life had become in the last four years? But she was the doctor, so she must have a good reason for rehashing my diagnosis and berating me again.

Obediently, I opened my mouth, straining to make a sound, but nothing came out except a puff of air as I exhaled. Dr. O'Rourke's irritation was obvious in her furrowed brow and the way she chewed on her pencil. This was our 168th session, and I was no closer to making a sound than I had been at the first. In truth, I hated to disappoint the doctor as much as I hated not being able to speak. She really seemed to care about me as a person, not just a customer who paid three hundred dollars an hour to stretch out on her couch.

"I'm not sure what we should do with you. I don't want to diminish the horrible thing that has happened to you, but it happened, and now you have to choose whether or not you are forever going to let that experience dominate and define your life."

Ah, her tough love, hard choices sermon. As earnest and compassionate as Dr. O'Rourke was, I was as lost four years later as I had been in the months after the accident. Swimming in circles in my kiddie pool of self-pity, hopelessness, and rage, I couldn't seem to find the ladder. There was no breakthrough looming on my horizon, at least not this year.

Writing everything on a pad of paper was inefficient and exhausting, so I used a voice-synthesizing device that spoke whatever I typed into it. Everything came out sounding like I was channeling Stephen Hawking, the famous English physicist who had lost his voice to ALS and used a similar device. I called it the Hawkie Talkie. A variety of voices and accents was available, from "female, English, mid-twenties" to "male, Midwestern, child." But the default voice, the robotic monotone with which it spoke my words, perfectly reflected the emptiness I felt. The kids at school found this incredibly entertaining, no matter how many times they heard it. As a result, I didn't tend to contribute much in class, furthering my metaphorical solitary confinement. Changing the voice setting to something more normal would be a no-brainer for most people. Why not make life a little easier? But stupid and stubborn, I refused to alter it. If I tried to fit in and still didn't, I would feel worse than I did having made no effort at all. By shutting myself off before anyone could slam the door in my face, I naively thought I was protecting myself. A classic "cut off your noise to spite your face" philosophy of life—not a recipe for success—just proof of what a total loser I was.

"BUT HOW CAN IT NOT INFLUENCE MY LIFE? MY FAMILY IS GONE, MY MEMORIES OF EVERY-THING THAT CAME BEFORE ARE HAZY. I HARDLY KNOW WHO I AM SOMETIMES."

"Well, as we've talked about before, over time your memory may improve. I had hoped hypnotherapy would have helped with that, but you are apparently immune to hypnosis. The most we can do is try again in a few months. I've usually had incredible luck putting my patients under. It doesn't make sense."

"IS HYPNOSIS MY ONLY HOPE?"

"It may just take time, or maybe some random event will trigger something in your mind, but the human brain is still very much a mystery, even to us so-called experts. The one thing I do know is that you were at a pivotal point in your development when this happened, so it may take longer. And please understand, I'm not saying that you can be who you were before. Everyone is influenced by experiences, so you will never be the person you would have become had you not lost your family, but you can become an equally wonderful person. And ultimately, you don't need to recover all your memories in order to recover. That is a key point. You can't lose sight of that."

"IS THERE A POSSIBILITY I'LL NEVER GET MY VOICE BACK?"

It was the first time I had expressed this concern to anyone, but after so long, I was beginning to realize that I could be stuck like this forever. My heart started to race.

"Don't think that. At the end of the day, *you* hold the power to heal your voice." Dr. O. reached across and put her hand over my heart. "It's hard for me to say this, but my methods have failed you, and now I think it's up to you. Only you can give yourself the permission to move on. I'm still here for you, but I think the time has come for you to explore your own inner strength. Your recovery rests inside of you." Folding her hands in her lap and leaning back against a cushion, Dr. O. said, "I'm afraid our time is up, but I'll see you in a month, just to check in. Introspection—that's my new prescription for you."

Chapter 3

"Does anyone want to add anything about the commercial uses of spectroscopy?" asked Mr. Ashton. Crickets. "Stephen . . . I mean, Sasha?"

Someone in the back row said, "Yes, Dr. Hawking, you must have something to say. Physics *is* your field of expertise. Maybe you could explain time travel to us, or aliens."

"FUCK YOU." The snickers were replaced by a chorus of "ooh."

Before I could be dismissed, I packed my books away and skulked out of the classroom as Mr. Ashton picked up the telephone on his desk. My bravado tended to come in brief spurts. Was he calling the principal or the school psychologist this time? It was not my first trip to the office. I knew the drill.

Sitting in my usual chair, I counted the linoleum floor tiles until the school gnome/secretary spoke. "The principal will see you now."

Balding and rumpled, with tiny reading glasses perched on the end of his bulbous nose, Mr. Carson was your stereotypical high school principal. "Good morning, Sasha. You've had a good run. It's been a whole week since you were last here."

I stared at the spot on the bridge of his nose where his eyebrows met.

"Such language is unbecoming. Your aunt and uncle are so well mannered. I just don't understand it. Should I wash your mouth out with soap? Maybe that would curb your sarcasm." Mr. Carson leaned forward, elbows on his cluttered desk.

"IF YOU WANT TO BE PRECISE, YOU SHOULD PROBABLY WASH MY HANDS, NOT MY MOUTH." I wiggled my fingers at him when I finished typing.

"What are we going to do with you, young lady? I'm sure Mr. Ashton just misspoke. Stephen and Sasha both start with the letter *s*. Don't you think you may have overreacted?" Mr. Carson looked beseechingly at me. Talk about leading the witness. Maybe he would let me off this time. Five visits to the principal, get one free.

"SO IF I CALLED MR. ASHTON MR. ASSHOLE, YOU WOULD CONSIDER THAT A SLIP OF THE TONGUE, PRINCIPAL CARSON, BECAUSE BOTH START WITH THE LETTER *A*?"

"I can see you're not in a very receptive mood this morning, Sasha. Perhaps an afternoon in detention will help you think more clearly." Sighing histrionically, the principal signed what must have been my hundredth pink slip and handed it across the desk. "We really have to stop meeting like this."

"D-I-L-L-I-G-A-S." Do I look like I give a shit, Principal Carson?

"I think you're very lucky I don't know what that means."

"T-Y-A-F-Y-S." Thank you and fuck you, sir.

"Well, you're welcome, I think. Go back to class, and try to have a better day . . . please. We're both getting too old for this." Mr. Carson flapped his hands in my general direction and turned back to his computer.

After-school detention was filled with the all the usual suspects, like a casting call from a 1980s teen rebellion movie, minus the mullets and Madonna bracelets. I took my seat by the window—regulars like me had "reserved" desks, like customers who frequented a neighborhood diner.

"Good afternoon, Sasha," said Mrs. Goodman, math teacher from eight to three, warden from three to five. With her closely cropped hair and a clutch of keys jangling on a retractable key ring hooked to her belt, she was straight out of a women's prison movie.

Leaning over my desk, she whispered, "Heard about your run-in with Mr. Ashton. Can't say I blame you. He can be a real jerk sometimes."

"THANKS, MA'AM."

Her breath reeked of cigarettes and black licorice, but I appreciated the support. She nodded knowingly. Apparently we were sisters in some mysterious sorority.

"Hey, Sash, what up? You look hot in your sweats." Jeff—or maybe Jed, I could never remember which—howled at his own lame attempt at humor.

"Come sit over here. It's lonely in the back." Paul patted the seat next to his.

Detention was primarily populated by jocks and hoods, kids with short fuses and minimal ambition—no National Honor Society officers or debate team standouts here. With their "fuck the system" attitudes, these degenerates were local heroes. Jeff/Jed and Paul, stars on the football and lacrosse teams and regulars at Mrs. Goodman's afternoon tea parties, definitely fell into this category. They wallowed in their roles as bad boys, lapping up the attention from their less daring classmates. Unlike most of the girls at Shoreland, I found their swagger repugnant and studiously ignored them, now burying my nose in my history book, pretending to be totally absorbed in the finer points of the First Amendment. What was so sexy about stupidity?

"Too good for us, huh?" Paul hissed, but I kept my eyes glued to the page. "You don't know what you're missing." He moaned and made kissing noises.

"You shootin' for a ticket to detention tomorrow, Welch?" Mrs. Goodman waddled down the aisle and stood, arms akimbo, in front of Paul's desk. I was grateful that she had distracted him.

"No, ma'am." Paul sat up and stared straight ahead.

"'Cause you know I'll be here, and there's nothing I'd like better than to spend another afternoon with my favorite juvenile delinquent." She leaned over his desk and batted her eyelashes. "Maybe you have a little crush, and you're just lookin' for an excuse to spend more time with me. Mmm? A little cougar action?"

Mrs. Goodman ran her tongue seductively over her lips, reminding me of a cow chewing its cud. Eighteen of the twenty after school detainees burst out laughing. Only Paul, his face crimson, and I were silent. Mrs. Goodman was the best.

Chapter 4

As part of my therapy, I kept a journal, writing down my thoughts, my feelings, my dreams . . . or rather, my one dream. For my seventeenth birthday, Charlotte and Stuart gave me a new journal, inscribing it: *Here's to lucky seventeen! This is your year, darling. Don't give up. We love you more than words can say. C & S.* By this time, even though I had been as silent as a cloistered monk for more than four years, we were able to joke about it, a little bit. I blew out the candles on the pale pink birthday cake with marzipan ribbons. It was far too pretty for such a melancholy occasion. We were sitting in front of the blazing fireplace, the mercury glass ornaments on the Christmas tree reflecting the dancing flames. Everything looked so perfect from the outside, but just under the surface, I was frustrated, damaged, and angry. I needed to pull myself together before my head exploded.

"Happy birthday, Sasha."

Charlotte and Stuart did their best to make it feel special and festive, but birthdays would always be bittersweet. It was bad enough that my family had died, but the fact that the anniversary of their death coincided so closely with my special day made a happy birthday a contradiction in terms. Stuart handed me a small blue Tiffany bag. In it was a gold necklace from which hung a tiny gold key. Were they sending me a not-so-subtle message that I alone held the key to my recovery, or was I being overly sensitive?

"What do you think? Very trendy, apparently. If you don't like it, we can take it back." Stuart was always practical.

"IT'S BEAUTIFUL. I LOVE IT. THANK YOU."

"We love you so much, and we'll always be here for you. Dr. O'Rourke called me yesterday and told me that she thought you needed a little break from therapy, a little time to yourself. So remember, if you need to talk, Stuart and I are always here to listen."

Charlotte held out her arms to me and I crawled into her lap, burying my face in her red cashmere sweater, trying to pretend that I wasn't a mute seventeen-year-old with no parents, only one friend, and a giant chip on my shoulder.

Stuart sat down next to us and rested his hand on my back. "It's going to be okay, Sash, I promise. You just have to give it some more time."

I nodded into Charlotte's sweater, even though I thought he was totally wrong. Stuart was a really good guy. He and Charlotte had been together since their first week of law school. They were a perfect match. They both loved being lawyers, felt totally fulfilled by their professions, and agreed that children wouldn't fit into their busy lives. But when I landed on their doorstep, barely a teenager, loaded down with more baggage than the *Titanic*, he had welcomed me with open arms and never looked back. While Charlotte had no choice to accept me—she was my flesh and blood—Stuart had no such connection. Despite that, he had quickly redefined his vision of his family and his future, finding a place for me in his home and his heart. In the middle of a sea of shit, Stuart and Charlotte had pulled me into their lifeboat, and I would always be grateful.

The day after Christmas, I met my best (and only) friend for coffee so she could give me my birthday present. She said it was something I really needed. Maybe she had bought me a new personality. I could only hope.

Jules—her real name was Juliana, but no one ever called her that—kissed me on both cheeks. "Happy birthday, babe." She had gone to Paris the previous summer and had adopted this European custom as her standard greeting. If anyone else did that, it would be ridiculously phony, but Jules managed to pull it off. "Did you get my texts and e-mails?"

I nodded and mouthed a thank you. Jules knew my birthday was really hard for me and that I liked to keep it low-key. We had met on the first day of nursery school, were milk and cookie buddies in kindergarten, penny partners in first grade, and best friends throughout. As we grew up, although we went off in totally different directions, we remained close. At least that's what she told me, because I really didn't remember much about our friendship beyond the fact of its existence. Into books and art, I could spend hours browsing through art anthologies at the library, lost in another century. Jules Harper, on the other hand, was head cheerleader and part of the theater crowd. She hated being alone and had a million friends, but I was still her closest. We were quite the odd couple, and I'm not sure why we meshed so well—maybe because there was absolutely no competition between us—but whatever the reason, I would never have survived without her love and support.

After the accident, Jules visited me in the hospital and then at home every day until I returned to school. Her over-the-top enthusiasm may have been the only thing that kept me from falling to the bottom of a well of despair. If she hadn't nagged me into reentering the stream of life, I might still be curled up in a ball somewhere.

"Sasha, I brought your homework. You have to do at least some of it. Come on. You don't want to end up repeating seventh grade, do you?" Jules had pointed to a pile of books and papers on the desk in the corner.

At that moment, I had planned never to leave my bedroom again, so whether or not I completed the seventh grade was irrelevant.

"Mrs. Walsh said if you read *To Kill a Mockingbird* and write a five-page paper about it, you can still get an A in English. That's good, isn't it?"

I had stared impassively at my best, and only, friend in the whole world. How could I have explained to her that nothing mattered anymore, least of all an A in English?

"Sasha, stop it. Don't ignore me. I know you hear me. I know you understand me. Please don't shut me out." Climbing onto my bed, Jules had stroked my hair and whispered in my ear. "I'm so sorry about what happened. I know how much you miss them. I love you so much. And no matter what, I'm not going anywhere, ever. We're sisters."

And she hadn't abandoned me for the last four years, through piles of legal pads covered with my illegible scrawl that passed for my side of the conversation, and hours of one-sided late-night phone calls when Jules would tell me what had happened on a date or at a school dance. She was my only link to the real world, and I lived vicariously through her. I melted when she described her first kiss, laughed silently when Jason Draper couldn't figure out how to unhook her bra, and cried to myself when I thought about how no one would ever kiss me or touch me like that.

Our whole friendship made no sense. Were I in her shoes, I doubt I would have had the patience to stick it out. As ill-fated as my life had been in certain ways, I was blessed to have

Jules, who had chosen me as her closest ally—as well as her pet project.

"I hope you like it." Wrapped in plain brown paper with a pink satin ribbon, my gift was clearly a book. "Don't open it here. Wait until you get home and then open it in your room."

Jules was an expert in translating my gestures, so when I tilted my head, shrugged my shoulders, and opened my eyes wide, she just laughed. *What?* I mouthed.

"It's something you need. You'll see. Trust me. I always take care of you, right?" That was true. In the last four years, Jules had been my advocate, my protector, and my champion. "Just make sure you're alone when you open it."

Gestures weren't enough. I pulled out my Hawkie Talkie. "WHAT DID YOU GET ME? A BOOK ON HOW TO BUILD A PENIS OUT OF OLD CAR PARTS?"

"Kind of. Don't worry. Text me after you open it, and let me know what you think. But enough about my fabulous gift. What did Dr. O. say at your birthday session?"

"SHE KIND OF FIRED ME. I THINK I'M HER ONLY FAILURE."

"What do you mean, fired you? I didn't think a shrink ever fired a patient. Couldn't that be dangerous? Wouldn't it be her fault if you slit your wrists? Did Charlotte stop paying her or something?"

"OF COURSE NOT. DR. O. SAYS I HOLD THE KEY TO MY OWN RECOVERY. THAT'S A DIRECT QUOTE. I THINK SHE'S JUST GIVEN UP ON ME."

"Maybe you're hearing it wrong . . ." Jules began.

"DEFINITELY NOT. WHAT DO I DO NOW? I CAN'T REMEMBER MUCH, AND WHEN I TRY, I GET A MIGRAINE."

"Well, she's the doctor. Buy yourself a giant bottle of aspirin and try to remember what happened the night of the accident and pretty much your whole life."

"GREAT IDEA. AND WHILE I'M AT IT, I'LL END WORLD HUNGER."

"I'm not saying it's going to be easy, just necessary. She wouldn't say that she thought you could do it if she didn't mean it. Would she?" For Jules, everything was simple and straightforward, no undercurrents, no hidden meanings.

"I'M NOT SO SURE ABOUT THAT. I THINK SHE'S RUN OUT OF SOLUTIONS AND SHE'S JUST PASSING THE BUCK."

"You need to have more faith in yourself. You're much stronger than you think you are. Maybe you need to start fighting for yourself."

"I ALREADY AM."

"Which I think might mean fighting *with* yourself." Jules sipped her coffee and stared pointedly at my talking machine.

"WHAT THE FUCK ARE YOU TALKING ABOUT? WHAT ONLINE SCHOOL OF PSYCHIATRY DID YOU GRADUATE FROM?"

"Don't be like that. I'm on your side. Remember? All I'm saying is that I think you've built a wall to protect yourself from something. The pain, the memories, and all that guilt about still being alive when they aren't. Maybe if you can break through that, you'll get your voice back."

"SO HOW MUCH DO I OWE YOU, DOCTOR?" I mimed writing a check.

The worst part was, Jules was right. Every time I looked in the mirror, I saw my sister staring back at me. She was the pretty one, the fun one, the one who should have lived. I was the expendable one, and yet here I sat, a useless lump of flesh who couldn't even ask for directions let alone do justice to the extra years I'd been given simply because I had been sitting on the right side of the car's back seat instead of the left.

"Don't be flip, Sash. I'm sorry, I probably shouldn't have gotten into it, especially on your birthday. Not fair. And you're right, what do I know?"

"IT'S OKAY. YOU'VE BEEN SO PATIENT WITH ME. ANYONE ELSE WOULD HAVE ABANDONED SHIP A LONG TIME AGO. I'M THE ONE WHO SHOULD BE APOLOGIZING." I opened my arms and we hugged, both of us crying.

Later that day, in the privacy of my room, I opened Jules's gift. It was a copy of *Everything You've Always Wanted to Know About Sex (But Were Afraid to Ask)*, by Dr. David Reuben. Inside the front cover she had crossed out the original inscription and written: *Dearest Sasha, You may have missed out on a few things, but read this and I guarantee you'll be more than caught up. You're seventeen—make it count. Your best friend, forever, Jules. P.S. Hide this well—if Charlotte and Stuart find it, I'll be on their shit list.*

Flipping randomly through the pages, I was startled by how many -isms there were in the world of sex: fetishism, voyeurism, sadomasochism, autoeroticism. Fortunately, chapter 1 was entitled "Beyond the Birds and Bees." I definitely needed a crash course. The stuff the gym teachers taught in health class was dull and clinical, while my aunt's infrequent and very sanitary efforts had always been prefaced by "When you're older, hopefully married . . ." I wanted to learn about the sex people had in the movies. I wanted to learn how to make a guy want me so bad he couldn't see straight.

I texted Jules. *Excellent gift. Thank you. I especially like the original inscription: "With love to my dear son—make*

sure you read this before your wedding night. Love, Mom."
Maybe I'm not as fucked up as I thought.

She wrote back: *Clearly just a loving mother looking out for her son. Sorry it's a used copy, but I found it at that cool vintage book store, The Last Word. Now you'll be prepared for your wedding night.*

Wedding night? I typed. *Isn't that jumping the gun? I'd be happy with getting felt up at the movies.*

Finding a boy who would put up with my shit show would be like winning the lottery. Finding someone who would stick around long enough to marry me would be a walking-on-water miracle.

Sounds good. As long as you have a goal. Happy birthday, Sasha! Now get reading.

Chapter 5

Kicking off my shoes, I tucked my feet under me at one end of my couch. As a regular at the Shoreland Public Library, I had acquired squatter's rights on one of the battered leather sofas in the sunroom off the main reading room. Charlotte and Stuart worked late in New York City at least three nights a week doing their lawyer thing, and I hated being alone in their concrete tomb of a house, just waiting to hear their key turning in the lock. The library was my haven. It was always filled with people, but since talking was frowned upon, it was the one place I felt like I belonged. I could enjoy a sense of companionship without standing out as the only one not carrying on a conversation. If my voice never came back, I could spend my life shelving books, unless of course I ended up baking fruitcakes or making lace in one of those convents where the nuns were required to take a vow of silence.

With a pile of architecture tomes on the cushion next to me, I settled in for another afternoon of browsing coffee table books filled with photographs of extraordinary sights in spectacular places I would probably never visit. I was the ultimate armchair tourist. Lost in photographs of the Cathedral of Santa Maria del Fiore, with a dome designed by Brunelleschi and a bell tower by Giotto, I was too busy imagining myself strolling across the Ponte Vecchio to notice that someone was standing in front of me.

"Excuse me, may I sit here?" He gestured at the empty third cushion.

I shrugged my shoulders in response. Rude, but I couldn't help myself. Although he was really cute, I knew that having a relationship with a boy was virtually impossible if I couldn't talk to him, so what was the point of attempting some half-assed form of communication, or even showing common courtesy? Along with all my other therapies, I was probably a candidate for some anger management classes. Besides, wherever he sat, I could enjoy the view, and since looking at a guy was the most action I could hope for, I found myself unable to make the effort to be nice, especially when there was no way he would reciprocate my admiration. Better to reject than be rejected. Better to be the sniper than the victim.

He had the body of a runner. His hair was long, longer than most guys at my school wore it, and I had a sudden urge to run my fingers through it. And he had this smile, like he knew a secret and desperately wanted to tell. Although I tried not to look interested, I stole quick glances as he sprawled at the opposite end of the couch, slouching low with his legs stretched out far enough to trip anyone who walked by.

Ballsy, making yourself so comfortable on my couch. Everyone here knows this is my corner. It's not like there aren't other pieces of furniture to sit on, I thought. What I really wanted to do was crawl into his lap and play with his messy ringlets, but that would only prove how out of touch with reality I was. Everyone knows you don't climb all over people you don't know, unless you're crazy.

Without a word, he stood and relocated to an enormous chair directly across from my couch. He dropped his backpack, causing the ancient, bespectacled librarian to turn around and frown in his general direction, and made himself comfortable, his legs draped over one arm of the overstuffed chair, not even glancing in my direction. Was the expression on my face that obvious? Was my shrug that offensive? Did I smell funny? Twisting my head a little to the side, as if I'd heard a noise and was turning to see where it came from, I sniffed at myself. Though I'd thought I wanted him to move, now that he had, I still wasn't happy. Peeking over the top of my huge book, I could see that he was smiling into the pages of his paperback copy of Sartre's *No Exit*, which, although a compelling story, had never struck me as particularly funny. There was something about this guy. I was hooked, but I knew it was a dead-end street, so I returned to my imaginary Italy vacation.

Unable to ignore the unnaturally cheerful stranger across from me, I finally gave up on Florence and gathered my things. In my hurry to escape, I let the enormous book on Italian architecture slip out of my hands. The thud caused everyone in the library to look up, except him. Wishing I could somehow melt into the floorboards, I stood there staring at my feet. He just kept grinning into his book, as if he were making a conspicuous effort to ignore me. I needed to go home, where no one could look at me or sit next to me or smile at me. So much for the library as sanctuary.

"Shhhhh," hissed the librarian.

It was already dark at five. Shivering in the biting January wind as I trudged down the steps, I realized I had stupidly left my coat on the back of the couch. How could a guy who barely looked at me throw me so far off balance? My punishment would be to walk home coatless. I was too embarrassed to go back for it—he might think I'd left it behind on purpose, like a dropped handkerchief in a nineteenth-century novel, a second chance to strike up an acquaintance. That wasn't going to happen. Instead, I took a shortcut through the park. The full moon reflecting off the snow made the ground glow, and the trees cast long shadows. A little bit spooky, but I was so busy dissecting my many inadequacies, I didn't take much notice. Besides, I wasn't afraid of the dark. There were so many other things to fear.

"Hey, Sasha, where are you headed?" Footsteps, more than one set, somewhere behind me.

Startled, I didn't turn around, just picked up my pace a little bit, although the path was icy and I was afraid I might slip if I started to run. The voice was familiar, just a boy from school, nothing to worry about. Seconds later, they were behind me, and then on all sides of me.

"What's the rush? You got someplace to go?"

The speaker was Jed/Jeff, my detention buddy, and the others looked familiar, although they were pretty much clones of each other with their nearly shaved heads and muscles bulging through their sweatshirts: Shoreland High School varsity football's finest. Changing directions, I continued to ignore them, but they surrounded me. Paul, my other detention playmate, scooped me up in his arms and carried me up the steps of the park's gazebo about twenty feet off the path. In the spring and summer, the gazebo was a popular gathering place for concerts, but it was deserted the rest of the year, and on a frigid winter evening it looked like an igloo. He put me down on the ice-cold concrete slab, surprisingly gently, and I scrambled to get to my feet. Not so gently he pushed me down on my back and straddled me, pinning my arms to the ground.

This was bad. First, there were four of them and only one of me. Even one-on-one, I wouldn't have stood a chance—I weighed half of what one of them weighed. Second, no one knew where I was or was waiting for me at the house. It would be hours before Charlotte and Stuart got home from work and realized I was missing. Finally, and worst of all, I lacked the ability to let anyone know I was in danger. No matter how hard I tried to scream, I remained dumb. Not even the most basic survival instinct could trigger my voice box. I was completely and utterly useless.

"Hurry up. I have to get home. My mom wants me to babysit my little sister tonight."

One of them looked at his watch. How ironic that he was in a rush to finish assaulting one girl so he could go home to look after another. The sound of a zipper being pulled down echoed in my ears.

"I'm not going to rush this, dude. You may like it fast, but I want to take it nice and slow."

"So, Sasha, this your first time? I'm guessing yes, looking at you. Don't be scared. Which one of us do you want to pop your cherry?" This from Paul as he sat on my chest.

"She doesn't talk, remember, so there's no way she's ever done it. I've never even seen her with a guy. But now that I think about it, she would be the perfect girlfriend—a rockin' little body and no whiny voice to ruin it. You want to be my girlfriend, Sasha? I bet I could make you scream." The one who had been standing out of my field of vision bent over my face, making kissing noises and licking his lips.

"You ever seen a cock up close? You ever touched one?"

"Stop fucking around, dickhead. I don't have all night, so if you're not going to get on with it, get the fuck out of the way, so I can get mine."

"Yeah, hurry up."

"Shouldn't we use something?"

"A condom? What the fuck for? You afraid you're going to catch something?"

"No, you asswipe. Cum is full of DNA. If she tells, we're fucked, and not in a good way."

"Ohhhh." I knew for a fact that Paul had flunked biology *and* chemistry. He put one finger under my chin and tilted my head back so I had to look at him. "You'd better not tell anyone, or else." If I hadn't been so scared, it would have been funny. Or else what? How could it possibly get any worse?

I struggled to free myself from under the two-hundred-pound gorilla. When he let go of my arms, I scratched at his face and tried to roll him off me, but it was like trying to move from under a pile of sandbags.

"Cool it, bitch. I think you drew blood with those claws of yours. Okay, dudes, I'm going first. I'm tired of holding her down."

He was like a cat playing with a mouse he had just caught, teasing me, wearing me out before he devoured me. With one quick motion he pulled my sweatshirt and T-shirt over my head. The frozen cement burned the bare skin on my back. Fumbling with the clasp on my bra, he gave up and tore the flimsy fabric, flinging the lacy bits to one side.

I closed my eyes, not wanting to look at them looking at me. Now was the time to go to my happy place, if I had one, which I realized I didn't. Exhausted from my escape attempts, which only seemed to amuse them, I decided to play possum. Maybe if I stopped playing their game, they would lose interest. It was my only hope. Jules carried pepper spray wherever she went, just in case. Why didn't I plan ahead like that? Fuck. How bad was it going to hurt, and how was I going to get home once they were finished? What if I got pregnant, or caught some horrible disease? What if they really meant that thing about "or else"?

Thirty minutes earlier I had been curled up on my library couch fantasizing about Italy, admiring a hot guy, and now I was about to lose my v-card to four Neanderthals posing as high school football players. Clearly, I was cursed. If only I had stayed in the library, I would be warm and safe and fully clothed. If I survived this, and part of me didn't want to, I would never let myself feel this vulnerable ever again.

"Nice tits." Jed/Jeff bent down and ran his hand across my chest, causing me to shiver, out of both cold and horror. No one had ever touched me there before.

"Look at her—she likes it."

"You moron, she's just cold."

Where was that superhuman strength people said they experienced when faced with a life-or-death situation? One person could lift a two-ton car, and I couldn't move a two-hundred-pound running back so much as an inch. I was no longer deliberately playing possum; I was completely paralyzed with fear.

"Hey, Sasha, what's the matter? No more struggle? It's more fun if you fight a little."

From the shadows came a new voice. "You wanna fight a little? *I'll* fight with you."

My eyes flew open. Springing from behind a bush and up the steps in one fluid motion, *he* stood with his backpack on one shoulder and a pair of nunchucks, chain rattling, dangling from his right hand. He was no longer wearing that secret smile, and his dark curls were tucked under a ski cap, but there was no mistaking it: my rescuer was the boy from the library. If he'd been wearing tights and a matching cape, I couldn't have been more surprised.

Paul looked slightly annoyed at the interruption, but he didn't move from on top of me. "Look, bro. There are four of us and only one of you, so I suggest you put away your little toy and keep walking, unless you want us to beat the shit out of you."

"As impressed as I am by your math skills, I'm not going anywhere. Let Sasha go . . . or else."

How did he know my name? Naked from the waist up, five boys looking at me, I was totally humiliated as well as terrified. Nunchuck Boy meant well, but, although he was as tall, he was half the width of one of the football players. He didn't stand a chance. Jed/Jeff lunged, but he was faster, the satisfying thwack of wood on bone and the clank of the chain echoing in the empty park, followed by a yelp of pain. Perhaps my fate wasn't sealed.

"Shit, man. That fucking hurts. Okay, I get it, you're a fucking karate master."

"But it's still one on four, dude," said one of the other geniuses.

"Damn straight," Jeff/Jed agreed. "We could still take you, even with your funky Jap sticks, but maybe you want to join us?"

His answer was another flick of his wrist. The chain seemed to move in slow motion, striking Paul in the ribs. Falling to the side, Paul gasped in pain.

"You don't hear so well. I told you to move so she can get up." My hero tossed his jacket at me. "Here, Sasha." I jumped to my feet and covered myself.

"I'm sure Sasha wouldn't mind one more. You can even have the honor of being her first, if you want. She's fresh meat." Jed/Jeff rubbed his head and smiled, still believing he and his friends had the upper hand.

"If I want to fool around with a girl, I don't need four other guys to hold her down. Do you assholes actually enjoy a good skull fracture? Don't you get enough of those on the field? No? Works for me . . ." Nunchuck Boy snapped his sticks to drive home his point.

My four attackers scrambled to the edge of the gazebo, backing down the steps, laughing nervously and holding up their hands to show they weren't going to make any more trouble. "Have it your way, you crazy fuck. You want to go Bruce Lee for robot chick, have her. She's frigid, anyway." They took off across the park, leaving us alone in the gazebo.

When we were alone, my knees gave way, and I fell to the ground. The whole world was spinning. He knelt beside me, careful not to lay a finger on me.

"Sasha, are you okay?"

I nodded, reaching for my clothes as he spoke, but my hands wouldn't stop shaking and I couldn't do it by myself. "Do you want me to help you?" he asked.

Again I nodded. Like a small child, I sat up, lifting my arms over my head as he dressed me, discreetly looking away as he pulled my shirt down over my chest.

"Don't worry. I've got you. My name is Ben, Ben Fisher."

My breath came in short gasps. Of all the times not to be able to talk. My mind was racing, filled with gratitude and questions and the sensation of his hands on my bare skin. *If you hadn't come along when you did, I don't want to think about what would have happened. But how do you know my name?* Where was my backpack? I needed a pen and paper, my talk box. I desperately needed to make him understand me.

"After you left the library I asked the old lady at the front desk about you. I feel kind of responsible for this mess—you only left because of me."

What are you saying? How do you know that? Who did you say you were? My heartbeat began to slow as my body warmed and I fully recognized that I was safe. Where was my Hawkie Talkie?

"Not that you should be walking home alone in the dark anyway, especially without a coat, and when you have such a rockin' little body, to quote a fool. Very tempting to those with not much self-control." This Ben person took my jacket out of his backpack and wrapped it around me. "Glad I noticed that you forgot your coat."

How do you know they said that to me? Were you watching from the bushes or something?

"No," he said. "I just got here."

We had been having a perfectly normal conversation, and I suddenly realized that even though I had said nothing out loud, this strange, brave boy had heard every word I thought. Had I hit my head on the cement? Was I unconscious? Was I hallucinating? *You know what I'm thinking.* This was a statement, not a question.

"Yes, I can read your mind." He said this simply, matter-of-factly, as if he were admitting to being able to play the guitar or drive a stick shift.

That's not even funny. There's no such thing. It was impossible to know what someone else was thinking. Maybe he was just incredibly observant and was reading my body language. *What's the trick?*

"As expressive as your body language was at the library when you shrugged your shoulders at me, I could hear what you were thinking."

What exactly do you mean, you can hear what I'm thinking?

"I can hear your thoughts, as if you're talking to me out loud."

All my thoughts?

"Every last one."

So that was why he was smiling into the book at the library. He knew all my dirty little secrets. Better not to go there right now.

Then you knew what was happening, and that's why you came after me?

It seemed perfectly natural, and yet it was otherworldly, having someone answer my thoughts as if I had spoken them aloud. For the first time in four years I could communicate without a pen or a computer. It was a miracle.

"I never thought you'd get in trouble on the way home. I just wanted to return your coat." I held up both palms to ask, what next? "Then I heard what you were thinking. You were terrified. I got closer, and then I could hear what *they* were thinking."

You got to me just in time. Another minute and . . . I couldn't even continue. I had been seconds away from catastrophe.

"Yes, good thing I distracted you."

What are you talking about?

"That's why you forgot your coat, isn't it?" He arched one eyebrow. My rescuer was flirting with me, at a time like this? More than a little inappropriate, but he *was* awfully good-looking. Or was he just being nice? It wasn't like I had any experience talking to boys. I would have to check with Jules.

I don't remember. Lying was clearly a waste of time, but I couldn't help it.

"If they had done more than tear off your shirt, I would've killed them." Suddenly he was being serious again. Was this guy crazy?

You could kill them? No offense, but you're kind of skinny. What are you, a superhero? Did you get bitten by a radioactive spider or something?

Ben laughed. "No, just a fourth-degree black belt. Lucky I have class tonight." He waved his nunchucks in the air. "When that creep bent over and touched you, I wanted to rip his hands off his arms. Who were those assholes, anyway?"

He reached behind me where my tattered bra lay in a crumpled ball, wordlessly picking it up and putting it in his pocket.

Thank you. I don't ever want to see that again. I shook my head, as if to erase the memory of having it torn off, feeling a strange hand grazing my breasts. *They're football players—Jeff or maybe Jed Colter, and Tom somebody, Paul Welch, and I'm not sure about the other one, Phillip Johnson, maybe. At school they're always together, and they all look alike, so I'm not even sure which one is which. Obviously not friends of mine.*

"Do you want to go to the police station right away, or do you want me to take you home first?"

I just want to go home. I'm not going to the police.

I wasn't sure about much, but I was sure about that. I felt ashamed, and somehow responsible for what had happened to me.

"Don't you understand? Are you in shock or something? Those dirtbags would have raped you if I hadn't shown up. They can't get away with that." Ben was right next to me, but he was shouting.

My rescuer was looking at me like I was insane. But actually, he looked pretty crazy, too—fists clenched, eyes wide. He was definitely more upset than I was at this point.

They could be charged with attempted rape, assault and battery, false imprisonment, maybe even kidnapping, since they carried me into the gazebo from the path. I rubbed the back of my head where it had hit the concrete. There was a big bump.

"What are you, a lawyer posing as a high school student?" He looked at me quizzically.

No, my aunt and uncle are both lawyers, so I guess I've picked up a few things. But if we go to the police, those creeps might turn around and sue you for assault, even if you were only defending me.

"I'm not worried about that." This guy was awfully sure of himself.

And all the attention—I'm enough of a mutant in school already. You don't know me yet, but you'll see.

"You don't look like a mutant. Are you some kind of alien?" he asked. That maddening smile was back. Was this more of that flirting thing?

Really, could we just forget about this whole nightmare? And I promise to be more careful in the future. Besides, maybe they weren't actually going to do anything. I managed a weak smile, wanting to show that it wasn't as bad as it probably looked.

"Well, they sure looked like they were about to do something terrible, and you don't even want to know what they were thinking." He shuddered and looked away for a second. "But whatever you decide. No pressure."

That's what I decide.

"You shouldn't let those assholes go free just because you think it'll up your freak quotient. How can anyone think you're strange just because you've experienced an unimaginable tragedy?"

His words were so heartfelt I wanted to cry. I had run through everyone's compassion a long time ago.

So the nosy Mrs. Olsen told you about me and my issues.

Mrs. Olsen, who had probably started working as a librarian when books were printed on animal skins, was both the custodian and receptacle of vast amounts of information in this small town, where everybody knew everybody. If you had any juicy secrets, Shoreland was probably not the best place to live.

"Yes, she told me about the accident. You've been through so much. I'm sorry about your family . . . and your voice," he said softly.

She's a little too chatty, the old bag.

In truth, I was glad Mrs. Olsen had spilled my guts for me. Retelling my tale to strangers was too painful, and therefore I avoided new people. But she had done my dirty work for me, and now this remarkable boy was leaning over me, his forehead wrinkled with concern about my well-being, having tactfully disposed of my bra and wrapped my coat tenderly around my quivering shoulders. She had done me a huge favor.

I just want to pretend it never happened, and from now on, I won't be so naive. Girls shouldn't walk alone through dark parks. It's not rocket science. Although I knew it wasn't my fault, I was still desperately embarrassed by my perennial helplessness.

"You should be able to walk wherever you want whenever you want, especially in a little town like this. Maybe I should teach you some self-defense moves." Ben put away his nunchucks, picked up my backpack, and helped me to my feet. "Do you think you're steady enough to walk home?"

I nodded again. I desperately wanted to talk, even though for the first time in a long time, it wasn't necessary.

So, can you read everybody's mind, or just some people's?

This was an extraordinary development. If there was such a thing as mind readers, what other supernatural fantasies could turn out to be real? Ghosts? Vampires? Time travel?

"Pretty much everybody's, although some more easily than others. I'm kind of like a radio, and the people around me are different stations, and some people have stronger signals than others. For some reason, your signal is really intense. I could hear you before I even saw you for the first time."

Were you born like that?

"I think so. When I was really little, I thought everybody heard what I was hearing. But when I was three, I heard my mother thinking about where she'd hidden the Oreos that she didn't want me to eat. I waited until she left the kitchen and then I ate the whole package."

That's handy.

"That's when I first realized I was different."

I wish I knew what everybody was thinking.

"It's not that great. People are mean, and most of the time, it's better not to know."

Really? But information is power, isn't it?

"Not always. When I was fourteen, I went to a girl's birthday party, a girl I kind of liked, and I thought she liked me. But I could hear her thinking that my nose looked like an eagle's beak and that my legs were hairy toothpicks."

That's terrible. He looked pretty good to me. I didn't mind his nose. It made him special, like the crack in the Liberty Bell.

"It was. I begged my parents for a nose job, but they said no, and I was afraid to talk to girls for almost a year. But I got over it, and the upside is I don't have to waste my time chasing after girls who aren't interested."

That's one way to look at it. Could he tell that *I* was interested? *Can your parents read minds?*

"Nope, just me. But my mother is definitely an unusual person. There's something mystical about her. You'll see when you meet her," he said, as if taking me home to his mother were the logical next step.

I didn't know what to say. Everything this very strange stranger had just told me was impossible, and yet I believed him without reservation. Despite his outlandish mind powers and his crazy martial arts skills, he felt familiar to me. On some level I didn't understand, I already knew him.

It must be really noisy, hearing everyone talking in your head all the time.

"It can be, but I've trained myself to tune it out when I want, so it's like low static most of the time. Sort of like having a wave machine inside my head. I don't know any different, so it doesn't bother me, unless I really need to concentrate, which isn't that often."

Then what do you do? I wanted to know everything about this incredible person.

"If I listen to music really loud, it drowns out most of the voices."

We were walking along like two perfectly normal people having a chat, and it was wonderful. I had completely forgotten the simple pleasure of conversation, learning about someone new, sharing my thoughts and opinions without the help of Stephen Hawking's robot voice. After four years of silence, I had stopped thinking about what I had been missing, and now it all came rushing back. Five blocks had never gone so quickly—we were standing at the end of my driveway, looking up at the stone and glass monolith that was Charlotte and Stuart's house. Even though my toes were numb and a light snow had begun to fall, I wanted to keep walking forever so I wouldn't have to say goodbye.

"Wow, that's where you live?"

Ben stood looking up at what Stuart described as a late twentieth-century homage to Frank Lloyd Wright. With its cantilevered wings, it looked as if pieces of the house were somehow floating in air. The house was at once incredibly modern but also very natural, almost part of the woods in which it sat.

It was an extraordinary building, unusual for Shoreland, which was full of old colonials and Victorians dripping with ginger-bread woodwork.

It's okay. It's kind of cold inside. Impersonal. You know what I mean? Come in with me. I'll show you. It's beautiful, but I like old things better—they're cozier.

Ben stood patiently as I dug for my keys at the bottom of my backpack, which he continued to hold. Perhaps I had finally met what Charlotte called the rarest of breeds, a true gentleman. It was like seeing a unicorn. There had to be something wrong with him. It was only a matter of time until I discovered his fatal flaw.

We entered through the front door that looked like a giant tree trunk. The interior was no less dramatic than the exterior, with soaring ceilings and walls of glass facing the backyard, which was really just a giant stone patio surrounded by tow-ering oak trees. Pale maple floors and sparsely placed leather and wood furniture made it look a little like someone had stolen half the contents. To me it was a lonely place, even when there were people in it. An enormous circular fireplace made of copper in the center of the living room was the focal point. I flipped a switch on the wall and the fire burst to life, instantly warming the room.

"Cool. Spontaneous combustion. This place is like some-thing out of a magazine."

We wandered around the first floor, Ben gaping up at the skylights and acres of white walls, punctuated by the occasional abstract painting.

This is home. But you see what I mean. It's not too homey. Taking off my coat, I went into the open kitchen and put the teakettle on the stove. *I'm still freezing. Do you want something hot to drink?*

Ben looked at his watch. "I have to go soon, but I can stay for a few minutes. Tea would be good."

He leaned against the kitchen counter, watching me measure out the tea, fill a pitcher with milk. We stood on opposite sides of the vast granite island, waiting for the water to boil. I crossed my arms protectively over my chest. Now that I was safely back home, and I had nearly accepted Ben's psychic ability, my mind was free to focus on my embarrassment. My ears felt hot, and my cheeks burned. Was there any possibility that this person had X-ray vision as well as super mind powers? At this point, I was ready to believe anything.

"No, I can't see through your clothes, silly. Who do you think I am, Superman?"

If you can see into my mind, I don't think it's much of a stretch to imagine you seeing through my clothes. And you did see me. I hugged my body even tighter. *I don't even know you.*

No one except the doctor had seen that much of me, and four years of being stranded on the social equivalent of a desert island had made me unnaturally shy.

"Don't be ridiculous. You have no reason to be embarrassed. It was only for a second, but yes, I did look at you, and you're beautiful." He smiled, showing even white teeth.

Beautiful was not an adjective usually associated with me, and having no idea how to accept a compliment, I stared at the steam rising out of the kettle.

"I didn't think you could get any redder, but you just did. Sorry. I'm a seventeen-year-old guy, and it's genetically impossible for me to look away from a half-naked girl. It's a fatal flaw, but I hope you can forgive me. Maybe if I take off my shirt for you, we can call it even."

Before I could think of a response, Ben removed his shirt, and his torso was just as I had imagined, looking like the giant

black-and-white photographs at the front of the Abercrombie
& Fitch store. An unfamiliar, but not unpleasant, ache radi-
ated in the pit of my stomach. I tried to suppress the thought
that I wanted to run my hands across his smooth chest. As
convenient as this ESP thing was, it was impossible to filter my
thoughts, and I couldn't hide these sudden and inappropriate
impulses. I'm sure he heard the whole thing, because that little
smile was back.

You can get dressed now. I suppose we're even.

Was he flirting with me again? My experience with the
male gender was virtually nonexistent. I had no brothers, my
father had been gone for four years, and Stuart was a rag-
ing metrosexual, whose hobbies ran to artisan bread baking
and German opera. He never missed Wagner's Ring Cycle at
the Met, all fourteen and a half hours of it. Until I opened
Jules's birthday gift, what little I knew of men had come from
her dating stories and the sex column in *Cosmopolitan* that I
sometimes read at the drugstore, an incomplete and inaccu-
rate education at best. Desperately in need of a crash course
in how to deal with the opposite sex, I just stared at Ben's
chest, trying to look as if his wasn't the first naked male torso
I had ever seen close up that wasn't made of marble. An image
of him in nothing but a fig leaf floated through my brain.
Something had clicked on inside me, and I wasn't sure what
to do with it.

My embarrassment was obvious, even to someone who
couldn't read minds, and I was grateful when Ben put his shirt
back on. "It's an incredible house, and I bet the views from all
these windows must be something, especially when it's snowing really hard. And it's kind of nice to live without too much
stuff distracting you. Very Zen."

My aunt and uncle like everything clean and simple. Not that it matters. They're hardly ever around anyway. All they do is work. Now I had to smile. *Thank you for rescuing me—this time from myself.*

Trying to look busy, trying to forget the image of Ben's ripped abs etched on my optic nerves, I took out mugs, spoons, and the sugar bowl. I fiddled with a package of shortbread cookies, carefully arranging them on a small glass plate, anything not to meet Ben's eyes.

"Is that your family?" Ben pointed at a framed photograph on the wall.

That was our Christmas card picture from the year they died. I liked knowing it was there, but I never looked at it.

"You look like your sister."

Liz was much prettier.

"That's not true. She was older?"

Two years. I didn't talk about my family with anyone, not even with Charlotte and Stuart. Sometimes I would catch Charlotte staring at that picture, or one of the other fifty or so she had placed around the house, but she would just smile sadly and shake her head. What was there to say?

Thoughtfully trying to change the subject, Ben said, "This is totally different from our house. We're renting an old salt-box colonial down by the beach. Whoever owned it before restored it perfectly. It's like stepping into a time warp. You'll have to come see it. There's something about you that's very old-fashioned. You would fit perfectly in that house."

My blood ran cold and I sank to the kitchen floor, fighting the blackness that was creeping into my field of vision.

"What's the matter? Did those creeps hurt you before I got there?" Ben sat down next to me and pulled me close to him, rocking me back and forth. "Maybe I should take you to the hospital. Is there a car in the garage we can use? Or should I call 911?"

I'm okay . . . really, I am. Taking slow, deep breaths, I concentrated on remaining conscious.

"Are you sure? You just went white as a ghost. What happened?" For all his mind powers, Ben was flummoxed.

7 Seashell Lane. 7 Seashell Lane. 7 Seashell Lane. My mind was totally blank, except for that.

"What? That's right. So you know it. It's got one of those landmark plaques on the front. My mom said it's one of the oldest houses in town." As he spoke, Ben gently rubbed my back, still believing, in spite of his ESP, that my fainting spell was a delayed reaction to getting jumped in the park.

I know which house it is, because it's my house. It's the house I grew up in. After my family died, I never went home again. When I got out of the hospital, I came straight here to live with my aunt and uncle.

"My mother said the house had a story, but she didn't want to talk about it, and I thought she meant something that happened a hundred years ago. Like Lizzie Borden and her ax."

I never even thought about what happened to it, not until this moment, never wanted to know, and Charlotte never told me. Now you're living in my house?

How many other memories had I barricaded up on the top shelf of the deep, dark closet of my mind? What a weird, random thing to meet the person who had moved into my old house, and under such insane circumstances. And why had I suppressed all the memories of the place I had lived in my entire life?

How long have you been living there?

"We moved in right before Christmas. Before that we were living in Italy. My parents were visiting professors at the

University of Florence last year, and we stayed on a few extra months. My father was researching a book, and when he finished we came back to the States."

How did you end up here, in this dinky little town, and in my house?

"We were going to get a place in the City, but my mom wanted a garden, and she saw some article in a magazine about the Shoreland Garden Club. And your house has a beautiful yard. It's overgrown, but my mom said all it needed was a little attention."

Unbelievable.

The dizziness had subsided, and my breathing returned to normal. A house was just a building. My home was with Charlotte and Stuart. No reason to flip out.

"Yeah, it's a weird coincidence. Maybe fate intended for us to meet. That's the only explanation I can think of," Ben said, tilting his head and looking directly into my eyes.

I felt as if he were staring straight into my soul. My heart skipped a beat, but I decided not to comment on his theory. Talking to boys was like learning a foreign language. Did that mean he was glad we had met? Did he like me, the way that boys like girls—an experience I didn't think I'd ever have—or did he suffer from white knight syndrome and was just happy to stumble upon someone in dire need of rescuing? Not knowing what to say about that, I just kept nattering on about the house.

I wonder what it looks like now. Where's all the furniture?

Had anyone lived there the last four years before Ben moved in? Now I was excited, but afraid as well. Although I wasn't in great shape, at least I was functioning, and I worried that digging up my emotional backyard might loosen my tenuous grip on my semi-normal life.

"All our stuff is in storage until my folks decide where to settle, so we rented it furnished, dishes and everything." Ben paused.

So he was eating off my plates, probably sleeping in my bed, a bed I hadn't even remembered I owned.

"I'm sorry—those are your things. I feel terrible, springing this on you, especially after what just happened in the park."

It's okay. And strangely, it was.

On one level, I was incredibly curious to go back home, but I worried that seeing the last place my family had lived, the last place we were together, safe and happy, would destroy any chance I had at recovering my voice. If I crossed the literal threshold into my old life, I feared I would end up rocking back and forth in the corner of some asylum, totally withdrawn from the world, my sanity irretrievable. Dr. O'Rourke was considered the best in the business, but she was no miracle worker, and if she hadn't been able to help me regain my voice thus far, I held out little hope that she could rescue me from the abyss I would fall into if I couldn't handle a journey into my forgotten past.

We sat on barstools at the kitchen counter, surprisingly at ease with each other considering the unusual circumstances of our introduction, chatting in our unorthodox way, Ben's lone voice resonating in the cavernous great room. Our conversation was spontaneous and effortless. The only downside, and it was a big one, was that Ben was picking up on *all* my thoughts, even the ones I wasn't consciously sending in his direction. No matter how hard I tried to keep those thoughts at bay, bury them deep in my frontal lobe, he must have been well aware of my attraction—not just to his mesmerizing smile and sculpted abs, but also to his sweetness.

He looked at his watch. "I'm sorry, but I really have to go. Thanks for the tea."

You're welcome. Thanks for defending my virtue.

What does one say to the person you've just met who saved you from a gang assault? A mere thank you seemed pitifully inadequate, but offering to be his slave for life would probably be a little over the top.

"My pleasure." Ben bowed chivalrously. "Seriously, are you sure you're okay to be alone? When are your aunt and uncle coming home?"

Soon. I'm fine.

I didn't want him to leave me, but he must know that, and he had to go, or wanted to go, anyway. Begging him to stay with me until . . . forever . . . sounded stalkerish, even to my inexperienced, desperate ears.

"I'll see you tomorrow at school. Um, I'm sorry we had to meet the way we did, but I'm glad we met. You know what I mean?"

He put his mug in the sink—gorgeous, brave, gentle, *and* tidy. Where was his halo?

I'm glad, too.

What I had thought was going to be the second worst night of my life had done a total one-eighty. Was this more than just a Good Samaritan following through on his good deed? Could my chronic bad luck finally be turning?

"And I'm sorry for blurting out the house thing like that. I had no idea." His expression was truly remorseful. "You've had quite an evening."

It's fine. You couldn't know. I didn't even know.

He hugged me briefly, and I leaned against him for a few seconds, absorbing his warmth, savoring his clean, male smell—all shaving cream and Irish Spring. I could've stayed like that for a month. Standing in the doorway, I watched him walk away, turning to wave before he disappeared behind a hedge. He was gone, and I was all alone again.

My near miss in the gazebo had left me feeling dirtier than I'd ever felt. I turned on the shower as hot as it would go and slowly undressed in the steamy bathroom, examining my naked reflection in the full-length mirror on the back of the door. Was I pretty? Was that why they came after me? Or was it just because I was so vulnerable? The latter, for sure. Tears flooded my eyes and blurred my vision as my body disappeared in the film of steam frosting the glass. Twenty minutes and a thousand gallons of scalding water later, I emerged, my skin the color of a freshly cooked lobster, and wrapped myself in a soft white towel. If nothing else, I felt like I had removed the top layer of skin and along with it any traces of those unwanted hands on my body. Unfortunately, I had also washed away all traces of Ben, and that made me sad. I wondered if he could read my thoughts all the way from Seashell Lane. I hoped so.

The front door slammed and I heard two sets of footsteps. "Sasha, we're home," called Charlotte.

As I stepped out of the bathroom in a cloud of steam, Charlotte walked into the bedroom.

"Sash, you don't need to use up every drop of hot water when you take a shower. Besides, you're going to burn yourself one of these days." She gave me a peck on the cheek. "We brought home Chinese food, so hurry up and get dressed before it gets cold."

Despite the enormous kitchen with miles of countertop, a commercial stove, and two huge ovens, our kitchen saw very little action beyond boiling water and the occasional bread-baking marathon. Charlotte and Stuart worked insane hours in New York, and a home-cooked meal was not high on their list of priorities. At seventeen, I was old enough to pick up the slack and probably should have been shopping and cooking for the family, but even going to the grocery store was traumatic for me. I was so afraid that someone would ask me a question and I wouldn't be able to answer without my machine, and then I would have to explain my mental illness, that I avoided most situations that required me to interact with strangers. Hurting but true. Consequently, we had become connoisseurs of takeout, and dinner from You Can't Fu Me was a regular fixture in our fast food rotation.

Stuart was at the kitchen sink, washing up for dinner—he could be a little OCD. Drying his hands carefully on a white linen towel, he looked less like someone preparing to eat dinner and more like a surgeon scrubbing up for an operation. He blew me a kiss.

"Hey, Sweets. What's up? How's Jules?"

Jules? We hadn't run into each other at school, as we only had a couple of classes together, and they didn't meet every day. I shrugged my shoulders. At home, I often resorted to exaggerated body movements to communicate. I had raised shoulder shrugging and eye rolling to a high art, and my aunt and uncle had become masters at interpreting the nuances of my various gestures.

"Wasn't she here this afternoon?" He gestured to the pair of mugs in the sink.

Charades were no longer going to work, so I grabbed my Hawkie Talkie and briefly described meeting Ben in the library and how he had walked me home, leaving out all the juicy, embarrassing, illegal bits.

Charlotte pounced. "You met a boy? Is he cute? He walked you home?"

I nodded in answer to each question.

"I knew it. It was just a matter of time. You see, I was right. This is going to be your year. Everything's going to change for you," Charlotte said, smiling broadly and giving me a hug. I hadn't realized that in her mind a boy was the cure for all that ailed me, or that she was clueless enough to believe that thinking about something could make it happen.

"HE LIVES AT 7 SEASHELL LANE."

Charlotte turned the color of the cardboard Chinese take-out containers. "The boy you met is named Fisher?"

More nodding. "WHY DIDN'T YOU TELL ME?"

As Charlotte stuttered, trying to find the right words, Stuart cut in. "Sasha, we spoke to Dr. O'Rourke at length about this, and she felt very strongly that if you didn't bring it up, we shouldn't go there. Charlotte and I weren't sure that was the right thing, but Dr. O.'s the professional, and when you never talked about your old house or anything in it, we figured she was right. According to her, your failure to recall anything meant that your mind couldn't handle it, and we didn't want to take a stand against your doctor and test that theory."

"I DON'T KNOW WHAT TO THINK."

It was like I'd just found a piece of a jigsaw puzzle that had been lost between the sofa cushions for four years. Shouldn't I be more worked up about this development? Shouldn't I be running over to Seashell Lane, looking for some clues to bring my foggy memory into focus? But instead of wanting to see my old bedroom again, I was way more interested in seeing Ben.

Alone in my bedroom I texted Jules.

I met a boy at the library today.
Cute?
Majorly.
Name?
Ben Fisher.

I know him. In my calc class. Total hottie, looks like one of those Roman statues you're always mooning over in your art books.

He kind of rescued me.

What???? she texted back. I could almost hear her yelling.

I'll e-mail you. Too long for text.

I laid out the whole sordid tale, leaving out the mind-reading bit. At some point I would tell her, but that was an in-person conversation.

Sasha, you have to go to the police!! How can you not tell Charlotte and Stuart? Ben's right. They would've raped you if he hadn't shown up. You can't let them get away with that. What if they come after you again? What if they attack someone else? You would feel responsible, wouldn't you?

Probably pretty selfish not to think of it the way Jules did, but I was practically a professional victim, and I didn't need everyone in the world to know that it had happened again.

I can't. It was the most embarrassing thing that's ever happened to me. I was half-naked and totally helpless. If I tell, I'll have to keep thinking about it. I just want to forget about it. Promise me you won't say a word to anyone, no matter what.

I promise. I think you're crazy, but I promise.

Thanks, Jules. I'll be fine. I just need to be more careful about wandering around in the dark.

Don't you dare blame yourself for what happened, Sasha. If you do, then I'll definitely tell. You're fragile enough as it is—more guilt isn't what you need.

Fine. No guilt.

So, is he nice?

Beyond sweet. Told me I'm beautiful. I blushed thinking about the naked part.

:) You are. So did he ask you out? Now Jules was sounding like Charlotte.

No. You think he might? It would have been weird if he had, after what happened.

Boys don't talk about looks unless they mean it. He must like you, or at least your boobs.

Funny. Cross your fingers for me.

My whole body's crossed.

Thank goodness you gave me that book. I might actually need it!

Trust me, Sash, you will.

Ben's appearance in my life was like a sudden onset of turbulence, and all my baggage was spilling out of my overhead compartments, no matter how hard I tried to slam them shut. The more I tried to shove my private thoughts to the back of my mind, where I hoped they might be hidden from his telepathic brain, the more intrusive those thoughts became, probably reaching Ben's supernatural ears as if I were shouting at him. No matter how hard I tried to concentrate on other things, every time I closed my eyes I saw Ben standing in my kitchen without his shirt, smiling that dangerous smile. My hormones, which had apparently been hibernating, had suddenly woken up. And like a bear after a long winter, I was hungry.

I fell asleep wondering who else knew about Ben's special powers. Was I the only person outside his family who knew, or was the inner circle much larger? Why did he tell me? He could have rescued me without disclosing his unusual talent. Maybe he thought I was special in some way, or maybe he thought a mute, social outcast would be the perfect person to keep his secret.

Instead of the usual nightly rerun of my personal catastrophe playing out behind my eyelids, I was bombarded with a spate of new images. Someone kept changing the channels. First I was wandering through an enormous hotel, ankle deep in water, barefoot, looking for a way out. Strange and vaguely disturbing, but a walk in the park compared to my usual nighttime viewing. Then I was in a dark, primeval forest, tree limbs reaching down to grab me, and I was dressed like a Disney princess, a cross between Snow White and Cinderella, meandering in circles, searching for a path to lead me out of the woods. It switched to a school, not mine, but larger, like a college campus, and I was wandering, desperately late for an exam in a class I'd never attended on a subject I knew nothing about.

When I woke up in the morning I wrote down everything I could remember—Dr. O'Rourke said that was key to analyzing one's dreams. She was right. When I looked at my notes, I realized that the common thread was the fact that I was lost. I didn't need Sigmund Freud to help me figure that out. I was lost—now if only I could start dreaming about how to find myself.

Chapter 6

Jules ran up to me as I stood at my locker. "Did you hear what happened?"

As I'd just arrived at school, and any number of things could have happened, I simply shook my head and widened my eyes. Jules leaned over and whispered in my ear. "Those creeps who jumped you in the park, all four of them, are in the hospital."

I tilted my head to the side and made a beckoning motion with my hand. A great opening, but not enough information.

"Apparently someone put something toxic in their jock straps, and their junk swelled up to, like, four times normal size. At the hospital, the doctors thought they might have to amputate, but they're better today, although I heard they won't be able to have sex for a year." By now Jules was laughing so hard I could barely understand what she was saying.

Head-tilting and blinking proving to be insufficient linguistic substitutes, I pulled out my robot ventriloquist machine. "DO THEY KNOW WHAT HAPPENED?"

"Nobody knows. They think it was some kind of prank, but because the locker room guy had already put their stuff through the laundry, the police have nothing to go on. Any evidence there may have been got washed away. It's a total mystery."

"I CAN'T BELIEVE IT."

"No worries about those assholes bothering you any time in the near future. *That's* good news."

I nodded. "KARMA'S A BITCH."

"Definitely." The first bell of the day rang. "I'll see you at lunch. I wonder if your statue boy has heard about this. Pretty funny stuff."

For someone who was so smart—Jules was taking AP calculus and AP French—she wasn't too swift. It hadn't even occurred to her that my savior was apparently also a vigilante. I needed to find him to see if it was really true or just some perfect, heaven-sent coincidence. The latter was unlikely, as no one but Ben and Jules knew about my run-in with the offensive line, and lucky coincidences were not my strong suit.

All day long, the engorgement of the four varsity athletes was the major topic of discussion in the hallways, the cafeteria, and, of course, the locker room. Everyone was grateful that the football season had already ended, so that the misfortune that had befallen these poor boys at least had no impact on Shoreland High's winning season. But lacrosse season was looming, and a prospective repeat state championship was at stake. It was a potentially disastrous situation.

Before the last bell, Principal Carson made an announcement over the intercom. "As I'm sure all of you have heard by now, several of our students were gravely injured as the result of a cruel and shocking practical joke. While I do not believe that any of our fine Shoreland students could be responsible for such a dangerous and devastating assault, I do hope that if anyone has any information that might lead to the apprehension of those responsible, that person would come forward. Someone has committed a heinous act against four innocent young men, and it is my earnest desire that such person or persons be brought to justice. Thank you, and good afternoon."

If I hadn't heard it with my own ears, I wouldn't have believed it. Four innocent young men, my ass. What was it that made some people think that athletic ability was synonymous with an elevated moral character? Even the principal seemed to believe that because these animals helped win football games they were automatically decent, honorable people, in spite of their regular appearances in detention. It made me want to tell everyone what they had tried to do to me the week before, but that could only get Ben and me into trouble. I had to hand it to Nunchuck Boy, he had it all covered—policeman, judge, jury, and executioner—all in one dreamy package . . . assuming that he was the one who had done the deed.

Ben was waiting for me on the front steps of the library after school. "Well? How'd I do?"

I can't believe you did that. What if you got caught?

I was starting to crush on him, and it wouldn't be good if he got arrested less than a week after we met. My make-believe love life would end before it had even begun. Could he have conjugal visits in prison even if we weren't married? Could I really fall in love with a possible lunatic who was into street justice?

He shook his head and laughed. "I know what everybody's thinking, remember? I had to do something. You're the one who refused to go to the police—you left me no choice." He took my backpack, opened the door to the library, and motioned me in ahead of him.

So it's my fault you went all Rambo on those morons? I didn't ask you to retaliate on my behalf.

"Don't feel guilty. It's not your fault."

It sure felt like it was my fault. *I didn't want or expect you to do anything, least of all take the law into your own hands. They almost had to have their things cut off.*

No matter how much I despised them and what they had done to me, I couldn't imagine hurting them back. I didn't have the stomach for revenge, I guess.

"So what if they did. Then they wouldn't be able to put them where they don't belong. Logical consequences. You shouldn't take your hammer out of your toolbox unless someone asks you to nail something. It's simple." For him, the matter had been resolved, justice had been done, and my honor had been salvaged.

Eww. Hanging a picture will never be quite the same for me. Thank you for that. What did you use, anyway? Are they really going to be okay?

What if Ben had caused permanent damage? What if they were sterile? Although they were prime physical specimens, they weren't too bright, so it was unlikely that any great advances in the world of science would be jeopardized if those goons couldn't father children, but still . . .

Ben stroked his chin. "It's an old family recipe—also makes a kickass chili. I think they should make a full recovery, although I've never used the stuff on people before, only ground beef."

You sound completely insane.

"If it makes you feel any better, it's totally organic, with no preservatives."

This was one big joke to him, and for a moment I wasn't sure if he was just trying to protect me, or if I was on the verge of getting involved with a sociopath. No, it couldn't be—he was too kind, and too handsome for that—and my four bullies were only being temporarily sidelined, just long enough to hopefully learn their lesson.

Remind me not to get on your bad side . . . or eat your chili.

We had been sitting on my sofa in the library sunroom for several minutes already when Ben jumped up. "Is it okay that I sit here with you? I don't want to invade your space or anything." He smirked at me.

Anyone who attempts chemical castration on my behalf is welcome to sit wherever he wants.

This couldn't be happening. I was joking around with the guy of my dreams, and I wasn't the least bit nervous. My only concern was that Ben was hearing everything I thought about him, not just what I wanted him to know, but there was no way around that. It was like the bathroom door of my mind was always open.

Chapter 7

A month had passed since Dr. O'Rourke had told me that I was a do-it-yourself project. Now I was checking in. I think she wanted to make sure that I hadn't come unglued, or more unglued, after stopping years of regular therapy. Ironically, for the first time in forever I was feeling slightly more connected, and all because of some stranger who should be wearing a turban and massaging a crystal ball at a carnival sideshow.

"So tell me more about this young man you met. What have you told him about your situation?"

Our hour, or more precisely, our fifty minutes, had only just begun, and Dr. O. was diving right into the deep end of the pool. My smorgasbord of recent issues would more than fill our session. But I had already decided that she didn't need to know everything about Ben. If I told her he was a mind reader, she would never believe me anyway—she would just call my aunt, prescribe some heavy-duty antipsychotics, or maybe even shock therapy, and increase the frequency of my appointments. If I told her that I had met him when he rescued me from a scrimmage with the Shoreland High School offensive line, she would insist on telling the police—assuming she didn't think I was simply delusional, which she might—especially if I paired that story with the mind reader information. And finally, she didn't need to know that Ben had moved into my old house.

She and Charlotte had decided early on that my psyche was too fragile to deal with memories of the old homestead, and I didn't want her to stop me from exploring my past by playing with my old toys or digging through the junk in my old basement, if at some point I decided to do so.

"I MET BEN AT THE LIBRARY. HE JUST MOVED TO TOWN AND SEEMS REALLY NICE. I TOLD HIM ABOUT THE ACCIDENT AND THAT I DON'T REMEMBER MUCH. IT DOESN'T SEEM TO BOTHER HIM THAT I CAN'T COMMUNICATE LIKE NORMAL PEOPLE. IN FACT, HE HANDLES IT SO WELL THAT WE DON'T EVEN NOTICE THAT I CAN'T TALK MOST OF THE TIME." Well, that was absolutely true.

Dr. O. was scribbling furiously in her notebook. Perhaps the good doctor could provide some advice on guys, since thus far she hadn't been useful for much else. Mute and motherless, I was ill equipped to navigate the murky waters of boy-girl relationships, but it had never mattered before Ben plopped down on my sofa. A product of parochial schools and repressive parents, my mom had never gotten around to demystifying the male gender before she died. And while I loved Charlotte to pieces, she was kind of a geek, and I couldn't imagine her instructing me on the finer points of getting to know a boy. Her courtship with Stuart had involved lots of chess matches and museum lectures, and what I needed to know was how to flirt without looking like an idiot and what to do with a guy in the back seat of a car, assuming I was ever lucky enough to land there. Jules's Monday-morning reports of her Saturday night adventures were always interesting, but her suggestions all involved me actually talking to a boy—not helpful. My birthday book was good, but it didn't explain the part that came before actual penetration, the getting-to-know-one-another messing around and the emotional stuff that went with all the groping. Thanks to Dr. Reuben, I was an expert on dozens of exotic sexual positions, but I wanted to know how to have a relationship, how the falling in love thing happened.

"That's excellent news, Sasha. He sounds like a very special young man." She didn't know the half of it. "By turning outward and developing new connections, you can begin to engage in life. Maybe your level of comfort with this boy is indicative of your readiness to make a recovery. What do you think?"

Dr. O. looked at me encouragingly, as if she could will me into mental health with her bright-eyed enthusiasm. Sometimes I wondered about the doctor's qualifications, in spite of her incredible reputation. Really, if it were that simple, I wouldn't still be sitting here, the impression of my ass permanently imprinted in her camelback leather sofa.

"MAYBE. I HOPE SO. CAN I ASK YOU SOMETHING ELSE?" She nodded again, her pen poised. I rarely asked her any questions, and she was clearly pleased with my newfound interest in therapy. It must have been a nice change from my usual pouting passivity. "WHY CAN'T I REMEMBER ANYTHING FROM MY LIFE BEFORE? I HAVE VAGUE FLASHES, BUT IT'S ALMOST LIKE I'M REMEMBERING SCENES FROM A MOVIE. AND WHEN I TRY TO FORCE MYSELF TO GO BACK, I GET A HEADACHE. WILL I HAVE TO GET MY MEMORIES BACK IF I WANT TO GET MY VOICE BACK?"

Since meeting Ben, I had become much more interested in getting to know myself, with the hope that I might become better girlfriend material, if by some remote chance he wanted to be more than my comic book superhero. And although I was still reluctant to rifle through my emotional closet for fear of what I might find there, I was at least a little bit curious about who I'd been before my world came crashing down. It was hard to imagine that Ben would stick around for very long unless I got my act together. He wasn't the kind of guy who had to settle for a fixer-upper.

"With you, Sasha, I'm afraid that speaking in terms of what has worked for other patients doesn't apply. For many people, remembering the events that led up to the traumatic episode triggers a flood of memories, and once the patient remembers, she can address the issues that have caused the particular psychic trauma, and the symptoms of the trauma—in your case, muteness—disappear. It's hard to say, as hysterical mutism is a very rare condition, and when it does occur, it doesn't usually last very long. Many people experience tragedies, but very few people lose their ability to speak as a result. Four years of silence is practically unheard of."

"SO I'M CRAZY AND WEIRD. IS THAT WHAT YOU'RE SAYING?"

"Not at all, Sasha. It's just that your reaction to the accident reflects the unique characteristics of your brain. While memory recovery may be the most common way to bring everything to the surface, I can't say that it's the only way. If you're unable to remember, perhaps you should try looking at this as an opportunity to start over. I firmly believe that you can speak again, even if your amnesia is never cured. You will simply travel a different road, but what difference does it make, as long as it gets you where you want to go?"

"SO TODAY IS THE FIRST DAY OF THE REST OF MY LIFE?"

"I know that sounds like something out of a drug rehab brochure, but at this point, I honestly feel you are, in a way, addicted to your silence. You use it to hide out from the world, to avoid dealing with problems and people. That's exactly what substance abusers do." Dr. O. put down her pen and paper and leaned forward, seemingly intrigued by her new theory. "Even though terrible things sometimes happen, the world is not such a terrible place. You're strong enough to handle anything that life throws at you, Sasha. Don't sell yourself short."

I had actually been feeling pretty good when I arrived, but now I was a junkie. Silence was my heroin.

"THAT SOUNDS BAD."

"Don't be upset. It's actually good news. Once you're willing to acknowledge that you're an addict, you're well on your way to recovery."

I didn't know quite how to take this revelation. Was Dr. O. going to send me to a twelve-step program to trade sad stories with fellow addicts in a church basement? I'd do it. Thoughts of Ben's arms wrapped around me for reasons other than protecting me from bad guys made me eager to try just about anything.

She glanced at her watch. "I'm afraid our time is up. Check back in a month, but feel free to call if you need me sooner. I think you're doing very well on your own, Sasha. And be good to this boy—he sounds like a keeper."

"I'LL DO MY BEST. BUT WE'RE JUST FRIENDS."

"That's how the best relationships begin, as friendships."

Dr. O. smiled and let me out the back door. I stood outside for a minute, trying to picture what kind of whack job would be sitting in my spot on the couch for the next hour, how loose my screws were in comparison with those of her other patients.

I hadn't gotten to ask her any questions about boys in general, although based on the fact that she hadn't helped me speak in four years, maybe I was better off learning about love, sex, and boys on my own. That and the fact that with her Coke bottle glasses and schoolteacher bun, she didn't look like she was getting any more action than I was. But wasn't there an old saying that those who can't, teach? There was always next month.

Chapter 8

I had never attended a single Shoreland High School sporting event. What would be the point? Watching normal, well-adjusted teenagers talking, laughing, and having fun didn't rank high on my list of favorite activities. As if I needed to be reminded about what I was missing. But now things were different, a little bit. Ben was running in some regional indoor track meet at a nearby college, and I almost felt like I belonged among the spectators. That, and I wanted to see him in his little running shorts. Jules and I climbed the bleachers, searching the crowd.

"Maybe now you'll come to a basketball game and watch me cheer. What do you think? Could you handle it?"

Jules had been incredibly understanding of my steadfast refusals to go to any games. Yet another example of how good a friend she was, letting me be selfish, knowing I wasn't capable of any better.

"MAYBE. WE'LL SEE HOW THIS GOES." Baby steps.

"There he is," Jules said, pointing to the center of the track. "Next to the supermodel."

Ben was standing beside a willowy girl with her hair pulled back in a thick ponytail, listening carefully to whatever she was saying to him. This chick belonged in high heels, traipsing down a runway with a spotlight trained on her golden mane, not surrounded by a bunch of sweaty teenagers in clunky sneakers and tank tops with numbers on them. Straight out of the pages of *Seventeen*, she had impossibly long legs, a Hawaii tan even though it was the middle of winter, and, apparently, plenty to say to Ben. And although I had no right to be jealous—our relationship was purely platonic—I felt a certain possessiveness toward him to which I knew I was not entitled. But I couldn't help it. The truth was that if Ben could read my mind as well as he said he could, he must know that I wanted him bad, and he was choosing to ignore my almost uncontrollable desire to wrestle him to the floor and stick my tongue down his throat. Even a social half-wit like me could take a hint, so I tried to hide my true feelings, with limited success, whenever he was nearby. If he thought about me as anything more than a charity case, he needed to be the one to make the first move. I was pretty desperate, but I wasn't quite ready to throw myself at him.

Did he even know I was here at the track meet? So far, my mind-reading friend hadn't looked up other than to stare into the eyes of the track star/lingerie model he was talking to. I decided to try an experiment. *If you can hear me, look up in the stands. I'm in the B section, about halfway up, black sweatshirt.* If he looked at me, I would know he hadn't tuned me out, made me part of the white noise that hovered on the edges of his consciousness. I leaned forward. Nothing. Then, with that exasperating smile on his face, he looked straight at me and nodded. What a tease he was. I felt like a fish being reeled in, but just as I reached the surface, my fate in clear view, the angler let out the line, sending me back into the muddy water, swimming aimlessly, not sure where I was going, desperate to see the sun again. Damn him. He looked away, still smiling, and the hook lodged even more firmly in my mouth.

After the meet, I wanted to rush onto the field, slip my arms around him, stake my claim, make sure that Miss Teen America knew she had some competition—not that I could really compete with her in the looks department, or probably any other way—but as usual I chickened out. Doing nothing was weak, but over the past four years, inertia had become a way of life.

"WE CAN GO. I'VE SEEN WHAT I'VE BEEN MISSING."

"It's not so terrible, is it? Are you finally ready to rejoin the living?" Jules asked.

She seemed to think that if I acted the part, everything would fall into place. Fake it till you make it isn't a bad philosophy, but I was a coward, and lazy to boot. Pretending I was having fun, pretending I felt like I belonged, required a tremendous amount of effort, and up until now I hadn't been motivated. Maybe Ben was my catalyst. Maybe I was ready to pretend to be normal so he would like me, and if Jules's reasoning was correct, I would magically *become* normal. The simplicity of her theory annoyed the hell out of me.

"I DON'T KNOW. IT'S NOT TERRIBLE. BUT I FEEL LIKE I'M A WHOLE DIFFERENT SPECIES FROM THESE PEOPLE. EVEN IF I PRETEND, I KNOW I'LL NEVER FIT IN."

Why was everything so hard for me? Why did I have to scrutinize every word, every look, and always find myself wanting? Maybe if I didn't think so much, I would be a happier person. Maybe I needed to stop living inside my head, but how?

"I think you'd feel that way even if you could talk. You're just different . . . and I mean that in a good way."

"THANKS. I GUESS."

"That's what I love about you—you're an old soul, as my mother would say. It's like you're past this garbage already. I know it's shallow and stupid to spend so much time looking in the mirror and wondering if some boy likes me. That doesn't mean I'm not going to do it, but I get how you feel. High school is just too, well, high school for someone like you."

If Jules only knew how much time I'd been spending in front of the mirror lately, analyzing my body parts—was my nose too big, were my breasts too small, were my eyes too close together, were my hips too wide—and wondering if a boy liked me. Unfortunately, on top of all my other difficulties, I had turned into the stereotypical high school girl, heavy on the angst.

Chapter 9

Every day he was waiting for me when school let out. This had to be more than a charity project masquerading as friendship, didn't it? Jules thought so, but she admitted it was tough to be sure—boys were unpredictable—and assuming something that wasn't true could be embarrassing if I started to buy into my own fairy tale. After instant messaging about it every night for two weeks, rehashing every word that Ben said to me, we still couldn't figure it out. Was he dense (impossible!) or just a tease?

As usual, Jules's advice lacked subtlety. *Maybe you should just attack him and see what he does. Then at least you'll know.*

I wasn't sure I was ready to take that kind of risk. *But if he doesn't reciprocate, then I've lost a really cool friend and made a total fool of myself.*

If I manned up and kissed him, and he didn't kiss me back, I would probably drop dead on the spot. It wasn't like I could pretend I was going to whisper something in his ear and accidentally landed on his lips instead. The risk was monumental.

My dad says it's impossible for boys and girls to be just friends.

So far I'm proving him wrong.

Not really—you're only being Ben's friend because you're chickenshit. You want more, Sash.

But if he doesn't want more, what I want doesn't matter, does it?

And so far, he was making it very clear he didn't want more. He knew exactly what I thought about him, and still he did nothing. Throwing myself under the Ben bus just to appease Jules and test her father's theory was not a strategy that appealed to me.

IDK.

So what would you do, Jules?

Maybe you need to drop a couple of hints. You could try dressing a little girlier. You look like a rain cloud.

Thanks. I was very defensive about my gray sweats.

Really. You have a great body, and we know B thinks so. Maybe you need to remind him what he's missing. He's already seen your tits. Show him some more.

Nice, J. I'll think about it. But sweatpants make me feel invisible and safe.

Not that safe—not enough to stop your jock friends from trying to score a touchdown in the park.

But that's about power, not sex.

It's about both, S. Anyway, back to B. If you want him to notice you, give him something to notice. And if all else fails, be bold. Nothing ventured, nothing gained.

Food for thought. GTG. See you tomorrow.

I went to bed and dreamt about running naked through the hallways of Shoreland High School; probably not the kind of bold Jules had in mind.

The next afternoon Ben was waiting for me in front of the school. "I don't want to go to the library today. Let's go for a walk at the beach. I feel like being outside." He took my backpack and led me over to his car. "You look nice, by the way."

Thanks.

Not having any better ideas, I'd taken Jules's advice and abandoned grey fleece for jeans. My sweater, although still grey, was at least not two sizes too big. They were part of my "just in case" wardrobe, purchased by Charlotte just in case I ever decided to dress like a girl. Thank goodness for her naive optimism. Well-outfitted, I was on the make, as much as I was capable. I was like a nun with a weekend pass from the convent.

The beach? But it's cold outside. And it looks like it might rain, or snow.

Why was I being such a baby, when being alone with him was what I wanted, more than anything? But he knew that already.

"Don't worry, I'll keep you warm."

There went those eyebrows. My heart skipped a couple of beats. Maybe this was it.

Oh yeah?

We had been flirting this way practically since we'd met, but nothing else was happening. We were stalled in the bantering stage. Despite Jules's suggestion that I take the initiative, under no circumstances would I ever make the first move, although sometimes I thought if I could do it just once, he might run with it. Unfortunately, way easier said than done. My fear of failure trumped my fresh-off-the-boat horniness.

"Yeah, I have an extra scarf and a really warm, ugly hat in my car. You'll be toasty."

Thanks. You bastard.

If he weren't so jaw-droppingly cute, I would hate him for teasing me when he had to know exactly what I wanted him to say and do to me.

"Tsk, tsk. Language, young lady. Not very becoming."

He shook his head as he opened the car door for me. His manners were from another century, and I found this old-world gentility totally hot. Dr. O'Rourke was right—he was a keeper—but did he feel the same way about me? Why couldn't he just let me in on the secret? How could I get him to lay his cards on the table—or on me—already? Every cell in my body was running out of patience.

I let off a string of internal profanities, just to assert my independence. *Shit, fuck, fuck, fuck, damn . . .* My naughty vocabulary was limited.

"That's pathetic. It's like listening to a baby trying out her first words." He laughed as we drove into the deserted beach parking lot. "Not a popular spot in February, I guess. I wouldn't recommend that you come here alone."

Don't worry, it would never occur to me.

We sat silently for a minute, watching the waves pound the beach, listening to the chain clank against the pole as the wind whipped the American flag. It reminded me of the chain on Ben's nunchucks, and I tried to push the memories of that evening down deeper. I didn't want to ruin the afternoon, which I was hoping would lead to something more than just a frigid walk and frozen fingers.

So, as long as I'm putting on this really attractive headgear, should we walk? I opened the car door, but the wind was so strong it felt as if someone were pushing it shut from the other side. *A little windy. Are you sure this is a good idea?*

Ben got out of the car and came around to open my door. When he reached in to help me out, I shook my head.

"What's the matter? You don't want me to touch you?" The way he said it, he knew that was definitely not the case.

I don't understand. What Jane Austen novel did you crawl out of? Opening doors, carrying my backpack, helping me out of the car. I know my memory is short, but I've never met anyone like you before. And does all this chivalry mean you like me—like me, or are you just pathologically polite?

Shit. I'd sworn I wouldn't beg, and yet here I was, practically on my knees.

Ignoring the last question, Ben said, "Don't you like having doors opened for you? I'm just doing what my mother taught me. Are good manners a bad thing?"

As we walked, he hooked his arm through mine, escorting me along the rocky beach path. I was grateful, as I felt like the wind might knock me over.

No, I like it. It's just different, I guess. You're like this with everybody, I suppose.

Didn't he see where I was headed with this? Did I have to hit him over the head with a club? Why was he torturing me? I wanted to be special, needed him to tell me that. But of course he saw everything, heard everything; he was just playing me like a violin, or he wasn't interested. Neither one was good.

"Don't think too much. Just enjoy the moment for a change." And with those words of wisdom, he stopped walking, put both his arms around me and held me close, my cheek resting against his chest. "I wanted to make you wait a little bit, just to be sure it's what you really wanted. You have so much going on inside your head all at once, I sometimes get mixed signals."

Is this enough of a signal?

I reached up—he was much taller—and wrapped my arms around his neck, pulling him down so our lips met. Jules gave excellent advice. Bold felt good. Go big or go home.

My first kiss was everything I had imagined and more. His lips were warm and soft, his hands on either side of my face, his thumbs stroking my cheeks, his whole body pressed up against mine.

We stopped to take a breath.

"So, how was your first kiss?"

There aren't words. I barely exist in most people's eyes, and no one has ever thought about me like this, ever.

I reached for his hand and kissed each of his precious fingers. Was this really happening to me? Had Jules's wardrobe advice been the tipping point? Was it really as simple as wearing clothes that fit?

"Well, *I* think about you like that. And tell Jules it wasn't the tight jeans that made the difference. You could've been wearing a garbage bag or a suit of armor—today was the day."

It's a good day.

"Was it okay for your first? Maybe I should've gone for some tongue to make it a little more memorable."

No, it was just right. Definitely has a place on my highlight reel. Maybe you can show me a few of your more exotic moves for my second kiss. And my third . . .

"Pushy. I like it."

We stared into each other's eyes for a few seconds, and I could feel myself getting lost in the intensity of his gaze. Then he kissed me again . . . with tongue.

Chapter 10

It was going to be a real live date. All I knew was that we were taking the train into New York City, but the rest was a surprise. Charlotte had insisted I wear a skirt that she proudly produced from the back of her closet—another piece in my "just in case" wardrobe.

"I knew he was going to ask you out, so I picked this up at Bloomingdale's. With black tights, you're going to look so cute. And you have to wear a little makeup, just mascara and eyeliner, maybe a little lipstick. It's a special occasion." She was more excited than I was, if such a thing were possible.

When the doorbell rang, the butterflies in my stomach almost flew out of my mouth. Until a few weeks ago, I had no illusions that a boy would want to spend time with me, unless he was carrying out some court-ordered community service. But the wind had shifted and now I was on deck, waiting for my turn at bat. The night before, Jules came over to give me a pep talk and some much-needed pointers.

"Do you know where you're going?"

"NO IDEA. HE TOLD ME TO DRESS UP—NO JEANS. HE'S PICKING ME UP AT TWELVE ON SAT-URDAY." I held up the skirt and she nodded her approval.

"That sounds like a matinee. He's definitely taking you to see a Broadway show. That happens to be a very cute skirt.

I didn't think Charlotte would go for something so short. Good for her." Jules lounged on my bed and watched me struggling to brush my hair with one hand and type with the other.

"IS THAT A GOOD FIRST DATE?" Jules went out on dates all the time, but no one had ever taken her to a show in Manhattan.

"Very good. Theater tickets are expensive, and you'll definitely go to dinner after. He wouldn't spend so much money if he didn't really like you."

"DO YOU ACT DIFFERENTLY ON A DATE THAN WHEN YOU'RE JUST HANGING OUT WITH SOMEONE?" I knew as much about the rules of dating as I knew about the ins and outs of Olympic curling.

"He obviously likes you the way you are, so just be yourself. You can manage that, can't you?" Jules asked, taking the brush from my clumsy hands.

"NOT EXACTLY SURE WHO I AM THESE DAYS."

"Just go easy on the sarcasm. You can be a little harsh sometimes, especially when you're nervous." She squinted at my reflection in the mirror, putting my hair up, taking it down again.

"NOTED. JUST A HABIT."

Jules didn't know that sarcasm was impossible with Ben. Pretense was out of the question. Should I let Jules in on the secret? Although I wanted to tell her, it never seemed to be the right moment, and I wanted Jules to get to know Ben first, without getting distracted by his gypsy act. And the more I thought about it, I realized I should probably get Ben's permission before disclosing his special power. As if she would even believe me. He would have to demonstrate—Jules was as skeptical as I was.

"IF HE'S SPENDING SO MUCH MONEY ON ME, DOES THAT MEAN HE'LL BE EXPECTING SOMETHING IN RETURN?"

I kind of hoped it did. What would dinner and a show cost me? Plenty, I hoped.

"Boys want something in return if they buy you an ice cream cone. But you should never, and I mean never, do anything out of obligation. Hasn't Charlotte had the talk with you?"

I shook my head. "EVERYTHING I KNOW I LEARNED FROM YOUR BIRTHDAY SEX BOOK, THE ADVICE COLUMN IN *COSMO*, AND A FEW ISSUES OF *SEVENTEEN* MAGAZINE FROM THE EARLY EIGHTIES THAT I FOUND IN THE BASEMENT."

"Well you're a little late to the party, but you're a quick study, so you should be able to handle it. I'll condense all my mother's speeches for you. Just the highlights from the Lucy Harper Book of Life Lessons. Maybe you should take notes. First, don't have sex until you're in college, if then. Second, oral sex is risky because you can catch a nasty STD, so don't think that's the easy way out."

"TMI."

"Third, boys will say anything to get you to mess around with them, so don't believe them when they tell you they love you or they'll die if you don't have some kind of sex with them. Fourth, don't drink or do drugs, because it makes you horny, fucks with your good judgment, and lowers your resistance."

"YOUR MOTHER SAID FUCK?" Mrs. Harper was a Sunday school teacher and wore seasonal appliquéd sweaters. Fudge, maybe, but fuck, never.

"I don't think my mother even knows what that word means. I just added that part for emphasis. Don't interrupt—now I've lost my place. Where was I? Oh, yeah. Lastly, if a boy really and truly cares about you, he won't pressure you, because he'll want to be with you for more than just a few minutes of heavy breathing and pelvic thrusting. Got it?" Jules took a deep breath. "That's the gospel according to Lucy Harper, PTA treasurer, woman of the world."

"SO WHAT DOES THAT LEAVE ME WITH? IS KISSING OKAY? OR WILL I CATCH SOME DISFIGURING DISEASE?"

This dating thing was far more dangerous than I had ever imagined. Jules had definitely taken the wind out of my sails.

"I left out my mom's mono/herpes speech. If she had her wish, I'd go out on dates wearing a body condom, if I went out at all."

"SO NO KISSING? WHAT'S THE POINT THEN? I MIGHT AS WELL JUST GO OUT WITH YOU." Having discovered the earth-shaking sensation of Ben's tongue in my mouth, I could hardly focus on anything else.

"You should be so lucky. You have to understand—Lucy's kind of uptight. And my dad's a doctor, an infectious disease specialist, no less. It's a lethal combination. But the way I see it, what's life without a little risk? I've kissed a few guys and I'm still here, so I think making out is fine. Don't you dare tell the parental units. I'll be grounded until menopause."

"ALL YOUR DIRTY LITTLE SECRETS ARE SAFE WITH ME. BEN LOOKS PRETTY CLEAN ANYWAY, DOESN'T HE?" We could take a shower together, just to make sure . . .

"Yes, he strikes me as someone with spectacular hygiene. Personally, I won't go out with a guy unless he flosses regularly and carries Purell in his pocket."

"AND I'M THE ONE WHO'S SUPPOSED TO BE LESS SARCASTIC?"

"Sorry. Thinking about my parents gets me worked up." Jules clenched her teeth.

"NOW I CAN'T STOP THINKING ABOUT BLOOD TESTS AND PETRI DISHES."

When I closed my eyes, I could see Ben and me making out, wearing latex gloves and surgical masks. Oddly enough, still hot.

"Forget that last part. You're not going to do any more than a little French kissing at most, so I think you're safe. Really."

✦

One minute after noon on Saturday the doorbell rang. Charlotte answered; she had posted herself steps away from the front door. Was she afraid Ben would change his mind and flee? He was definitely prompt—that was a good sign. From my room, I could hear Ben chatting with my aunt and uncle. All perfectly normal, except this was the first time a boy had ever come to pick me up. Standing in front of my mirror, I gave myself a silent lecture. *This isn't any different from all the other times you've hung out with him. He must like you if he's taking you to the City for the whole day. Jules said so, and she knows. Calm down. Your palms are getting sweaty.* I took one last look in the mirror. *He must be into freaks, because you're no beauty. Shut up. I'm not saying anything you don't already know about yourself. Not now.* Was I turning into a split personality, on top of everything else?

"Sasha, Ben's here."

Charlotte could barely contain her excitement about my first foray into the world of normal teenagers. In a way, her enthusiasm made sense. When my parents died, she became responsible for a thirteen-year-old head case. Going out on a real date, with a real boy, was so wonderfully healthy, and like me, Charlotte probably hadn't believed it would ever happen.

Ben gave me the once-over. "You look so pretty in real clothes."

I nodded and curtsied. *Fuck you, mister.*

"That's what I always tell her. Ben, maybe you'll be the one to talk Sasha out of her sweats."

Charlotte, oblivious to her own double entendre, continued chattering away.

"I'd love to try, Mrs. Thompson." He raised his eyebrows in my direction, biting his lip.

Big talker. Would you like to skip the City and go to a motel? I'm game.

"Have a wonderful time. Enjoy Manhattan. You must be special, Ben, because she never wants to go to the City with us. Sasha, don't forget your talkie box."

Dutifully, I picked it up off the table; not that I needed it. I kissed Charlotte, and Ben took my hand.

When we were safely in the car, Ben turned to me. "Your aunt does have a way with a phrase, and you're the one who's a big talker. What do you know about motels anyway?"

In the movies, that's where people go to have sex during the day.

"Ah, sounds romantic. Maybe next weekend. I already have today all planned. Or we can do the motel thing on the way home, if you're still in the mood." He kissed me, his tongue tickling mine, his hands in my hair.

That feels so good it hurts. He was kissing my lips, but I could feel it deep inside me. I was aware of every nerve in my body firing in rapid succession, my blood rushing through my veins.

He lifted his head and looked past me. "Your aunt and uncle are watching us."

Both of them? That's embarrassing. I put my hands over my face.

"No, it's not. Charlotte thinks it's wonderful that you've found a boy who appreciates how beautiful and special you are. That's a direct quote."

That's gross.

"She's thinking she'd better have the talk with you, as soon as you get home, based on the way I'm kissing you."

That's even worse. Charlotte's version of the birds and the bees would likely involve an elaborate explanation of how flowers pollinate.

"Your mother never explained the facts of life to you?" There was a note of surprise, and maybe a little worry, in his voice.

You mean the stork? Yeah, I know all about that.

"Very funny." He tilted his head. "You do know where babies come from, don't you?"

Are you trying to tell me there's no stork? Then it's definitely the cabbage patch. Did I come off as such an innocent? Did that mean I was a bad kisser?

"Ha ha. It's just that your history is a little unusual, so you could've missed a few things." He started the car, the tires crunching over the gravel driveway, and waved at Charlotte and Stuart, who ducked out of sight. "Don't be so insecure. I wouldn't be kissing you if I didn't like it."

I had a big sister, and I have Jules, so I'm not totally clueless.

An hour later, as we walked through Times Square, I held onto Ben for dear life. New York City was noisy and crowded and overwhelming. But it felt good to be buffeted by the people, to hear Ben shouting at me over the din of the cars and the thousands of voices all babbling at once. I felt alive and excited to find out what was going to happen next. We crossed the street and stopped in front of a theater. The marquee said *A Chorus Line*.

"Charlotte told me that this was your favorite show, that you've seen it three times. Do you remember?" Ben was watching me carefully, as if looking for some flicker of recognition in my eyes.

I shook my head. *Nothing.* Did I even like musicals? Inside the theater we settled in our seats—sixth row orchestra. Ben handed me my ticket. "A souvenir." The price on the ticket was $161.

These tickets are too expensive. You shouldn't be spending so much money on me. Jules had said theater tickets were pricey, but this was ridiculous. Upside: anyone who spent that much money had to be expecting something in return.

"Why not? I think you're worth it."

But a hundred and sixty-one dollars?

"Don't worry. I have plenty of money. I worked all last summer. My parents have made some wise investments over the years and published a few books. No one is going without shoes so we can come to the theater." He draped his arm over my shoulder. Even through my sweater, my skin tingled.

But even so, I feel funny. Jules said . . .

"What did the wise Jules have to say?"

Ben didn't know Jules beyond calculus class, and I was a little worried they wouldn't hit it off if they tried to get to know one another. Each seemed suspicious of the other, as if each were an interloper in the territory that was me. If I wanted them to be friends, I needed to be careful about how I portrayed her to him. But when someone is reading your every thought, diplomacy goes out the window.

She said that boys expect something in return when they spend money on a girl, and you're spending a ton of money on me. I wished I hadn't gone down this road, but there was no way I could keep any secrets from Ben anyway. Was he on his way to hating my best friend? *And she said I should never do anything out of obligation.*

"Wise words from your guru. Jules isn't wrong. Most boys look at a date as the first half of an exchange. He buys dinner, and she's dessert." So maybe we *would* be stopping off at a motel on the way home. "But I'm not like that . . . and I know that disappoints you a little bit, doesn't it?"

Stop showing off. I already know you know what I'm thinking.

"Sorry, but your mind is like a porn site, and I know that you're hoping I'll jump you in the car on the way home."

I blushed mightily and looked around, hoping no one had heard that last part. There was an elderly couple in front of us, and I could swear the wife was trying to listen in on our odd one-sided conversation.

It's totally unfair. I have to wait for you to tell me what you're thinking, if you feel like it.

"So you want me to tell you?"

Duh. It was like we were playing poker and he could see all my cards—no contest.

Ben leaned over and whispered, "I think you're pretty cute. And I didn't bring you to the theater so you would feel like you owed me. Are we clear?"

Clear. And a little bummed out. I wanted him to say out loud all the things I was thinking.

"Don't worry, we're thinking exactly the same thing."

I guess I have to trust you on that.

"You do. Anticipation makes it better. I promise." The lights dimmed, and the music swelled. Shifting in my seat, I wondered how I was going to sit still for the next two hours. "You'll make it." He rested his hand lightly on my thigh.

Not if you leave your hand there.

"You're just going to have to suffer, because the hand stays."

He moved it up an inch or two for good measure. From the waist down I was on fire, and he thought it was funny. There must be something wrong with me, because Ben seemed totally unflustered, in spite of all the flirting.

The music must have seeped into my brain, because about ten minutes into the show, I suddenly knew every note. Mouthing the words, I got lost in the story, almost, but not quite, forgetting about Ben's hand resting on my leg.

Thank you so much. I did love this show. It's perfect.

Closing my eyes for a second I could see my mother, sitting between Liz and me, waiting for the music to start. That second when the theater was so dark I couldn't see my hand in front of my face, right before the orchestra started to play . . . it was thrilling and a little bit scary, holding my breath, waiting for that first note. How amazing to feel that again.

You can't imagine what this means to me. Although I tried to blink back the tears, one escaped and fell on Ben's hand. *How stupid. I'm sorry. Happy tears, I swear.*

"I know, and it's not stupid," he whispered, and he looked at me, his own eyes glistening in the darkness, tenderly kissing my cheek.

After the curtain went down and the lights went up, we sat quietly as the theater emptied around us. *How did you know this would make me remember?*

"I didn't, but in my own life, so many memories are tied up with music. Charlotte wasn't sure it was a good idea to bring you. She was afraid it might upset you. But I thought it was worth a shot. You're not *that* unstable, and every little thing you remember is another piece of your puzzle back in place."

Although he wasn't asking me directly, he clearly wanted to know if the show had triggered anything significant. But other than a few flashes of a trip to the theater five years earlier, there was nothing major. It would take more than sequins, top hats, and catchy lyrics to fix me, but it was a thoughtful gesture.

Every little bit helps. One of these days. He nodded encouragingly and squeezed my knee.

As we strolled through the lobby, Ben insisted on buying me a souvenir T-shirt and coffee mug. "If that feeling starts slipping away, put on the shirt and drink out of the mug, and you'll remember the excitement you felt when the lights first went out."

I don't need a shirt to jog my memory. I'll never forget that feeling ever again.

"What about that feeling you had when my hand was on your thigh?" Ben put his arm around my waist as he steered me along the crowded sidewalk to our next destination.

I still have that, but you know that already, don't you? You want me to tell you how much I liked it? Is that it?

My face must have been scarlet, and I was perspiring in my wool tights, even though the temperature was barely above freezing.

"Pretty much. I love that you're so innocent but you're so . . ." His hand strayed down my skirt and he patted my rear end.

I think horny's the word you're looking for. Our conversations were so open, which probably would never happen if I actually had to say those kinds of things out loud. What girl would ever have the nerve to tell a guy she was horny?

As fearless as Jules was, I doubt even she had ever been so candid with a boy.

"Don't worry. I don't take credit for that. You're ready—I just happened to come along at the right time. Lucky me."

But it is you. It would be unimaginable to feel that way all the time, unconnected to any particular person. How awful—like an itchy rash that wouldn't go away. *It's not just hormones. I think I can tell the difference, in spite of my lack of experience.*

"You need to start thinking about something else, because we're both thinking the same thing, and every time I look at you, I want to kiss you." We were standing at a corner, waiting to cross, surrounded by a swarm of humanity, but Ben seemed oblivious, saying these incredibly intimate things.

A middle-aged woman in jeans up to her neck and a Big Apple sweatshirt turned to me and said, "Young lady, you need to hang on to that boy. In forty years, Vern has never talked to me like that."

She grimaced and gestured at the man next to her. In a Budweiser cap and NASCAR jacket, he didn't look like a master of seduction. As if to prove her point, he opened his mouth, simultaneously burping and revealing half a dozen gray teeth tilted every which way, like headstones in a neglected graveyard.

As usual, I just nodded. Ben laughed. "Thank you, ma'am. I hope she listens to you."

The light changed and we crossed in unison, moving like a vast school of fish. *Your smooth talk even works on the bingo crowd. Impressive.*

Ben sighed. "That did it. Thinking about Vern and his wife in their double-wide doing the nasty—I'm cured, at least for a little while." His hand started to cup my butt again, but I swatted it away.

I'm glad you find my skirt so appealing, but if you keep touching me like that, I'm going to melt inside these clothes. I'm officially changing the topic. Where are we going?

"Our reservation isn't for another couple of hours, and we're too young to hang out in a bar, so we're going to wander around."

Ten minutes later we walked through the Art Deco doors of the Empire State Building. *I've never been here before. You're an excellent tour guide.*

"You'll always remember your first trip to the top. Even if you can't figure out everything that happened in your life before, you can still make all kinds of new memories. And I have lots of good ideas."

Oh really. Back seats, motels, secluded beaches . . .

"And not all of them involve being alone with you—I swear."

Standing behind me at the back of the crowded elevator, Ben slipped his hands under my coat and ran them across the front of my skirt, pulling me against his hips. "Sorry about that. You're pushing against me, and it just happened." His lips were next to my ear, and between whispers he nipped at my earlobe.

I should slap you for that. The people in front of me are pushing me back against you. I can't help it. And you're pulling me. What I really wanted to do was turn around and climb him like a koala bear in a eucalyptus tree.

"So you don't like it when I do this?" His hand slid under my sweater, stroking my bare skin.

Stop it. I was so lightheaded I thought I would faint.

"It's a long elevator ride, and you're standing in front of me, so close you're practically behind me. What else am I supposed to do?" His breath was quick in my ear.

Talk about the weather? School? You don't have to put your tongue in my ear at every opportunity.

The elevator came to a stop suddenly, my stomach catching up with it a second later. Ben quickly pulled his hands from under my clothes.

"I kind of do. Come on. We definitely need some fresh air."

The winter wind whipped at our faces as we looked at the City spread out below us, sparkling jewels sprinkled on black velvet. How many millions of people were behind all those lights? For the first time in I don't know how long, I thought about the rest of the world—that with or without my disability, I could be a part of it. In fact, I *wanted* to be a part of it. Like a flower blossoming after a very long winter, I felt renewed. Perhaps it was just the surge of adrenaline I experienced every time Ben touched me, or the effect of his powerful pheromones, but whatever the cause, it felt like I was on the precipice of something wonderful, and I was excited.

Ben stood behind me, pointing out various landmark buildings, burying his face in my hair, nuzzling my neck. While people around us commented on the biting cold, I felt blissfully warm. The heat between us was more than just figurative.

"Have you seen enough? It's time for dinner. You must be starving. I forgot to get you any lunch."

I was going to comment on that. Very neglectful. You'll have to be punished. I leaned back against him, not wanting to let the cold air rush between our bodies.

"You definitely shouldn't let me off the hook. I need to be punished. When can we start?" he whispered in my ear.

Turning me around so I was looking up at him, he kissed me hard, ignoring the fifty or so people milling around us. I loved that he was so uninhibited. Always a jealous witness to other people's public displays of affection, I much preferred being a participant.

Ben was no better behaved on the ride down, but I had given up trying to stop him, and decided to enjoy all the attention. Curbside, he hailed a taxi, and minutes later we were standing in front of the maitre d' at Mario's, a stereotypically Italian restaurant in Greenwich Village.

"Good evening. Reservation for two under the name Fisher."

"Right this way, sir, miss."

It was like being out with a grownup. Ben was so self-assured, so handsome and serious looking in his blue blazer. Any minute I would wake up on the couch at the Shoreland Public Library, having dreamed every enchanting moment I'd spent with this Prince Charming with the magic tongue. The restaurant was dark, with lots of red leather, and tiny votive candles scattered on the tabletops. It screamed romantic interludes, handholding under the table, and lots of Chianti. How did I end up here?

"I brought you here for a reason. Not just the risotto, which is amazing, but for something else." Ben gestured to a shiny black baby grand piano in the corner.

Don't tell me you're a lounge singer as well as a mind-reading sprinter.

"Nope. Continuing the theme of the day, which is music, in case you missed it—the Empire State Building was just a last-minute addition—there's a guy who sings here on Saturday nights. Standards mostly, lots of show tunes. I hope you like it, even though it's kind of old-fashioned. I love this stuff."

Why doesn't that surprise me?

He was probably also a connoisseur of black-and-white movies, drank scotch instead of beer, and did a mean fox-trot.

"I prefer the waltz, and I don't really drink, except a little wine. I did live in Italy, after all. My favorite movie is *Notorious*, which *is* kind of ancient—1946." Ben shook his head and took my hand. "You're making fun of me. Do you think I'm too old for you?"

I definitely like the vintage manners, so I guess I can put up with you, as long as you don't fall asleep before dessert. What time do you have to be back at the old-age home?

We settled on mushroom risotto and veal something. Food was irrelevant. The way I felt, I didn't care if I ever ate again. Ben ordered for us, in Italian, of course. The waiter turned out to be from Florence, and after a few minutes of conversation, he disappeared, returning with special treats from the kitchen, bowing and saying, "*Buon appetito.*"

It was like having dinner with a famous actor or politician. Anyone else would come off as a snob, but Ben was totally sincere and completely unaware of his own specialness. He was naturally suave, and I was under his spell.

Do you always get treated like a celebrity?

"I'm a voice from home, that's all."

Sitting back, looking around the room as I munched on calamari, I noticed that we were the youngest people in the restaurant by at least twenty years. It wasn't that I minded being the only one here who still slept with a retainer, but it made me think. Was I mature enough for Ben? He was perfectly at ease here, with the fine food, the clinking wineglasses, and the seductive light of flickering candles. More accustomed to takeout pizza, diet Coke in a can, and the operating-room glow of Stuart's eco-friendly kitchen light bulbs, I was feeling way out of my league in the midst of all this urbane sophistication.

Just then, a man in a tuxedo sat down at the piano and started to play and sing. I had experienced more new things in this one day than I had in all of the last four years. What else did Ben have planned? I couldn't begin to imagine. Closing my eyes, I let the music wash over me. Life was good.

"Are you okay? My mother thought I was overdoing it with theater *and* dinner." Ben reached across the snowy white tablecloth and took my hand. "Maybe she was right."

I love everything about today. After such a long time, I worry I may never talk again, but since I met you, it doesn't matter so much. I can still be happy, thanks to you.

Even in the restaurant's dim light, I could see Ben blanch until he was nearly as white as the tablecloth. "But . . ."

Don't freak out. It's not like I've picked out a china pattern.

I hadn't meant to overwhelm him with my appreciation or some implied statement of lifelong dependence, but it wasn't like I could keep what I was thinking secret from him anyway. The color failed to return to his cheeks. How could I fix my latest blunder?

I'm not proposing or anything. Chill. For someone who could hear all my thoughts, he wasn't a very good listener.

"I just worry that you'll give up, that's all." He took a fork-ful of tiramisu and fed it to me. "You deserve only good things, and I don't want you to miss out."

Before you came along, the only thing I was missing was a real life. You rescued me that night in the gazebo, and every day since. I know now that I'll be okay, whatever happens with my voice. Lifting his hand to my lips, I turned it over and gently kissed his palm.

"I just want you to be happy, to live a full life." He had suddenly gotten very serious. "That's the most important thing."

Sounds like a toast. I held up my cappuccino cup, trying to lighten the mood. *Cheers. And thank you for the most perfect day of my life.*

Chapter 11

As usual, no one was home. A note on the kitchen table reminded me that tonight was a bar association dinner in the City. Charlotte and Stuart wouldn't be back until late.

Dear Sasha,
Do your homework. Leftover pizza in the fridge. Make sure the doors are locked and turn on the alarm before you go to bed.
Love,
Charlotte

The only sound was the tick of the mantel clock and the hum of the furnace. I led Ben by the hand into my room and pushed him down onto my bed. Stretching out next to him, I pulled off his sweatshirt, then his T-shirt, kissing the hollow above his collarbone. This was a calculated risk on my part. We had done some kissing, but except for the occasional wandering hand, that was all. It was still hard for me to believe that a guy, especially a normal (except for the mind-reading thing) and incredibly cute guy, could possibly be into me. In the back of my mind, in spite of all his reassurances, I worried that our whole relationship was just an extended pity party, no matter how many sweet nothings he whispered in my ear. I hoped not, but sheer desperation trumped any pride I might have had. He reached up to put his arms around my neck, and I made my move. His heart beat fast under my fingertips as I stroked his chest, moving lower, lightly tickling his stomach, and finally slipping my hand inside his jeans.

"Stop." Ben pushed me off and sat up.

But why? You like it. I put my hand on his bare chest and stared pointedly at the bulge in his pants. *You don't really want me to stop, do you? Let me make you feel good.* Was that sexy, or did I sound like a bad actress in an X-rated movie?

"No, I'm not going to be your fuck buddy when you can't even speak to me. Or is a blow job some new kind of speech therapy?" He put his fingers around my wrist and moved my hand from his chest to the bed.

What just happened? Please don't be mad. You know I would talk if I could.

"I'm not mad, Sasha." He sure looked mad, but maybe I just needed to make him understand the reasons behind my apparently ill-conceived attempt at romance.

It's just so good to feel something, to feel how warm your skin is, to feel your heart beating under my hand. When I first stopped talking, people tried so hard to help me, to bring me back. But after a while, everyone gave up. And when they stopped talking to me, they stopped touching me. You're the first person who's made me feel human, who's made me feel anything, in such a long time. Can you understand that?

"I get that part. But going downtown? A simple thank you would've been plenty."

I'm sorry if that was the wrong thing to do. I thought you liked me like that, not just as friends with a few benefits. I thought you would like me to do those things to you. Shit.

I had totally screwed things up, as usual. Ben knew how I felt about him, and now I had no idea how he felt about me. Was he really angry, or just shocked? Disgusted? Turned off? This was a very uneven playing field. How could I have so completely miscalculated his reaction?

We lay silently next to each other for a few minutes. I tried to make my mind go blank. The harder I tried not to think about anything, the more scattered and outrageous my thoughts became. First I thought about literal blank slates, but then I was writing on them, dirty words, which made me think about what I had been about to do. Ben must have thought I was a total slut. And what would Jules's mother have to say? Fudge, probably. My social development had come to a grinding halt when I stopped speaking, which meant my ability to relate to boys was seriously stunted. So although I wanted to show him how much I cared, I had absolutely no idea how to go about it without coming across as a skank, and an incompetent one at that.

"I get it. Your boy-girl communication skills haven't evolved normally. How could they? But you kind of startled me. I do like you in that way. You know that."

Gratefully, I nodded and put my hand over his. He didn't pull away. A good sign.

"I'm incredibly physically attracted to you. It's fairly obvious, isn't it? When I should be doing homework, I'm fantasizing about what you look like naked, and you're the star in all my wet dreams." My face turned the color of boiled beets. "Is that better? You always want to know what I'm thinking. Can you handle it?"

I shrugged.

"Maybe it's not so great to know what the other person is thinking all the time."

So if you like me that way, then what's wrong? Relief that I hadn't burned all my bridges flooded me, but I knew there had to be a big "but." *When we were in the City, you couldn't stop touching me. What changed in the last few days?*

"About that. I'm really sorry if I led you on. My behavior in the City was over the top, but you looked so good in that little skirt. And it was just an incredibly romantic day. I kind of got carried away."

Feeling me up in the elevator of the Empire State Building? Only an idiot would think that actually meant something.

"I've definitely been sending you mixed signals, and that was wrong." He may have been contrite, but where did that leave me?

A girl could get ideas. The wrong ones, according to you. This evening wasn't going at all as I'd planned. Leave it to me to misread all the flashing lights and neon signs.

"You're absolutely right. My attraction to you made me stupid, and for that I can't apologize enough."

I accept your apology. Can we move on? I'll keep my hands and my mouth to myself until you're ready.

Now that he had admitted what an asshole he was being, I could afford to be a little sarcastic. All that talk about how ripe I was, when he wasn't ripe for anything but a bunch of yakking. If I wanted to have a chat, I would call Jules.

"Moving on is exactly what I'm trying to do."

Yay for you.

"You need to let me finish."

Fine. Finish.

"Even though the physical thing is really important, it's not enough, at least not for me."

But we're already good friends, and until today, we'd hardly done anything but talk and kiss. You're my best friend, other than Jules, and that's only because I've known her forever.

Like a desperate defendant, I argued my case, hoping that if kept talking I would hit on the words that would make him recognize what we had together. My already fragile ego was beginning to crumble, and the tears welled up, ready to spill over.

"Exactly, we haven't done much yet—and then just now—talk about zero to sixty in under ten seconds. Trust me, slow is better."

We haven't exactly been moving at the speed of light. I knew—or rather, Jules knew—plenty of kids in our class who hooked up on the first date. By comparison, Ben and I were engaged in something closer to a nineteenth-century Victorian courting ritual. *You need to figure out what the hell you want from me, and until you do, you need to keep your goddamn hands off my ass.*

"Sasha, I'm really sorry."

Stop saying that. It's not helping. Why couldn't he just shut up and kiss me? It wasn't like I really wanted to go down on him. I was only trying to be thoughtful. Now that I knew what a priss he was, I probably should have bought him a bouquet of daisies instead.

"Fine. All I want to say is that you don't need to do stuff like that to hold my interest. How could you think that's what I wanted from you?"

Why did the only teenage guy with principles have to be the one lying on my bed? There was something seriously wrong with him, but I still wanted to win him over. In total panic, I vomited all the words I had left, hoping the sheer force of my explanation would be enough.

I'm really sorry. You're right, I definitely overstepped, but I'm sure I can figure this out. Just give me a little time. This relationship stuff is totally new for me, and you make me feel like I'm going to die if you don't touch me. I've never felt like that before. I moved too fast. I get it. But you know it's not just your body I'm interested in, don't you?

The whole thing was really kind of funny if you thought about it. The *guy* was telling the *girl* to put on the brakes, tuck it back in, keep her hands to herself. But laughing was the last thing I felt like doing.

"I understand what you were trying to do, but getting the order of the bases right isn't the real problem. You're buried under a mountain of issues, and until you dig yourself out from under them, it wouldn't be fair to distract you from that."

You don't distract me. In fact, you help me stay focused. Even I was getting nauseated by my puppy-like fawning.

"In the last few weeks, you've clearly discovered sex—congratulations—and I've enjoyed being a part of it, more than you'll ever know. Now you need to discover how that fits in with the rest of you. And most important, you need to rediscover your voice." He rested his index finger on my lips.

You've been leading me on with all your meaningful glances and good manners and that thing you do with your tongue. Trust me, it's your fault.

"I agree with you. It's totally my fault. But that doesn't change our situation." If I was a puppy looking for a belly rub, he was a dog with a bone. Enough already.

So now you want to be my shrink? Rediscover my voice? What the fuck do you think I've been doing for the last four years? Playing solitaire?

Where did all his psychobabble come from? He had obviously changed his mind about me, about us, but what had triggered it? It had to be what I said in the restaurant—I scared him away with all my sloppy gratitude. But he wasn't perfect either. What kind of guy panics when a girl tries to stick her hand in his pants? Most guys would say a quick prayer of thanks and get naked, but instead I was trying to justify my actions to a purity ring salesman.

Ben kept going. It was like he had this speech in his pocket, and he was going to deliver it, no matter what. "Because of my special ability, you're allowed the illusion of normalcy when we're together, but there's nothing normal about it. It would be selfish of me to stay with you now—in the long run you would suffer. You deserve to have a regular life. You deserve to laugh out loud at the movies, whisper 'I love you' at just the right moment, say 'I do' at your wedding, and sing lullabies to your babies. You shouldn't go through life without a soundtrack."

Now you've turned into a fucking greeting card commercial. Weddings? Babies? I'm seventeen years old, and yes, I'm seriously screwed up, but don't flatter yourself. I wouldn't marry you if you were the last man on earth. That wasn't true, but the fact that his tongue was flapping instead of dancing with mine was pissing me off. *You're being a fucking jerk.*

"You're so beautiful, and the fact that you're kind of damaged and vulnerable makes me want to take care of you—just make it all better, right now. But you'll never get better if you quit trying because I'm easy for you to be with."

Every word he said after "beautiful" was just noise. No one had ever felt that way about me, and if he walked out the door, no one might ever feel that way again. He was slipping through my fingers, like sand at the beach, and there was nothing I could do to stop it. Throughout our argument we had remained only inches apart on my bed. Now he leaned over me, his face hovering so close to mine that his features were a blur.

You just told me to stop the heavy breathing, and now you're going to kiss me? You're more messed up than I am.

But whatever he was doing, I liked it. Ten seconds ago I was ready to punch him in the nose, and now . . . maybe he wanted me as much as I wanted him, and he couldn't control himself. That sounded ridiculous even to me, but a girl could hope. I reached up to wrap my arms around him, pull him down on top of me, but he grabbed my hands and pinned them above my head. This was playing out way better than any script I could've written. Now that he'd vented, we could get back to business.

"Just be quiet for a minute. You're thinking too loudly." He licked his lips, and then mine. "You like that?"

No. Don't. Stop. What's wrong with you? I opened my mouth to his tongue and intertwined my fingers with his, as if I could make him stay if we were tangled in knots.

"Just proving a point." Slowly he ran one hand down the front of my shirt and slipped it inside the waistband of my sweats. "Should I keep going?" His voice was a whisper.

My insides were molten, and if not for my skin to contain me, I would have been a steaming puddle on the bed. But after a few seconds of bliss, Ben withdrew his hand. I reached down, trying to make him put it back, but he pulled away, looking self-satisfied and perfectly controlled. Bastard.

That is so wrong. Why did you stop? It's not fair to start something if you're not going to finish it. I didn't know exactly what finishing it involved, but whatever was going on, I was just getting started.

"You want me to make you feel good?"

The weight of his body on mine made me feel safe, but his words were going in circles. Hadn't my body just been screaming *yes*?

Isn't that kind of where you were headed? You said you were proving a point. I think I missed it. Show me again. Now I was beyond mad, really horny, but mad too.

"So you're angry, are you? Why? Because I disappointed you, didn't fulfill your expectations?"

Well, yeah. You touched me, where, I might add, no one has ever touched me before, and I really liked it, and then you stopped after five seconds. Disappointed is a good word for it. So is frustrated, desperate, aching.

I tried to sit up but he pushed me back down, kissing me on the lips again. I wanted to hit him, among other things.

"You taste really good. I'm going to miss that." Suddenly he sat up. "Dig yourself out, Sasha. Do the work—I promise I'll make it worth your while. Now I have to go, because if I stay another minute I'm afraid I'm going to force you to live out one of those fantasies I mentioned, which you would probably like, but which would undo everything I just said." He kissed me platonically on the forehead. "As much fun as we have together, I'm not good for you right now. We need some time apart so you can focus on you. I'm getting in the way. Think about it. In your heart, you know I'm right."

You don't know what you're talking about. I've been focusing on me for the past four years, and I've been miserable. Now I'm actually happy, except for the last fifteen minutes. You're the best thing that's ever happened to me. So much for dignity. The tears won out and poured in rivers down my cheeks, making damp polka dots on the quilt. *Please don't leave me.*

Ignoring my tears and silent pleas, Ben stood and walked slowly to my bedroom door, not turning around as he opened it. He paused in the doorway. "I'm really sorry if I hurt you. I didn't mean to jerk you around. I should have controlled myself better. I hope you can forgive me someday."

Never.

I looked around for something to throw at him, but he was gone before I could grab a book from my nightstand. How could I hate him at the same time I was falling in love with him? More than anything I wanted to run after him and throw my arms around him, make him finish the story he had started to write with me. I hoped he didn't hear that, although of course he had, and I could almost see his Mona Lisa smile as I heard the front door slam.

Chapter 12

"Sasha, some flowers were just delivered for you. Come see."

Flowers? The only person who might have sent me flowers on Valentine's Day had conveniently dumped me two days earlier. Charlotte must be mistaken. Sasha Black wasn't such an unusual name. The delivery guy had obviously come to the wrong house.

An enormous wicker basket sat on the kitchen counter, filled with an arrangement that could only have been put together by a blind florist. There were at least a dozen different kinds of flowers, in every color of the rainbow, vying for attention in a bed of moss. In its own way it was beautiful, and it certainly reflected the chaos that was going on inside me, but it was definitely not your typical Valentine's Day offering—no long-stemmed roses and baby's breath. At least he cared enough to send flowers, and he definitely had a sense of humor. The card said, *A mess of flowers for a hot mess. Get to work. I'm waiting.* There was no signature, but it was obvious. He was as subtle as a sledgehammer. I quickly stuffed the note in my pocket.

Charlotte was barely able to contain herself. "Is it from Ben? What does the card say? I've never seen anything quite like that. Whoever sent that has very unusual taste, I must say."

"UNUSUAL IS AN UNDERSTATEMENT. AND THEY ARE FROM HIM, BUT WE'RE TAKING A BREAK. I SHOULD HAVE TOLD YOU BEFORE."

"A break? You just started going out, and he really seemed to like you. I thought you had a wonderful time in the City. Did something happen?"

Charlotte's indignation on my behalf was slightly comforting, although I sometimes wondered if she was a little too invested in my emotional well-being and social development. Becoming my default mother when she had no prior experience must have been terrifying, but I think she occasionally took her role a little too seriously. Not only was I miserable for myself, but now I felt like I was letting Charlotte down. It was too much pressure.

"APPARENTLY MY NOT TALKING WAS MORE OF A PROBLEM FOR HIM THAN HE THOUGHT. HE SAID HE'D COME BACK WHEN I GET MY VOICE BACK, WHICH WILL PROBABLY BE NEVER."

As disappointed as I knew she was, it was a relief to finally tell Charlotte. Her vicarious thrill over my shiny new love life was hard to take even when things were going well, and in the two days since the breakup, I'd been lying to her whenever she asked about Ben, which was all the time. At least I could stop pretending I was happy.

"You poor baby. I really thought Ben was different. He seemed to have the maturity to handle your little problem. Do you want me to talk to him?"

Typical of Charlotte to characterize more than four years of psycho silence as nothing more than a little problem. And even more typical of Charlotte to believe that she could solve the problem by intervening on my behalf. She was a lawyer to her very core—a settlement conference with the opposition was all that was needed to bring the two sides together.

"Talk to whom?" Stuart grabbed his travel coffee mug off the counter. "Char, we're going to miss the train. Get a move on." Charlotte didn't answer, just hugged me, but Stuart wasn't about to give up so easily. "What's going on, ladies? Who are you going to talk to, Charlotte? And who sent those crazy flowers? Honey, is there something you want to tell me? Do you have a secret admirer? That idiot at Fitzgerald & Green? The one with the Italian suits and the bad toupee?"

"SHE'S NOT GOING TO TALK TO ANYONE." I stamped my foot for emphasis.

"Would someone catch me up, please?" Stuart stood, cup in one hand, briefcase in the other, looking back and forth between Charlotte and me, totally baffled.

"Ben broke up with Sasha, and now he sent these strange Valentine's flowers to her. I thought maybe if I talked to him, I could straighten everything out. He seemed like such a nice boy. So reasonable, so grown up for his age. I'm sure it's just a simple misunderstanding." Charlotte's voice was impatient—she was clearly eager to execute her not-so-well-thought-out plan.

Stuart shook his head and glared at his wife. "Charlotte, Sasha's not six years old, and Ben is not some boy who put gum in her hair or stole her lunch money. When will you learn that you cannot fix everything by talking it out? Some things just are."

Thank goodness I had an ally. Not a morning person, Stuart didn't usually have much to say before he and Charlotte caught their train, but for me he was making an exception, and I was grateful for his support.

"Maybe if I talked to his mother . . ."

"Don't you dare. Life is not a broken plate—you can't just glue it back together. Stay out of it. If this boy is destined to have the unique pleasure of being part of our Sasha's life, then it will work out that way, and you poking your nose where it doesn't belong will only make such an outcome impossible. This is one of those situations in which you have to let nature take its course."

"That's your opinion, Stuart. I just want to know what happened, and perhaps offer up a dose of common sense. Young people can let their emotions get the best of them, you know." Hands on her hips, Charlotte wasn't ready to give up.

"If you were paying attention, you'd see that it's Sasha's opinion that you butt out as well." I nodded vociferously, although it upset me that I was the cause of a rare disagreement between my aunt and uncle. "Mind your own beeswax, Charlotte, and let's get out of here. We've already missed our regular train. Shit, now we'll have to catch the local." Stuart held the door open for Charlotte. "Bye, Sash. Love you."

Charlotte's shoulders slumped. At least she knew when she was beaten.

"Goodbye, sweetie. I'm sorry. I just wanted to make it all better. You know that. Don't worry, I'll keep my big mouth shut. This mothering stuff is much harder than practicing law."

She kissed me on the forehead and rushed past Stuart as he rolled his eyes in my direction. *Thank you*, I mouthed.

At school, I hoped and dreaded that I would run into Ben. But since he knew where I was at all times, it was up to him to either seek me out or avoid me. When the last bell rang, it was clear that he didn't want to see me. Head down, I trudged through the crowd of happy normals. My brief foray into the world of light, guided by Ben, was over, and now I returned to my home in the shadows. Now that I'd tasted the good life, mine seemed that much more drab and pointless. Damn him.

"You look like shit." Jules fell into step beside me. "What's wrong?"

I stopped and dug my Hawkie Talkie out of my backpack. "HE DUMPED ME."

"Is that why you've been avoiding me for the last couple of days? I thought maybe you dumped *me* for *him*. I was giving you a pass since it's your first time around the block. That's rough. I'm surprised. He doesn't look like the type to cut and run. Especially after your big date. It sounded perfect."

"I THOUGHT IT WAS PERFECT TOO. STUPID ME. BOYS SUCK."

"How'd he do it? Facebook? Text?" Did the logistics really matter at this point?

"NO, HE'S A GENTLEMAN. HE DID IT IN PERSON."

I spilled the whole foul anecdote, including how I attacked him and he rejected me. It sounded even more pitiful in the retelling.

"That's harsh. But what made you think going down on him was the right thing to do?" Jules made a retching noise and stuck out her tongue. I guess that meant she had never attempted it. Why didn't I talk to her before I decided to get creative?

"I DIDN'T REALLY THINK IT THROUGH. WE WERE ALONE, AND I WANTED TO MAKE HIM FEEL GOOD. THAT WAS ALL. I WASN'T CONSIDERING ALL THE MORAL RAMIFICATIONS."

"And truthfully, what sane guy would turn that down? Hard to imagine not only refusing, but giving you the ax on top of it. Most guys would drop trou in a heartbeat. He's definitely an odd one." But he had been *my* odd one, and I loved him, and now I had fucked it up royally.

"I MISS HIM."

"It's kind of funny, actually. Six weeks ago you'd never kissed anyone on the lips, let alone anywhere else. I'd say that's real progress, even if you're having a temporary setback." Jules giggled and poked her tongue against the inside of her cheek.

"THAT IS SO DISGUSTING, JULES, AND I DON'T THINK IT'S TEMPORARY."

"Why? From what you told me, Mr. Hands-Off-My-Junk didn't really break up with you. He just wants you to get your shit together before he commits. Can't argue with his reasoning."

"WHOSE SIDE ARE YOU ON?" I had hoped for more sympathy from my best friend.

"I'm on your side, and so is Ben, if you'd bother to listen to what he said."

"DO YOU KNOW WHAT DAY IT IS TODAY?" I traced a heart in the air and scowled.

"I have to admit, dumping you—well, sidelining you, really—right before V-day is kind of bad form. Even though he said it wasn't permanent, his timing was pretty lousy. It's cold-blooded, I'll give you that."

"BEYOND LOUSY. TODAY WAS SUPPOSED TO BE MY FIRST REAL VALENTINE'S DAY EVER, WITH A REAL LIVE BOYFRIEND. IT'S WORSE THAN IF HE'D NEVER COME NEAR ME."

Ben had gone from being the most thoughtful guy in the world to the most insensitive. Couldn't he have waited until after Valentine's Day? Couldn't he have given me a heart-shaped box of chocolates and a dozen red roses, and then discarded me?

"Maybe he just forgot the date. I don't think boys focus on Valentine's Day the way girls do. It's really a holiday for us, not for them."

"DID HE HIRE YOU TO DO PR FOR HIM? YOU'RE MY BEST FRIEND. YOU'RE SUPPOSED TO BE ANGRY AT HIM, NOT MAKE EXCUSES FOR HIM."

"You're right. He's a no-good, rotten bastard, and you're well rid of him. Is that better?"

"MUCH. SO HOW DOES HE LOOK? I HAVEN'T SEEN HIM AT SCHOOL AT ALL." Now that Jules was mouthing the right platitudes, I could ask the important questions.

"He looks good. Still cute, and built. Maybe a little sad, but it's hard to tell. And not that I want to make you more miserable than you already are, but that model chick from the track team has been sniffing around. I didn't think it was an issue, because I thought you guys were hard at it."

"SHE DOES HAVE THE ADVANTAGE. SHE CAN TALK TO HIM. AND SHE LOOKS LIKE SHE SHOULD BE POSING FOR *VOGUE* INSTEAD OF GOING TO HIGH SCHOOL." I was so fucked, and I'd done it to myself, so it wasn't like I could wallow in self-pity, which, although useless, was at least a distraction.

"But he likes the way you look, or at least he did, so don't get so hung up on the beauty queen. Have you tried running into him by accident? Maybe if he sees you, he'll remember how much he cares." Jules looked proud of herself for coming up with this ridiculously simple solution.

"HE'S REALLY GOOD AT AVOIDING ME." I still hadn't told Jules that Ben knew what I was thinking as I was thinking it, so unless he wanted me to find him, it wasn't going to happen. "IF HE'D CHANGED HIS MIND, HE

COULD JUST COME TO MY HOUSE . . . OR THE LIBRARY. HE'S DONE WITH ME. IT'S OVER."

"From what you've told me, whether or not it's really over is up to you, right?" I didn't answer, just glowered. "He told you that if you found your voice, he'd be waiting with open arms. Isn't that basically what he said?"

"SURE. I'LL TAKE CARE OF THAT THIS AFTERNOON. EXCEPT FOUR YEARS OF THERAPY DIDN'T HELP, SO MAYBE IT'S NOT SO SIMPLE AS YOU TWO LOSERS THINK IT IS."

Jules, who had held me up through the worst of it, knew better than anyone how hard I'd worked. And I knew I shouldn't be so rude to her. If she bailed, I would be completely rudderless.

"I know. I'm sorry. It's not easy, but it's definitely worth it, don't you think? *He's* definitely worth it." Jules flexed her muscles, pointed at her stomach, and then wiggled her tongue lewdly.

She had a point. Just thinking about him made me feel that delicious ache all over. In four years, I had never felt so motivated to get my life back on track.

"MAYBE YOU'RE RIGHT. BUT HOW?"

"I have no idea, but we'll figure it out. I'll help you."

One of the things I loved most about Jules was her lack of stubbornness in comparison to me. Saying sorry came easy for her, even when she was probably right, and her ability to indulge me while at the same time helping me focus on the big picture had made our fight fizzle before it got too heated.

"YOU WANT TO COME IN? YOU HAVE TO SEE THESE FLOWERS."

The fragrance of all those blooms filled the house. "It smells like a flower shop in here."

"THAT'S EXACTLY WHAT IT LOOKS LIKE."

Jules buried her face in the basket, taking a deep breath. "It's perfect."

"WHY? BECAUSE IT'S A METAPHOR FOR MY LIFE?" I handed Jules the card Ben had sent, now crumpled from having spent the day in my pocket.

"He's funny. Well, it is, kind of, but don't you see what he's done? In the Victorian era, flowers were used to send messages. Every kind of flower had a different meaning. I think he's sending you a message. That's totally something he would do, considering he acts like he's visiting from another century."

"ARE YOU SURE HE DIDN'T JUST ORDER THE DISCOUNT LEFTOVER BOUQUET?"

"I don't think so. We already know one thing: he's definitely not cheap." Jules opened up Charlotte's laptop, which was sitting on the counter. "There you are. FlowerSymbols. com. Let's see, what's in here?"

"GLADIOLAS, PEONIES, PINK TULIPS, WHITE CHRYSANTHEMUMS, IRIS."

"Okay, glads stand for strength of character, pink tulips are symbols of caring, white mums mean truth, and iris are faith and friendship. You see?"

"MAYBE, BUT NOT TOO ROMANTIC A SELEC-TION. NOT EXACTLY A LOVE LETTER."

"What else is there? You've only named a few. That looks like a forget-me-not, which symbolizes memories."

"SUBTLE."

"I see one red rose, right in the middle, and red roses stand for love, passionate love, so there. It was just a semi-dumping."

"I FEEL SO MUCH BETTER."

I was being sarcastic, but in truth, I did feel better. If Ben cared enough to go to the trouble of sending a secret message in flowers, maybe he really meant he would wait around while I got my act together. The only questions now were whether such a thing was possible, and if so, how long would it take?

The next day, I had one of my check-in appointments with Dr. O. Like Charlotte, she was surprised and more than a little upset about the demise of my short-lived love affair.

"That's a shame, Sasha. But from what you've just told me, his decision to leave you was based on his concern for your well-being over the long term. I don't believe your connection with him has been severed as completely as you think."

"HE BASICALLY SAID HE WOULD COME BACK IF I STARTED TALKING AGAIN. SOMETHING ABOUT HOW IMPORTANT IT WAS FOR ME TO SAY MY MARRIAGE VOWS OUT LOUD AND SING TO MY CHILDREN."

"A little melodramatic, perhaps, but I see where he's coming from. This young man is focusing on the distant future, perhaps because he sees something in you that makes him hope you could have a future together. Have you thought about it that way?"

"IT'S HARD TO THINK ABOUT ANYTHING ELSE, BUT AFTER FOUR YEARS, DON'T I HAVE TO START CONSIDERING THE POSSIBILITY THAT I MIGHT NEVER SAY ANOTHER WORD?"

A few months ago, the thought that I may be permanently mute was enough to send me into a cold sweat, but now I felt oddly in control. That had to be a good sign. Mentally, I felt healthier than I had since this nightmare began, even though Ben was giving me the semi-cold shoulder.

"That's certainly a very mature attitude, but I don't think you should ever give up—not after four years, or even fourteen years, if it came to that. But what I think Ben is suggesting, and what I have been trying to say as well, is that your focus should shift toward your future and the potential that lies there, rather than getting lost in the dark corners of your past."

In fact, Ben had told me just the opposite—that I *should* be spending my time unpacking my emotional steamer trunk, not shoving it overboard unopened. Because Dr. O'Rourke had spent more than four years sometimes pushing me to remember, assuring me that my future would be built on the foundation of my past, and other times saying I could start over right now, I wasn't sure what to think. But either way, whether I looked backward or forward, nobody was offering any magical cures. If there were drugs to remedy everything from baldness to bubonic plague, why wasn't there a pill or a potion to fix me?

"I'M BEGINNING TO THINK IT'S JUST GOING TO BE TOTALLY RANDOM IF IT EVER HAPPENS. MAYBE IF I GET HIT ON THE HEAD? YOU COULD WHACK ME OVER THE HEAD WITH ONE OF YOUR PAPER-WEIGHTS. WHAT DO YOU THINK?" On a bookshelf in her office was an extensive collection of Venetian glass paper-weights—tiny fish swimming through crystal, millefiori, and incredibly realistic flowers encased in glass spheres.

"An unorthodox treatment, for sure, and something I cannot in good conscience do." Had she considered it briefly? "The Hippocratic oath dictates that I 'do no harm.' Giving you a concussion and possibly a subdural hematoma would most certainly violate that promise. But if you're interested in random approaches, what would you think of taking a Rorschach test?"

"INKBLOTS? I THOUGHT THAT WAS JUST IN THE MOVIES."

"No, it's very real. Many people discount its value, but I've occasionally gleaned some useful information from it. It's worth a try, don't you think? And way safer than hitting you over the head with a hunk of glass."

"WHY NOT?" Nothing to lose at this point, and we still had thirty minutes to kill.

Dr. O. removed a stack of large cards from a filing cabinet and sat down next to me on the sofa. She handed me the one on top.

"Different people see different things. There are no right or wrong answers. Just tell me what you're seeing and feeling when you look at each of the cards."

"THAT'S IT?" I remember reading somewhere that Rorschach inkblots were actually sexually explicit representations of male and female anatomy. Peering at the first picture, I decided that my nonexistent sexual IQ must have affected my ability to see what was in front of me. "IT LOOKS LIKE TWO PIGLETS KISSING."

"Okay." Dr. O. jotted that down. I pointed to the pigs' ears and the place where their snouts met. Was the doctor trying to suppress a smile? What else could it be?

"How about this next one?"

"THAT'S TWO PEOPLE WITH THEIR HANDS PRESSED TOGETHER, ABOUT TO KISS."

"Anything else?"

"THEY'RE WEARING RED SKI MASKS."

If I'd known she was going to show me these, I could have looked them up on the Internet to make sure my answers were normal. Now I was just being honest, which in my case probably meant totally deviant.

"Fine, and this one?"

"TWO PEOPLE LOOKING AT EACH OTHER, LIKE THEY'RE ABOUT TO KISS." Why were they all the same?

After I had evaluated all ten cards, all pictures of people or animals kissing—except for the ninth one, which looked like a man's torso—Dr. O'Rourke sat back and looked over her notes. "Fascinating. I'm really supposed to engage in an involved and specific evaluation of your responses before I offer an opinion, but off the top of my head, I would have to say that except for your inability to speak, you seem to be a totally normal teenager."

"REALLY?" I found that hard to believe.

"Absolutely. Your interpretation of the inkblots suggests a preoccupation with male-female relationships, which is what one would expect from someone your age. Sex is a primal urge that manifests during puberty, and although your problem has hampered your social progression, your natural desires are still there. Based on your limited sexual experience, you see people kissing. Pretty textbook stuff. If you were more sexually savvy, you might perceive something more graphic."

"SO?"

I was in heat, and I'd barely rounded first base—I already knew that—but what to do about it, especially with Ben out of the picture? If there was no pill for my muteness, maybe there was a pill I could take to make that wonderfully awful feeling go away. Without someone to share it with, it was nothing more than an annoying distraction, like an itch in the center of my back that I couldn't quite reach.

"It's very simple. You need someone to rock your world." She smiled indulgently at me.

"IS THAT A MEDICAL TERM, DOCTOR?" Dr. O'Rourke, in her tweed skirts and sensible shoes, didn't look like someone who had ever had her world nudged, let alone rocked.

"You need a guy, and if Ben isn't the one, then you'll find another one. He may be the first boy who's shown an interest, but he most certainly won't be the last. With or without your voice, you're intelligent, beautiful, and funny. Just have faith."

As much as I wanted to believe her, I knew that Charlotte was paying her a ridiculous amount of money, and that made me question her sincerity. It was her job to bolster my self-esteem, and if she had to tell a boatload of lies to do that, so be it. Telling me I was dull, unattractive, and hopeless wouldn't serve anyone's interests, even if it were true.

"EASIER SAID THAN DONE."

"Nothing worth having is ever easy, my dear. I'm afraid our time is up. See you in a month, Sasha."

Great. The world famous psychiatrist said I needed someone to rotate my tires. How was I supposed to go about making that happen? Were there escort services for adolescents? Teen gigolos? I would have to check the Internet. Maybe if I told Ben that the doctor had recommended some male companionship as part of her treatment, he might agree to a pity make-out session. Maybe if she wrote me a prescription he would go for it. Something to consider.

That night I dreamt we were back together, and I could talk, and the sky was a ridiculously vivid shade of blue. I woke up disappointed and lonely, but it was still way better than dreaming about screeching brakes and burnt rubber.

Chapter 13

A week later, I woke up after dreaming about Ben for the umpteenth time. We were walking on a beach, but it was warm and sunny instead of cold and rainy, and we were talking and laughing, splashing in the shallow water. Just like a commercial for a vacation in the Bahamas.

Suddenly I knew exactly what to do. The house was still—my aunt and uncle worked so hard during the week that they often slept until noon on Saturdays—and I tiptoed out, gently shutting the great slab of a front door behind me. It wasn't a long way to my destination, but it was too far to walk. Although I had a driver's license, I avoided getting behind the wheel much as I dodged any activity that involved my behaving like an independent, almost-adult. But this was important.

Ten minutes later, clammy hands gripping the steering wheel, I pulled off the road onto the narrow shoulder separating asphalt from the woods beyond. A deep gash still scarred the tree where the Volvo had crashed into it. Like me, the oak had never fully healed. At the base of the tree were some faded, withered bouquets of flowers and one fresh bunch of white tulips. No brown edges or wilted blooms; they couldn't have been there for more than a day. When I got closer, I saw a note peeking out of the cellophane. It was a poem.

Fear and betrayal, a heavy load,
A winter night, an icy road,
Nothing left for me to hold,
They can't go home,
But one does live,
And though she burns,
Should she forgive?

Fear and betrayal? She burns? Was "she" me? In my hand was a poem written by the person who had taken my family. Was that possible? Or did someone have a very sick sense of humor? Stooping in the dirt, I tore at the plastic wrapping around a bunch of dead flowers. Another poem, typed on pale blue paper, which was now brown and wrinkled from exposure to the weather. I sat down in the dirt, my mouth dry, my heart racing.

Love and death,
One last breath,
Blood and pain,
What do you gain?
Because of a tree,
No one goes free.

There were seven short verses, each one more bizarre than the last. At the top of four of the slips of paper was the anniversary date of the accident, and the rest had the dates of Mom's, Dad's, and Liz's birthdays. Who would do such a thing? What little I knew of the accident was that it had been a single-car crash. The police report was short and to the point: no other cars, no witnesses, cause of accident listed as excessive speed on an icy, snow-covered road. Simple, straightforward—case closed. This made no sense. The Shoreland Police Department was no CSI, but still.

I texted Jules. *I'm at the accident scene, Old Farm Road. Please come ASAP. I need you.*

Although I was sure I had woken her, she texted back almost immediately. *Ten minutes. Stay calm.*

True to her word, Jules pulled up ten minutes later in her bright red Mini Cooper as I sat hyperventilating in the front seat of Charlotte's car, my forehead resting on the steering wheel. Seeing my best friend was enough to stave off the rising nausea, and I looked up with grateful tears in my eyes. How many times had she ridden to my rescue in the last four years?

"Sasha, what's going on? What are you doing out here? You refused to come here when Dr. O. suggested it, and now at seven o'clock on a Saturday morning? Are you okay?"

She opened the door, bent down, and wrapped her arms around me. I started to cry, tears coursing down my cheeks, my body shaking with the effort.

After a few more minutes, the tears slowed, and Jules stood up. "Scoot over. Better?"

I nodded and reached for my voice box. "THANK YOU FOR COMING. I'M SORRY I WOKE YOU."

"Not a problem. But what are you doing here? It's freezing. What were you thinking?"

I handed her the stack of poems I had collected.

"What are these?" She flipped through the pile. "Where did you get them?"

"THEY WERE INSIDE SOME BOUQUETS OF FLOWERS."

"Who wrote them?"

"IT SOUNDS LIKE IT WAS THE PERSON WHO CAUSED THE ACCIDENT."

"What the fuck? But the police said there were no other cars. The Volvo just skidded on the ice and hit the tree." As Jules described it, my dream of the crash started playing in my head and I ground my fists into my eyes. "I'm sorry, Sash."

"MY FATHER DIDN'T JUST SLIDE INTO A TREE. THERE WAS ANOTHER CAR." I shook the squares of paper.

"How could the police miss that?" Jules's voice was incredulous.

"THE EARLIEST DATE ON THE NOTES IS THE FIRST ANNIVERSARY OF THE CRASH. THE INVESTIGATION WAS LONG OVER BY THEN."

"I guess that makes sense, but it doesn't say much for the cops in this town. Weren't there skid marks from the other car?"

"WHO CARES? DON'T YOU SEE? WHOEVER WROTE THESE POEMS KNOWS WHAT HAPPENED THAT NIGHT."

Jules got out of the car and went over to the tree, where she rubbed the wounded trunk with her gloved hand. She picked up the bunch of white tulips lying at its base.

"These flowers are perfect. It's brutal out here, but they're not frozen yet. This person was just here."

"THAT MAKES SENSE. MY DAD'S BIRTHDAY WAS YESTERDAY."

"It's simple then. When's the next birthday? We just have to stake out this tree, and we'll catch him."

Jules paced back and forth in front of the tree as she spoke. I could practically see the wheels turning as she formulated her grand plan.

"I CAN'T BELIEVE THIS IS HAPPENING."

"But Sasha, don't you see? This is good. This is what's supposed to happen. You're here, in the middle of it. You're standing up to your pain, and you're still upright, you're still breathing. No lightning bolt has shot from the sky to strike you down where you stand. You're on your way to getting your voice back, and getting Ben back." Jules's glass was always half full.

I opened and closed my mouth. "NOTHING."

"You can't expect miracles, you dunce. Give it time. Rome wasn't built in a day, right?"

"I SUPPOSE." How long did it take to build Rome? I was in a hurry. "WHAT SHOULD WE DO NOW?"

"First thing, we need to take these notes to the police. They'll be able to track this person down, figure out what really happened," Jules said as she stared at the slips of paper.

"NO." I shook my head violently.

"Why not? What do you have against the police? Don't you want to know who wrote these?"

"I DO, BUT IF THE POLICE ALREADY DECIDED THERE WASN'T ANOTHER CAR, THEY'RE PROBABLY NOT GOING TO EMBRACE THE THEORY THAT THERE WAS."

"You think they won't admit they made a mistake?"

"THEY'RE NOT GOING TO WANT TO PROVE THEMSELVES WRONG. BESIDES, IF THEY START HANGING OUT HERE, THEY'LL SCARE THIS PERSON AWAY AND WE'LL NEVER KNOW."

"Maybe. So you want to play detective? Do we set up a hidden camera or something, or should we just hide in a tree?" Jules took a few steps into the woods. "Whose birthday is next?"

"LIZ'S IS IN A COUPLE OF WEEKS."

"You should call Ben and tell him what you found. He'll be so proud of you for facing your fears, and maybe he can help us find this guy." Jules nodded encouragingly. She seemed more desperate to get Ben and me back together than I was.

"I DON'T WANT TO SEE HIM NOW. I'M NOT READY." Once I had figured this out, I could walk proudly up to Ben and tell him, in my own voice, what I'd done, all on my own, for myself.

"All right, you're the boss." Jules shivered. "Let's get out of here. You can buy me breakfast—that's the price for waking me at dawn on a Saturday."

"I'LL MEET YOU AT PJ'S. ALL THE PANCAKES YOU CAN EAT. HOW DOES THAT SOUND?"

"And bacon?"

"AND BACON."

As I drove to the restaurant, my shoulders felt a little less stooped, and the sky looked a little brighter. The clouds were lifting, at least for the moment. Could a few bunches of flowers and some crummy poetry be the light at the end of my tunnel?

PJ's had been serving breakfast to Shorelanders for more than eighty years, and no matter what the hour, it was always packed with high school kids. For that reason I usually stayed away, but I knew it was Jules's favorite place. The aroma of maple syrup, coffee, and bacon greeted us before we even got inside. Maybe I should rethink my decision to steer clear of this place—I did love pancakes. But as we made our way to a booth in the back, we passed a few kids who happened to be in my physics class.

"Hey, Professor Hawking, how're things in detention? Any scientific breakthroughs lately? Loved your special on the Discovery Channel."

No pancake tasted that good.

Chapter 14

The smell of freshly brewed coffee welcomed me as I climbed into the front seat and quietly shut the door. It was 4:15 in the morning, but it felt like the middle of the night. Jules handed me a steaming paper cup.

"It's not a real stakeout without coffee and doughnuts."

"OF COURSE NOT."

The dramatic aspect of our quest to catch the mystery poet in action appealed to Jules's theatrical bent. I was surprised she hadn't given us each cop names, although it was still early.

"Did you know that the Creepy Cruller opens at 4:00 A.M.?" She was way too chipper, considering she was not naturally an early riser.

"HOW MANY COFFEES HAVE YOU HAD THIS MORNING?"

"I had two double espressos while I was waiting for the chocolate ones to come out of the oven. They're your favorite, right? Why do you ask?"

I put my hand on her leg, which was bouncing up and down in time to the song on the radio, and nodded at her fingers tapping the same beat on the steering wheel.

"YOU'RE JUST A LITTLE HYPER, ESPECIALLY FOR SO EARLY."

"I guess I am." She took a deep breath and exhaled slowly.

"JUST A TAD."

I hoped the caffeine would wear off soon. If she was this fidgety, she might fall out of the tree.

"Sorry," Jules sang. "Are you okay? Being that it's Liz's birthday and everything?"

"IT'S WEIRD. ON HER BIRTHDAY WE ALWAYS WENT TO THAT GERMAN RESTAURANT DOWN-TOWN. WE ATE SCHNITZEL AND STRUDEL AND THERE WAS FOLK DANCING."

I hadn't thought about that place since the accident, but in the last few months memories had begun to float in, like bits and pieces of a boat washing up on shore long after the shipwreck. Part of me wanted to go back to the Alpine Vil-lage, to try and remember more, maybe feel closer to Liz, but I wasn't sure I could handle it.

"That sounds like a total geek fest. So not your sister."

"EXACTLY. I THINK THAT'S WHAT MADE IT SO COOL. SHE LOVED IT."

Liz would have been nineteen if she had lived. I won-dered what she would look like, where she would have gone to college, whether she would have a boyfriend. Would we still be close, or would she have left me behind when she went away to school? So many questions that could never be asked or answered. Maybe I should put away my detective hat and leave the past in the past. But looking over at Jules, I realized there was no backing out.

"WHAT ARE YOU WEARING?" Jules was dressed in brown coveralls and a matching cap. "ARE YOU PLANNING ON CHANGING THE OIL BEFORE OR AFTER THE BIG STAKEOUT?"

"You're a riot. There's a matching set for you in the back seat, smartass. This way we'll be sure no one can spot us in the trees." She tapped the side of her head. "Success is in the details."

"I THOUGHT GOD WAS IN THE DETAILS. YOU'VE WATCHED ONE TOO MANY EPISODES OF *LAW & ORDER: SVU.*"

"I'm just being logical. We're going to park down the road a ways and approach through the woods." She had it all worked out.

"YOU FORGOT THE CAMOUFLAGE NETTING."

"No, I didn't. It's in the trunk."

Her father was an avid hunter, so I shouldn't have been surprised that Jules would be so knowledgeable and well equipped. I rolled my eyes. If she made me put shoe polish on my face, I would have to hit her.

"If we're going to do this, we're going to do it right. We have to be invisible."

"OR AT LEAST CRAZY."

"I got you your chocolate doughnut. Now let me have my fun—and increase the chance of catching this guy. Leave your coffee in the car."

"WHY CAN'T I TAKE MY COFFEE? IT'S 4:30 IN THE MORNING. I NEED CAFFEINE."

"The same reason you can't take your Hawkie Talkie—we're trying to blend in with the woods, so no unexpected smells and no unexpected noise." Jules handed me a pen and a small pad of paper. "If you have something to say, you'll have to write it down."

"UNEXPECTED SMELLS? THAT'S RIDICULOUS. WE'RE NOT TRACKING A BEAR. AND IT'S PITCH DARK. HOW WILL YOU SEE WHAT I WRITE ON THE PAD?" She pulled out a tiny flashlight and cupped her hand around it. "NO NIGHT VISION GOGGLES?"

"Daddy wouldn't let me borrow them. They cost a fortune, and he was afraid we'd break them."

I should have known. "FINE. LET'S GO, GENERAL."

Huddled next to each other in the crotch of a tree, shrouded in netting, we each peered at nothing through binoculars. A squirrel scurried across a branch overhead and I flinched, almost falling from our precarious perch.

"Careful, you'll break your neck," Jules whispered, grabbing me around the waist.

I scribbled on my pad. **Sorry. Just nervous. What if one of the squirrels mistakes our heads for giant acorns?**

"Relax, I think the squirrels know the difference."

Two hours later we folded our camouflage netting and limped back to the car, our legs numb from sitting still for so long. At least we hadn't been attacked by rabid chipmunks. Our flower-leaving bard had failed to show. Not that I'd really expected it, but somewhere, deep down, I had hoped it would be that easy.

"NOW WHAT?" I sipped my cold coffee and gnawed on a doughnut. "WHOEVER IT IS FORGOT MY SISTER'S BIRTHDAY."

"You can't be ready to give up after one mission."

"MISSION? SHOULD I BE SALUTING WHEN I TALK TO YOU?"

"I'm just saying it's a little soon to throw in the towel."

Jules took a swig of coffee and removed her cap. Even in a dirt-colored mechanic's jumpsuit, she was still the head cheerleader who never wanted for a date on a Saturday night. Her flawless skin glowed, and I wondered, as I had so many times, why she bothered with me.

"AND WHY ARE WE SO SURE THAT THIS FLOWER DROP ONLY OCCURS UNDER COVER OF

DARKNESS?" Spending the afternoon with Chip and Dale was way more appealing than huddling in the dark, not sure what was about to crawl up my leg.

Clearly a stupid question, based on the look Jules threw my way. "Because whoever is leaving the flowers is a killer and wouldn't dare show his face in the daytime."

"I SUPPOSE THAT MAKES SENSE, BUT I'M NOT CONVINCED IT'S GOING TO MAKE ANY DIFFERENCE IN THE END."

"Have you totally forgotten why you're doing this?" Yawning, Jules put the car in gear and slowly headed back toward town.

"I KNOW. MY VOICE. BUT AFTER SO LONG I CAN'T BELIEVE ANYTHING COULD REALLY MATTER." When I was feeling discouraged, I tended to wallow in it.

"First of all, it's not just your voice you're trying to get back. What about your twenty-first-century Roman god? You can't have forgotten about his tongue already. I mean, the way you described him to me, *I* can practically taste him."

Oh yeah, kissing. I nodded.

"Having kissed a few guys, I can tell you he sounds like a rare talent—worth working for. Don't give up so easily."

"YOU'RE RIGHT. I NEED TO THINK LONG TERM, BE POSITIVE. SO TOMORROW MORNING, SAME TIME, SAME DOUGHNUTS?"

"I was thinking tonight. It's still Liz's birthday, right up until midnight. I'm up for it if you are." We pulled into my driveway just as the sun rose over the trees.

"OKAY. WHAT HAVE WE GOT TO LOSE? THANKS FOR EVERYTHING. I FEEL BETTER."

In spite of Jules's overzealous attention to details, it was obvious that all she wanted to do was help me get what I wanted. Knowing how sincere she was, I could easily forgive her over-the-top approach.

"Wear all black. I'll bring stuff to blacken our faces."

"WE'RE NOT GOING BEHIND ENEMY LINES."

"No complaining allowed. I'm in charge of makeup and wardrobe. Be ready at 2200 hours, Corporal, or else."

I gave her a hug and climbed out of the car. "YOU NEED TO DO MORE THEATER STUFF AT SCHOOL, OR MAYBE LESS. BYE. DON'T TEXT ME. I'M GOING TO BED."

"Sweet dreams. Remember the tongue." Jules saluted and sped away.

✦

"I feel it. Tonight's the night," she said as I climbed into the car, my feet crunching on an empty doughnut box and four cardboard coffee cups.

"JUST BECAUSE YOU SAY IT DOESN'T MEAN YOU CAN WILL IT INTO HAPPENING."

"Don't be so negative. Remind me to throw that crap out when we get back. It's pretty disgusting, isn't it?"

The car seemed to know its way to the spot down the road from the wounded tree. We marched quickly and soundlessly through the woods. I was getting into the whole paramilitary fantasy, imagining us on a top-secret mission deep in enemy territory. If we stepped on a twig, we would give away our position and be taken prisoner. When the interrogators threatened me with death unless I talked, I would just smile knowingly.

After about an hour in our tree, I must have dozed off, because I opened my eyes to the glare of headlights when the rumble of tires on the dirt by the side of the road woke me.

Jules put her finger to her lips, and we carefully climbed down from our branch, trying to get close enough to glimpse a license plate. We hadn't discussed what we would do if someone actually came to leave flowers, and now we looked at each other, eyes wide, afraid of what would happen if we were discovered. If this was the murderer of my family, he might kill us and hide our bodies in the woods to avoid having to pay the price for his wretched crime. The closest thing we had to a weapon was the tiny diamond emery board that Jules always carried since she stopped biting her nails. It was unlikely we would be able to file anyone into submission. As we got closer, I could see that it was a van, not a car, and it had writing on the side. It said Shakespeare's Flowers, and underneath, "A rose by any other name . . ."

Suddenly Jules ran toward the van, yelling, "Stop!" just as a balding, slightly overweight man stepped out with a bouquet of white tulips.

Dropping the flowers, he threw his hands in the air. "I don't carry any money in my truck. There's twenty bucks in my wallet in my back pocket. Take it. Don't hurt me. I've got a kid." He tossed the keys he was holding into the dirt. "Here, take the van too."

Jules stopped in her tracks and I caught up with her. "We're not going to rob you."

"Then what the hell are you doing? You almost gave me a heart attack." When the man realized his muggers were a couple of teenage girls in matching jumpsuits, he sheepishly lowered his hands and picked up the dropped flowers. "What kind of crazies are you, hiding in the woods?"

"We wanted to know who brought the flowers and poems."

"What? I deliver a bunch of white tulips to this spot a few times a year. That's all I know. I get paid extra to deliver them at midnight. You'll have to talk to my boss if you want to find out more." Gently placing the bouquet at the base of the tree, he climbed back into the truck and rolled down the window. "You two shouldn't be wandering around in the middle of the night. It's not safe, for you or anybody else, for that matter," he said, putting one hand to his chest. "You scared the shit out of me."

"Thank you, sir, and I'm sorry we frightened you. It's just that my friend's family was killed in an accident on this spot, and we're trying to find someone who might know more about what happened."

"Oh, that's terrible. Good luck, then, and I'm sorry about your family. Call my boss in the morning. His name's Mike Grant. Maybe he can help you."

As he pulled away, leaving us choking on a cloud of dust, Jules jumped up and down. "We did it. It worked. Sasha, this is huge. We're going to figure out what happened that night. Can you believe it?"

I shook my head and stared at the cellophane-wrapped bouquet. Maybe I really was on my way to a breakthrough. Tears silently streamed down my cheeks, and I put my head on Jules's shoulder. In the light of our little flashlight we stood holding each other. After a few minutes, I picked up the bouquet, and we walked back through the woods. Finally, we were making some progress.

"So what does this one say?" Jules started the car, and I unfolded the most recent poem and read it out loud.

"LIFE IS TRANSIENT,
DEATH IS FOREVER. LIKE YOU,
I AM LOST FOR WORDS."

"Is that a haiku?"

"IT IS." But it wasn't the fact that our mystery poet was branching out beyond simple rhyming that caught my attention.

"It's not bad. I like haiku. Using only a few words is very dramatic."

Sometimes Jules missed the forest for the trees. "THANK YOU FOR YOUR INSIGHTFUL LITERARY ANALYSIS, PROFESSOR HARPER. BUT DIDN'T YOU HEAR? WHOEVER WROTE THIS KNOWS ME, KNOWS THAT I'M MUTE."

"We live in a small town. Lots of people know you don't talk, don't they? It's not exactly a deep dark secret, Dr. Hawking."

"IF YOU WEREN'T DRIVING, I'D PUNCH YOU."

"It's true. The fact that the person who wrote this poem knows you don't speak doesn't get us anywhere." Jules seemed awfully sure of that fact, but I wasn't totally convinced.

"I SUPPOSE YOU'RE RIGHT. BUT MAYBE IT MEANS THIS PERSON IS FROM HERE, NOT SOMEONE WHO WAS JUST PASSING THROUGH."

Who would cause a terrible accident and drive away without even calling an ambulance? A criminal fleeing after committing a crime? A drunk driver? A kid? A drunk kid? The possibilities were endless.

"I'll give you that, but local still means we're talking about thousands of possible suspects. If we were CSI, we could do paper and ink analysis, but I think that's beyond us." Jules was clearly disappointed that we were so technically limited.

"MAYBE THE GUY AT THE BARD'S BUDS WILL HAVE SOME ANSWERS."

"How long did it take you to come up with that?"

"IT JUST CAME TO ME. IT'S GOOD, RIGHT? LET'S GO BACK TO YOUR HOUSE AND GET SOME SLEEP. ALL THIS SLEUTHING IS EXHAUSTING."

"Sounds like a plan, Nancy Drew."

✦

Shakespeare's Flowers was a half-timbered Tudor storefront in a strip shopping mall two towns away from ours. Kitschy was an understatement, and I wouldn't have been surprised if the owner had greeted us wearing knee breeches and a codpiece. Fortunately, the Disney details only extended to the architecture. I stood next to Jules, biting my lower lip, desperate to speak for myself.

"Good morning. How may I help you, ladies?" said a blondish man in Levi's and a work shirt.

Jules stepped forward, chest out, trying to make herself look taller. "We're looking for Mike Grant."

"That would be me." He looked at us expectantly, and I gave Jules a nudge.

"We're investigating a possible homicide, and we need some information about the flowers and poems left at the site of the accident on Old Farm Road in Shoreland. Your delivery driver said you could help us."

Way to go Jules Harper, cheerleader/cop. She was doing an uncanny impersonation of Horatio Caine on *CSI: Miami*—entertaining, but unlikely to get us very far. I glared at her, but she was deep in character, and, short of slapping her, nothing was going to stop the interrogation.

"Oh, really?" Mike Grant said, flipping through a stack of receipts on the counter.

This wasn't going to be so easy. I nudged Jules again and scribbled the words **Cool it, Sherlock** on the palm of my hand.

"Yes, sir," Jules answered in an unnaturally deep voice.

"May I ask the reason for your interest? It's against company policy to share information about my customers, and you two don't look like you're here in an official capacity. Do you by chance have a search warrant?"

He smiled to let us know he was willing to play along, but his eyes were cool. This guy wasn't going to reveal his favorite flower, let alone the information we were looking for. Jules had wanted us to dress like we were going on a job interview, but I had refused, thinking such details wouldn't matter. But now we looked like a couple of kids playing Encyclopedia Brown, sticking their noses in where they didn't belong. We were like a bad Nickelodeon TV show. I would definitely hear about this later. I guess Dr. Hawking was going to have to come out. Furiously I typed my appeal. It was our only hope.

"FOUR YEARS AGO MY FAMILY WAS KILLED WHEN OUR CAR CRASHED INTO THAT TREE ON OLD FARM ROAD. I VISITED THE SCENE OF THE ACCIDENT FOR THE FIRST TIME A FEW WEEKS AGO AND FOUND THE NOTES AND THE FLOWERS. I'D ALWAYS THOUGHT THAT OUR CAR JUST SKIDDED ON THE ICE, BUT THESE POEMS MAKE ME THINK THAT IT WAS SOMEONE ELSE'S FAULT. I'M JUST TRYING TO FIND OUT WHAT REALLY HAPPENED AND WE THOUGHT YOU MIGHT BE ABLE TO HELP." I held my breath.

"I'm so sorry, miss . . ." Face contorted with empathetic grief, Mike Grant looked like he was about to cry. Bingo.

"I'M SASHA BLACK, AND THIS IS MY FRIEND JULES HARPER."

Taking both my hands in his, he said, "I had no idea. I'm so sorry. What a terrible tragedy. Were you very seriously hurt? The injuries must have been severe to cause you to lose your voice."

This was embarrassing, but if there was a possibility this man might help us, I owed him an explanation. "I HAD NO PHYSICAL INJURIES, BUT I HAVEN'T BEEN ABLE TO SPEAK SINCE THE ACCIDENT. IT'S CALLED HYSTERICAL MUTISM. AND I HAVE AMNESIA. I'M JUST TRYING TO GET MY LIFE BACK TOGETHER."

Short of handing over my medical records, that was everything. I might as well lay it on thick if it might improve our chances of getting a name.

"That's horrible—orphaned and so severely traumatized."

"WE'RE SORRY TO BOTHER YOU, BUT WE HOPED YOU MIGHT HAVE SOME INFORMATION THAT COULD HELP US FIND THIS PERSON. IT WOULD MEAN SO MUCH TO ME TO KNOW WHAT REALLY HAPPENED THE NIGHT THAT MY FAMILY WAS KILLED."

My eyes filled up with tears. Everything I was saying was true, and the tears were real, but I felt like I was manipulating this poor man with my sob story.

Jules, sensing his vulnerability, jumped in. "That's exactly why we're here, sir. Sasha's doctor has said that she may be able to recover her voice and her memories if she can remember the minutes around the accident. If we can figure out exactly what happened, Sasha might be cured. It's been a four-year dead end, until we found the flowers."

There was nothing to add to that, so I just nodded earnestly and squeezed Mike Grant's hands, which were still clutching mine.

"As I said before, I make it a practice of respecting the privacy of my customers . . . but under the circumstances . . ." He took back his hands, rubbed his eyes, and sniffed.

"THANK YOU, SIR." *Please don't change your mind.*

Opening a filing cabinet behind him, Mike removed a large manila envelope and dumped its contents on the counter. "I really don't know much, but I'll show you what I have." He carefully laid out thirteen identical business-size envelopes, all typed, with no return address. "A few times a year, I receive an envelope containing three hundred dollars in cash, a poem, and a note instructing me to place the poem and one dozen white tulips at the base of the tree on Old Farm Road. The notes are never signed, so I have no clue as to who the sender might be. I delivered the flowers myself the first time, but after that I just sent a driver. It was strange, I'll admit, but truthfully I didn't think about the possibility that this person could be a criminal." Mr. Grant looked like he was worried that he might be in trouble, what Stuart would call an accessory after the fact. "I just thought it was somebody's relative. I never even looked at what was written on the pieces of paper."

"JULES, LOOK AT THE ENVELOPES."

They were light blue, like the stationery, and postmarked all over the world, a stamp collector's dream—London, New York, Zurich, Berlin, Barcelona, Florence, Venice, Rome. My mystery poet was either an airline pilot or an international spy.

"Nearly every one was sent from a different city. And you have no idea who this person could be?" Detective Harper was back. She picked up an envelope and held it up to the light. Was she looking for fingerprints?

"None. I don't even know if it's a man or a woman. Based on the postmarks, I'm assuming the person isn't local, but no one has ever called to confirm a delivery or ask about the cost. Three hundred dollars is way too much for the size of the order, but there's no way I can get in touch to offer a refund."

"NOW WHAT?" I turned to Jules. After a promising start, the trail had run cold.

"You're too easily discouraged, Sasha. We're just going to have to do some digging. Let me copy down all the cities and the dates. They might be significant, taken as a group. Mr. Grant, thank you for all your help. Here's my phone number—if you remember anything else or you get some more information that might help us, could you give me a call?"

Now Jules really did sound like a police inspector. I waited for her to whip out a business card, but she just wrote her number on the outside of the manila envelope.

Standing on the sidewalk outside the store, my resolve continued to wane. "GREAT. NOW WE'RE LOOKING FOR A NEEDLE IN A HAYSTACK THE SIZE OF THE WHOLE WORLD."

"You are such a downer. I think the fact that this person travels so much narrows things down considerably."

"DEFINITELY. I'M THINKING RUSSIAN SPY OR ART SMUGGLER. MAYBE WE SHOULD CALL INTERPOL."

"There's no use talking to you when you're in a mood. I'm taking you home. You can read your sex book and fantasize about Ben. He's a big part of your reason for doing this—remember? Keep your eye on the ball."

"IN THAT CASE, DON'T YOU MEAN BALLS?"

"Exactly my point. With talk like that, it's obvious you're in desperate need of a tongue down your throat and a hand down your pants." Jules kept a straight face, but I could see she was about to crack up.

"YOU THINK?"

Would Ben ever kiss me like he had before? I worried I would never feel his arms around me again, and that made me more depressed than my lost voice ever had.

Chapter 15

"How are you doing, Sasha?" Dr. O. sat, pen poised over her legal pad, waiting for me to announce some major breakthrough.

"I FEEL GOOD. NO PROGRESS ON THE TALKING FRONT, BUT I FEEL LIKE I'M MOVING IN THE RIGHT DIRECTION."

"In what way? Any progress with that boy? Did you get back together?"

"NO, NOTHING SINCE HE TOLD ME HE LIKED ME BUT HE FELT LIKE HE WAS GETTING IN THE WAY OF MY GETTING MY VOICE BACK." It was easier to talk about it with her than with Charlotte.

"And how does that make you feel?" Classic softball shrink question. I expected more from the illustrious Dr. O'Rourke.

"IT MAKES ME FEEL LIKE SHIT."

Dr. O. raised her eyebrows. I usually made an effort to control the language when I was with her, but she was annoying me. Since I couldn't tell her about how Ben's supernatural talent had played such a significant role in our relationship, we weren't going to get very far with this line of inquiry.

"Understandable. But you must see that someone with your condition has more complex issues than most teenage girls, and it would have to be a very unusual boy to be able to handle them over the long term, no matter how mature."

If any boy had the stuff to cope with my issues, Ben was the one, but even with his extraordinary gift he didn't have the patience to deal with me.

"SOMETHING ELSE DID HAPPEN. I VISITED THE ACCIDENT SCENE."

Dr. O. stopped writing and looked up. "Interesting. What made you decide to do that after all this time?"

She was probably annoyed with me for not having done it years ago when she recommended it. But better late than never.

"I DON'T KNOW. I JUST WOKE UP ONE DAY AND DECIDED IT WAS TIME TO GO THERE. IT WASN'T THE SNOW AND ICE THAT MADE OUR CAR HIT THE TREE." I tossed it out there, expecting a spectacular reaction, but she just went back to scribbling on her yellow pad.

"What makes you say that?"

"SEE FOR YOURSELF." I handed her a few of the poems. "THESE WERE TUCKED INTO BOUQUETS OF WHITE TULIPS THAT SOMEONE LEFT AT THE BASE OF THE TREE."

"Goodness." After scanning each one, Dr. O. took a deep breath. "Are there more?"

"I HAVE SEVEN OF THEM, BUT THERE WERE THIRTEEN ALL TOGETHER. I DON'T KNOW WHAT HAPPENED TO THE REST."

"How do you know how many there were if they weren't all there?" Dr. O'Rourke asked.

"JULES AND I TRACKED DOWN THE FLORIST AND . . ."

She cut me off. Finally, I had sparked some interest. "Tracked down?"

"IT WAS JULES'S IDEA. WE CAMPED OUT IN A TREE AND GOT LUCKY. THE GUY FROM SHAKE-SPEARE'S FLOWERS CAME BY IN THE MIDDLE OF THE NIGHT."

"Fascinating. So what did you find out?" Dr. O. stared at my fingers as I furiously typed answers to her questions.

"WHOEVER CAUSED THE CRASH DOESN'T WANT TO BE FOUND. NO NAME, NO RETURN ADDRESS, PAID IN CASH, AND POSTMARKS ON THE ENVELOPES FROM ALL OVER THE WORLD. PRETTY MUCH UNTRACEABLE."

"What do your aunt and uncle think about this?" she asked.

"I HAVEN'T TOLD CHARLOTTE AND STUART YET. SHOULD I? IT WOULD PROBABLY JUST UPSET THEM, AND UNTIL I KNOW SOMETHING, WHAT'S THE POINT?" Charlotte would be angry with me if she knew I was keeping such a major secret, but truthfully, what difference would it make? "IT'S NOT LIKE MY FAMILY WOULD BE ANY LESS DEAD IF WE KNEW EXACTLY WHAT HAPPENED."

"That's true. A very mature attitude. And if you need to talk, you always have me. So does that mean you haven't gone to the police?"

I shook my head. Maybe she was worried they would sub-poena my medical records and arrest her for stealing Charlotte and Stuart's money for the past four years.

"THE POLICE AREN'T GOING TO WANT TO INVESTIGATE A CASE THEY CLOSED FOUR YEARS AGO. ACCORDING TO THE REPORT, ICE CAUSED MY

FATHER TO LOSE CONTROL OF THE CAR. I COULD
FIND A SIGNED CONFESSION UNDER THAT TREE,
AND I DOUBT THE SHORELAND POLICE DEPART-
MENT WOULD ADMIT TO BEING WRONG." Not that I
had anything against local law enforcement, but their skills ran
more toward directing traffic at weekend tag sales and handing
out parking tickets.

"You're probably right about that. At this point, so many
years after the fact, it's probably best to leave things be. As you
so succinctly said, it's not going to bring your family back. It
seems to me that looking forward is your best strategy. Maybe
knowing that your father didn't do anything wrong is enough
for you. Do you really need to know all the details?"

"I DON'T KNOW."

"Have you considered the possibility that this poet is some
weirdo who's making stuff up, trying to draw attention to
himself?"

Dr. O. leaned forward, as if trying to read my thoughts in
my eyes, probably trying to see if this new information had
made me any nuttier. I had been worried that she would insist
we call the police with the information Jules and I had found,
so that they could solve the mystery and provide me with some
kind of closure. Weren't psychiatrists all about closure?

"BUT WHY WOULD SOMEONE PRETEND TO
BE THE PERSON WHO KILLED MY FAMILY? THAT'S
EVEN CRAZIER THAN I AM."

"Just throwing it out there. This world is full of all kinds of
unusual people, as you well know. So now what are you going
to do?"

"I HAVE NO IDEA, BUT I'LL FIGURE IT OUT."

For the first time, I really felt like I *was* going to figure it out. And the fact that Dr. O. didn't seem to have all the answers didn't matter at all.

"That sounds like a good idea. Just keep in mind your goal—getting your voice back. It's easy to get distracted, and your friend Jules sounds like someone who likes projects. You don't want to get so busy playing Sherlock Holmes and Dr. Watson that you lose your focus."

"JULES GETS CARRIED AWAY SOMETIMES, BUT SHE WANTS ME TO GET MY VOICE BACK AS MUCH AS I DO." I seemed to spend a great deal of time defending my best friend's good intentions.

"And what about your boyfriend?" Dr. O. looked at her watch but didn't say anything. We were almost out of time, thank goodness.

"HE'S NOT MY BOYFRIEND ANYMORE."

"But he would be if you could talk to him, isn't that correct? It's all about the talking. Keep that on the front burner. At this point, I think memory recovery might be overrated, especially in your case." She didn't need to rub in the fact that I had a lousy memory. "Okay, I'm afraid we have to call it a day, but I think you're getting there. Keep it up—move forward, Sasha. That's where your future is."

"YES, MA'AM." Did Dr. O. really just say that?

"By the way, I'm going to a medical convention next week, so I'll be out of the office. If you need me for anything, you can e-mail, and I'll get back to you as soon as I can."

"I'LL BE FINE." I picked up my backpack and opened the exit door.

"You're right, Sasha, you will be." Dr. O. smiled warmly and went to open the front door to let in her next victim.

Chapter 16

"I've been waiting for you."

Ben's mother opened the front door before I was even halfway up the walk. How did she know I was coming? How did she know who I was? During the weeks Ben and I had been dating, I hadn't met his mother. And although he had said he was the only clairvoyant in the family, he did say that his mom was magical, whatever the hell that meant. The closer I got to my old front door, the more I realized just how bad this idea was. Seven Seashell Lane was no longer my home, and Ben was no longer my boyfriend.

"I'M SASHA BLACK. I'M SORRY TO BARGE IN ON YOU LIKE THIS. I SHOULD GO."

Just as I had suddenly had the urge to return to the place where my family had died, I had woken up that morning with a desperate need to go home again. For whatever reason, my addled brain was telling me to return to the nest. But what little confidence I'd felt when I set off on my latest quest dissolved as the dreadful monotone that stood in for my voice echoed in the chill late afternoon shadows; such a contrast to Mrs. Fisher's lilting, almost musical voice. Turning around, I was practically in the street when I felt a hand on my shoulder.

"What are you doing, Sasha? Don't go. You're supposed to come here. I want you here. Ben wants you here, even though he doesn't know it yet."

She knew the magic words. At the sound of Ben's name, I turned around and looked into eyes the exact same color and shape as Ben's. We had not spoken to each other at school, and he never came to the library anymore. Glimpses across the cafeteria, down a hallway—that was all I had seen of him in the last month. Seeing someone up close who was so close to him made me miss him even more. Maybe he was here. No one was peering out from behind the curtains, but perhaps my exile was almost over.

"BEN WANTS ME HERE?" I wanted to hear her say it out loud again.

"He wants you to get better. He's having a difficult time right now. Your breakup was hard on him."

She made it sound like *I* had broken up with *him*. Now I knew Ben was a freak. What teenage guy had heart-to-hearts with his mom about his love life? Had he filled her in on the specific circumstances that had led to that breakup? As weird as this family was turning out to be, I couldn't imagine that kind of openness. But the possibility that my blow job blooper was fodder for dinner table conversation in the Fisher household made me want to run fast and far.

"IS HE HERE NOW?"

Please be home. I crossed my toes inside my shoes. At the very least, he could tell me exactly how much his mother knew about us.

Ignoring my question, Mrs. Fisher asked, "Did Ben tell you anything about me?"

"JUST THAT YOU AND YOUR HUSBAND ARE UNIVERSITY PROFESSORS, AND THAT YOUR HUSBAND IS WORKING ON A BOOK."

"Nothing else?"

I shook my head. Maybe Ben had lied to me. Maybe Mrs. Fisher was a card-carrying telepath and was testing me.

"I'm surprised. I wonder why. I guess he wants you to do this all on your own." She was almost talking to herself at this point. Definitely not a mind reader. Ben had been telling the truth. Thank goodness.

"WHAT DIDN'T HE TELL ME? ARE YOU LIKE BEN? DO YOU READ MINDS?" I had to ask, just to be sure. "WHAT AM I SUPPOSED TO DO ON MY OWN?"

"No, I can't hear your thoughts. Only Ben has that particular gift. But we're an unusual family, and I don't think it's a coincidence that our paths have crossed."

In her long skirt and dangly gold earrings, she resembled a gypsy fortune teller more than a college professor. "REALLY?"

Was this woman merely eccentric, or was I on the verge of something momentous? Maybe Mrs. Fisher could help me find the mysterious murdering poet, help me figure out what to do when I did. A crystal ball seemed as good a solution as anything Jules and I had come up with so far.

"I do. When we were moving back to the States, we weren't sure where we should live, but when we walked into this house—your house—it spoke to us, and I knew we had to start the next leg of our journey here."

"YOUR JOURNEY?" Did that mean they weren't staying in Shoreland?

"I feel the spirit of your family in this house. Do you think you might be ready to do a little spiritual spelunking, Sasha?" Crazy *and* alliterative.

"I DON'T KNOW."

"Sit for a few minutes. It's okay. You're a little afraid of me. I see it in your eyes. Please don't be. I'm not as strange as you think I am." Maybe Mrs. Fisher really was a mind reader. She sat down on the step and patted the place next to her.

I sat down next to Ben's mother on the front steps of my old house, just like I used to do with my own mother when I came home from school. Biting my tongue, wanting to cry at this unexpected peek into my past, I looked up at Mrs. Fisher, half expecting my mother to be staring back at me, but it was just the hippie cat lady, and I breathed a little easier. Maybe just being in my old house would be enough to get the memory ball rolling. Buoyed by this nutsy woman's off-the-wall enthusiasm, I almost believed I was ready to face it.

"I'm so sorry about the loss of your family. There is no greater tragedy. But your survival speaks to your strong spirit," she said, smiling sadly.

"NOT SO STRONG. I STILL NEED FOUR TRIPLE-A BATTERIES TO SPEAK, AND I BARELY REMEMBER MY CHILDHOOD. I'M AFRAID OF EVERYTHING. AS YOUR SON HAS TOLD ME, I'M A MESS."

"Ben doesn't really believe that, and neither do I. Besides, you're not so fearful as you once were."

"WHAT DO YOU MEAN?" I hadn't told anyone other than Dr. O. about the poems and flowers, and she was bound by doctor-patient privilege. And Jules had sworn she wouldn't spill it.

"You forget, dear girl, your thoughts speak louder than words." For a few seconds, she rested her hand on my head.

"BEN? HE HASN'T SAID A SINGLE WORD TO ME IN OVER A MONTH." Thirty-six days, actually, but I didn't want his mother to think I was obsessed with her only child.

"He may not be speaking to you, but he's keeping tabs on you. He hasn't left you, even if it looks that way." Was this quirky woman just being kind, or was that really true? I desperately wanted to believe her.

"HOW? HE TOLD ME HIS ABILITY ONLY WORKS AT CLOSE RANGE AND HE'S BEEN AVOIDING ME."

"As far as you know." One eyebrow went up, just like Ben's.

"BUT I'VE ONLY SEEN HIM AT A DISTANCE AT SCHOOL AND NEVER ANYWHERE ELSE."

"I don't want to say that Ben has been stalking you, but he does make the occasional nocturnal visit. Your mind is apparently very active right before you fall asleep."

"OH."

I felt hot all over, and I knew my face was bright red. Most nights before I dozed off I spent fantasizing about Ben being in bed with me. I hoped he had exercised some discretion and conveyed only relevant information to his mother, which hopefully did not include my mental reenactments of various examples in Jules's sex book. It was hard to tell from her face exactly what she knew. From now on, I would have to revise my bedtime routine.

"You've visited the scene of the accident—that took tremendous fortitude. And you know that someone caused the crash that killed your family. That's tremendous progress, don't you think?"

Another more pressing thought occurred to me. Now that I was making a concerted effort to heal my psyche, maybe Ben would come back to me. His mother would vouch for my sincerity and diligence on my mission to recapture the power of speech. How could he say no when I was doing exactly what he wanted?

"WHAT TIME IS IT? I HAVE TO BE SOMEWHERE AT 4:30."

That wasn't exactly true, but I needed to be alone, to sort out all this new information, and I needed to figure out how to tell Charlotte about the poems. And Ben wasn't here.

"It's time, then. Do you want a ride home?" Mrs. Fisher stood, brushing off her skirt.

"I DON'T MIND WALKING AND I COULD USE THE FRESH AIR. IT'S NOT FAR."

"If you like. Ben won't be home until much later, but I'll tell him you were here. Although I suppose he probably already knows that." Maybe she was a mind reader after all. "You're not ready to see him anyway."

My face fell. "BUT I'M TRYING. ISN'T THAT ENOUGH FOR HIM? DOESN'T HE CARE?"

"Yes, Sasha, he does, very much." She spoke with such conviction, I had no choice but to accept what she said.

"THEN YOU'LL TALK TO HIM FOR ME?" It was unlikely that Ben's own mother would agree to be my advocate, but it was worth a try.

Mrs. Fisher shook her head. "Please try to understand. Ben is taking the long view. You have your whole life to have a relationship with him, or some other young man. But that will only take place if you work out your relationship with yourself."

Mother and son apparently subscribed to the same life philosophy, which meant, at least for now, I was on my own. Damn.

Chapter 17

"Look."

Jules dropped a newspaper page in my lap as I sat on my old couch in the library sunroom. I enjoyed my afternoons there less since Ben had given me the boot, but I had no better place to go, and there was always the hope that he would sit down next to me just as he had that first day. So here I sat, looking at a monograph of Italian Renaissance painting, staring at Botticelli's *Birth of Venus*, daydreaming about Ben.

"TEENAGE GIRL GIVES BIRTH TO TWINS IN BACK OF TAXICAB. FASCINATING. ARE YOU TRYING TO TELL ME SOMETHING?"

I handed back the piece of paper without looking up. She had interrupted my daydream right at the good part.

"No, you idiot, the article underneath that. The reading at Bookends tonight. 'Derek Moore talks about his new book, *In Verses Veritas*, a story of one man's journey toward personal truth through poetry.'"

"SO?"

Jules sighed melodramatically at my failure to jump on board her thought train. Sometimes she assumed I thought about things exactly the same way she did, and when I wasn't able to finish her sentences, she was frustrated.

"Look at the picture on the cover. Don't you see it?" She held the newspaper about an inch from my face.

"IT'S BLURRY, BUT IT LOOKS LIKE SOME KIND OF FLOWER."

"Not just any kind of flower—it's a white tulip." She jabbed her finger at the fuzzy newsprint photograph of the book cover.

"AGAIN, SO WHAT? I DON'T THINK OUR MYSTERY POET HAS THE EXCLUSIVE RIGHTS TO PURCHASE WHITE TULIPS." With her typical enthusiasm, Jules had jumped from a single coincidence to full-on indictment. In my mind, she had soared over the Grand Canyon of conclusions. "IF A GUY WROTE A BOOK ABOUT FORGIVENESS, IT WOULD BE PERFECTLY LOGICAL TO PUT A WHITE TULIP ON THE COVER, SINCE IT'S NO SECRET THAT TULIPS REPRESENT FORGIVENESS. ANYBODY CAN LOOK ON FLOWERSYMBOLS.COM."

"I know, but I have a feeling. Just come with me."

She pulled at my arm, and the enormous book spread across my lap crashed to the floor. The librarian cleared her throat and shook her head.

"YOU'RE GOING TO GET ME KICKED OUT OF HERE, AND I DON'T HAVE ANYPLACE ELSE TO GO." Jules had caught me in a low moment.

She patted my head. "Poor homeless girl. Did Charlotte kick you out of the mansion? You can come live with me, but first we're going to this bookstore."

I gathered my things. Jules was relentless, and once she'd made up her mind, it would be easier to rewrite history than convince her otherwise.

The bookstore was jammed when we arrived. Whoever this guy was, he had a following. Every chair was filled, so we stood at the back with a dozen other people, barely able to see the man with a beard and long hair sitting in a big leather chair. After a few minutes, a middle-aged woman dressed in tie-dye from head to toe picked up a microphone.

"Welcome, everyone. What a crowd. Apologies to those who have to stand, but it'll be well worth it. Derek's insights into the human spirit are without parallel."

Jules elbowed me and whispered, "It looks like we fell into a Woodstock reunion."

We had to be the youngest people in the room by at least thirty years.

Why are we here again? I scribbled on my notepad.

"Poems, forgiveness, white tulips, murder," she hissed. "Just listen. It takes patience to be a good detective."

Remember, Sherlock, we're not real detectives.

"Good evening. My name is Derek Moore, and I have a terrible secret. Four years ago I committed a crime, and I never told anyone."

Jules shoved me so hard I almost fell over. Now he had my attention. Could we have backed into it? I started to sweat. Was I looking at the person who had changed my life forever? In my mind, I had imagined someone classically evil, with slicked-back hair and a little black mustache curled up at the ends—not a Jesus lookalike in cowboy boots, torn jeans, and John Lennon sunglasses.

"What I did doesn't matter now. I've made peace with my transgression, and rehashing what I've done wouldn't accomplish anything. And that leads into what I want to talk to you about, what I've written about: forgiveness. Forgiving yourself for your own wrongs, and forgiving others for their shortcomings. Anger, whether at yourself or sent out into the world, only brings you down, only reduces the quality of your life. It's a poison that will slowly and surely kill you. How do you dispel that anger? I'm here to tell you—poetry. I cannot emphasize enough the power of words to heal."

My muscles cramped up, and my handwriting was barely legible. **You think this is the guy? What do we do now?**

"I don't know. Shhh."

Jules was listening intently—what she was waiting for this guy to say, I didn't know. Did she expect some kind of confession? To me, he was just spouting clichés, preying on the human need to feel better about ourselves, to get things off our chest and move on.

I wrote Jules another note and shoved it in her face. **His speech is pretty generic. Say you're sorry, in stanzas, and move on.**

Now that the moment was at hand, I wasn't sure I was ready to face the person who had killed my family. Jules grabbed the pencil out of my hand and gestured toward the speaker.

"Just listen," she whispered. Either she was gathering evidence I couldn't identify as such, or she was totally into the bullshit this crackpot was spewing.

Mr. Moore was staring off into space, almost preaching to the rapt crowd. I had to hand it to him; he was polished. He spoke totally off the cuff, no notes.

"Even something as serious as murder can be forgiven. There is no offense which our Lord does not forgive, and therefore there is no wrongdoing which we ourselves cannot forgive."

Before I could grab Jules's sleeve, she had taken off for the platform, climbing over the aging flower children if she couldn't squeeze between them.

"Citizen's arrest, citizen's arrest!" I followed the trail she had blazed but before I could reach the front of the room, two security guards had grabbed her. "Arrest him, not me. He killed my friend's family. He just said murder should be forgiven. He's talking about running a car off the road and killing three people."

Although there had to be a hundred people in the room, you could have heard a pin drop.

Derek Moore sat motionless in his chair, legs still casually crossed, seemingly unfazed, not even looking at Jules as he addressed her.

"Miss, I'm afraid I have no idea what you're talking about. Could someone please handle this interruption so that I may continue? Young lady, you are not only misguided, you are rude."

I reached out to Jules, but the security guards, having patted her down to make sure she wasn't packing heat, were already hauling her toward a side door. A minute later we were on the sidewalk. Jules stood, gasping for air, rubbing her bruised arms. I pulled out my voice box.

"WHAT THE FUCK IS THE MATTER WITH YOU? ARE YOU TRYING TO GET US ARRESTED?"

Before she could answer, the earth mother who had introduced Derek Moore emerged from the side door. "Are you high?" Kind of a funny question from someone who looked like she'd probably spent the last five decades stoned. "I should call the police." Didn't she mean pigs?

Jules pulled herself together and stood nose to nose with Miss Yasgur's Farm 1969. "That man in there killed my friend's family. He ran them off the road in a snowstorm four years ago. I don't know whether he was drunk or stoned or what, but he wrote some poems, and he left them at the tree with white tulips, and we figured out it was him."

Jules had clearly gone off the reservation. I knew what had happened and *I* could barely follow what she was saying, she was talking so fast.

Expecting the woman to pull out a phone and call 911, I was shocked when she started to laugh. "That's a fascinating story, but quite impossible."

"But the picture of the tulip and the poems and all this crap about forgiving yourself for committing a crime. It has to be him," Jules insisted.

She had a wild look in her eyes, and I put my hand on her arm, hoping she would come back down to earth and just stop talking before we got into more trouble. I still hadn't told Charlotte about the poems, and I was beginning to think I didn't want to.

"MA'AM, I'M REALLY SORRY ABOUT THIS. MY FRIEND IS A LITTLE UPSET." Since when had I become the voice of reason? "WE'RE GOING TO LEAVE NOW. SORRY FOR EVERYTHING."

"Oh, you poor thing." My frantic typing and robotic voice seemed to take the hysteria down a notch. The Hawkie Talkie was incredibly powerful—everyone who heard it instantly started oozing sympathy. Maybe it wasn't such a nasty little device. It was turning out to be quite useful. "She's talking about your family, isn't she?"

I nodded, trying to squeeze out a tear. If this woman had planned on calling the police, maybe she would take pity on the head case and her mute friend. We made quite a pair, and I couldn't imagine anyone with an ounce of compassion who would want to make trouble for such a damaged duo.

Laying her hand lightly on my shoulder, she said, "I'm so sorry for your loss, but there is absolutely no way Derek Moore could have caused the accident."

"Why do you keep saying that?" Jules had recovered her voice and was about to relaunch her trek down her twisted road to reason, but thankfully the woman cut her off.

"He couldn't have run a car off the road, because he doesn't drive. Derek Moore has been blind since 1972. The pigs—I mean, the police—sprayed him with some kind of tear gas at an anti-war rally, and he was allergic to the chemicals. He never recovered his eyesight."

Jules's jaw dropped. Finally, she had run out of things to say.

"WE'RE GOING TO GO. SORRY FOR THE TROUBLE WE CAUSED."

I took Jules's arm and dragged her to her car, digging the keys out of her pocket and letting us in. Just as we got inside the sky opened up, and we sat perfectly still, listening to the rain pound on the roof.

"YOU DIDN'T READ THIS WEIRDO'S BOOK, DID YOU?"

"Nope."

"BLIND FOR THIRTY YEARS. HENCE THE SHADES INDOORS." I wanted to laugh at the ridiculousness of what had just happened, but Jules was embarrassed enough already.

"I'm so sorry. I just had this feeling. When I opened the newspaper, there it was. It was like fate." Jules shook her head and then rested it against the steering wheel. "I'm really sorry."

"IT'S OKAY. YOU WERE JUST TRYING TO HELP. BUT MAYBE NEXT TIME YOU COULD DO A LIT-TLE RESEARCH BEFORE WE MAKE A SCENE AND ALMOST GO TO JAIL."

"Point taken."

"IT'S ACTUALLY KIND OF FUNNY. YOU LOOKED VERY GRACEFUL, HURDLING OVER THE HIPPIES. GAZELLE-LIKE."

"Thanks." Jules let out a giggle.

It *was* kind of comical, especially since we didn't end up behind bars. If she'd laid a hand on Derek Moore, I'd probably be calling Charlotte to bail her out on an assault charge.

"CITIZEN'S ARREST? WHERE DID YOU COME UP WITH THAT?"

"I think I saw it on an episode of *CSI: Miami*." Jules looked at me and broke out laughing. That was one of the best things about Jules—she didn't dwell.

Chapter 18

A church bell in the distance rang four times. "The school building is closing in fifteen minutes. It's time to go home, kids, as much as you love this place. But chin up, you get to come back, bright and early tomorrow morning." Mr. Carson fancied himself a comedian and liked to use the school's PA system to share his talent with the student body.

I put my notebooks in my backpack and left the library, heading for the locker room. Charlotte had texted me twice to remind me to bring my gym clothes home for a bath before they walked back to the house on their own. Everyone else had apparently left for the day, and I could hear the rhythmic tick of the oversized black and white clocks that hung all over the school. Hopefully, the gym wasn't already locked. No games were scheduled on Wednesdays.

As I rounded the corner, a voice startled me. "Hey there, Sasha. Long time, no see."

Out of the boys' locker room paraded my four tormentors. I had not seen them up close, nor had they spoken to me, since our rumble in the park. With Ben in my life, I'd no longer felt the need to act out, so I hadn't been to detention in ages.

Eyes down, I thought I could make it to the safety of the girls' locker room, but they followed me through the swinging doors. Like the rest of the school, it was deserted. Just my luck. A student body of close to a thousand, and the building was empty except for the five of us.

"Wait up, cutie. What's the rush?"

Like pack hunters, they surrounded me and I stood, my back against a bank of lockers, wondering how I managed to end up in such an awkward position with these goons not once, but twice.

"Were you worried about us? We're all better now—you wanna see?" Jed asked.

I didn't answer, just stared past them, wondering if I tried to run, how many seconds it would take for them to catch me.

"We know it was you who put that shit in our jock straps," Paul said.

I shook my head, my palms already damp with sweat.

"Who else would do that to us?"

Trying to breathe normally, I shrugged.

"What about that fuckface with the chucks?"

Shrugging and shaking my head at the same time, I stared at the ceiling.

"You don't look too sure about that. BTW, where is he? Isn't he usually two steps behind you?" Tom asked.

Not knowing what else to do, I shrugged again. I looked as idiotic as they sounded.

"While we're waiting for him, maybe we could try to finish what we started. No hard feelings." All four guffawed. "Well, maybe a few . . . hard . . . feelings." Paul put his hand on his zipper.

The locker room was closer to civilization than an empty park in the middle of winter, and I figured if I didn't show my fear, I could get out of this latest calamity on my own. Maybe. I held up my middle finger.

"That's right. I'm glad we're thinking the same thing. Except I like to call it making love."

Jed took my hand, kissed my fuck-you finger, and put his other hand on the crotch of my sweats. All the blood rushed from my head and I saw stars. This couldn't be happening again. And while I did have pepper spray this time, it was buried uselessly at the bottom of my backpack.

With his thumb, Jed rubbed me through my pants and whispered, "You like that. I can feel how hot you are."

If I fainted now, would that scare them away? Or would I simply get a concussion when my head hit the floor?

Sneakers squeaked on the linoleum outside the door, and I prayed that it was a lacrosse player returning to retrieve a forgotten stick. *Turn left, not right.* The door swung open.

"So how are the four foreskins of the apocalypse this afternoon?" Ben stood there, nunchucks in hand, smiling broadly.

Déjà vu all over again. I slid down to the floor, all feeling gone from my legs.

"Told you," Paul said. It was probably the first time he'd ever been right about anything. "You're late. So, Sasha was just telling us what you did to us."

Ben glanced over at me, and I shook my head slowly.

"I don't know what the fuck you're talking about," Ben said.

"I kind of think you do," Jed said. "And now it's your turn to get burned."

"Nice rhyme. You're a poet *and* a detective," Ben said.

Before Ben could cock his wrist, Paul had grabbed his arm and twisted it behind his back. The nunchucks clattered to the floor. Without Ben's sticks, we were fucked.

His voice still as smooth as glass, Ben said, "I just saw the security guard around the corner. He'll be coming through here any minute."

"Go ahead, yell for help. I want to hear you scream like a little girl," Paul said. "Right before I break your fucking arm."

He shoved Ben to the floor. I hoped Ben knew enough to stay there.

"Help!" Ben called, but I didn't need to be a mind reader to know that there was no security guard around the corner.

Pounding their fists into their palms, Paul and company looked like the Sharks right before they started their dance rumble with the Jets in the first act of *West Side Story*. They were so busy thinking about reorganizing Ben's facial features that they had completely forgotten about me, which didn't matter, because I was cemented to my spot in front of the lockers. Drawing his ham-sized fist back, Paul punched Ben square in the nose. Blood sprayed everywhere. Until that moment, I didn't think anything bad could ever happen to Ben. He was always ten minutes ahead of everyone else, but now he was curled up on the floor, blood streaming from his nose.

I had to do something, or at least try. Whether or not he loved me, whether or not he ever came back to me, I would do anything for him. Already on the floor, I extended my left foot, hooking the nunchuck chain with the toe of my shoe. Slowly, trying not to attract attention, I pulled my leg back in. Hoping I could actually do what needed to be done, I grasped the wooden handle the same way Ben did, jumped to my feet, and started swinging wildly. Fortunately, we were all pretty close together, so it didn't matter that I wasn't aiming, or that my eyes were closed. There was the unmistakable thunk of wood connecting with someone's kneecap. I swung the nunchucks over my head and down. *Crack.* Either I'd split someone's skull open, or I'd broken Ben's sticks. When I opened my eyes, Paul and Jed were on the floor, one clutching his knee, the other shielding his bloody head from further attack. The other two were already halfway out the door.

I bent over Ben. His eyes were nearly swollen shut, and his nose wasn't quite in the center of his face anymore. I had fantasized endlessly about being near him again, his face inches from mine, but this particular scenario had never occurred to me. At least he was here, and even though he hadn't been able to repeat his knight in shining armor act, he was definitely still tuned in to my brain channel.

Are you okay? He looked anything but okay.

"I'm sorry," he murmured. "And thank you."

Sorry for what? I cradled his head in my lap.

"I'm the one who's supposed to save you, and you ended up saving me."

Rescuing me from bad guys isn't your life's work. And even Superman needs a little help sometimes.

Grabbing a towel from an open locker, I soaked it in warm water and started mopping the blood off Ben's face. *Does that hurt?* I blotted gently around his nose, afraid I was making it worse.

"I'm fine," he said, and pulled himself up to a sitting position. This guy did not like being rescued.

You don't look too bad. I was lying, and of course Ben knew it, but I didn't know what else to say. *And look at them. They look way worse.* Paul and Jed had struggled to their feet and were limping out of the locker room without saying a word. If they had been dogs, their tails would have been between their legs.

"You're a magnet for those jerks," Ben said.

They were after you this time. I was just the opening act. Dumb as they are, they figured out that either one or both of us tried to neuter them.

"I'm really sorry. If I'd known . . . I should have thought it through, but truthfully I thought they were too stupid to figure it out."

Stop apologizing already. Can you stand up?

"Really, I'm fine." He stood up and rubbed his wrist. "Not broken, just sprained." Going over to the mirror, he inspected his no longer perfect face. "You think my mom will notice?"

Nah. You look great. As far as I was concerned, his nose could be sticking out of his chin, and he would still be beautiful.

"You look pretty good, too." Ben pinched the thick gray fabric of my sweats and whistled.

You're not looking at me these days, so why should I dress up?

"You should wear whatever you feel like. But you're irresistible, even in baggy sweats and a ponytail."

You're a regular comedian.

We had bonded over a bloody nose and fighting sticks. He got beaten to a pulp while he was trying to help me, and I ended up saving the day. It was a good place to start over.

"Come on. I'll take you home." He picked up my backpack. It almost felt like it had before he had dismissed me from his life. "I have my car today."

Don't you think you should go to the doctor and have someone look at your nose? I can walk home, or I can go with you.

"Let me drive you. It's on my way, and I don't need a doctor. It doesn't hurt at all." His voice was firm—the perpetual grownup who never needed to be taken care of.

Before I could do any more protesting, my backpack was on the back seat and he was standing holding the car door open for me. Why did he have to be in charge all the time?

What happens if they come after us again? They know what we did.

"We won't have to worry about them too much longer." He smiled mysteriously, and then winced in pain.

What does that mean? Don't take this vigilante business too far. You're too pretty for prison, even with your new nose.

I reached over and stroked his curls. At least he didn't pull away. I missed having someone I could "talk" to.

"Do you really think I'd break the law?"

I'm pretty sure putting poison chili seasoning in someone's underwear is illegal.

"Semantics. I'm actually talking about doing a little crime prevention this time. The four wise men are going to buy some drugs next week—pot, roofies, Ecstasy. They do a little dealing on the side for pocket money instead of a paper route."

How do you know that?

Ignoring my stupid question, he continued. "As soon as they get the stuff, I'm going to tip off the principal, and they'll all be arrested and expelled."

You're sure?

Would it be as easy as Ben claimed? The principal loved his winning varsity thugs. It was hard to imagine Mr. Carson would end up playing a key role in their downfall. It seemed more likely he would look the other way or try to pin it on somebody else, someone less vital to the Shoreland High athletic program.

"Positive. In a few weeks Jed's going to be sitting in a jail cell, worrying about losing his own virginity to some guy named Cheech. Plucking your flower is going to be the last thing on any of their minds."

He started the car and drove in silence, taking the long way home, occasionally looking over at me. I stared out the window, trying to push my thoughts deep down and far away, out of my conscious mind, in the vain hope that Ben couldn't hear how much I wanted him to hold my hand, take me in his arms, carry us back to where we'd been before. His hands remained on the steering wheel, so either he was ignoring me, or I had successfully erected a mental brick wall. It was almost certainly the former.

"Here you go."

At the top of the driveway, he reached across me and opened the door. I refused to take the hint. He sighed and turned off the engine, got out of the car, retrieved my backpack, and opened the car door from the outside. Catatonic, I sat staring at my hands folded in my lap. One, two, three . . .

"Sasha, get out of the car."

I was behaving like a stubborn child, but I was prepared to do anything that would delay his leaving even for a few minutes, even if I looked like a fool doing it. Good attention is better than bad attention, but bad attention is better than none at all.

"Sasha, I can read your mind, remember? I know exactly what you're doing." He reached out his hand to me. "I'm flattered. Now get out of the car."

If I get out of the car, will you stay with me for a little bit? I don't want to be alone. Now I was being immature and manipulative, but desperate times called for desperate measures.

Ben shook his head. He was as stubborn as I was, the bastard.

"I heard that."

I have no reason to clean up my language, since you're not talking to me anyway. Why won't you come inside? Pleeeese? Definitely not too proud to beg.

"You know very well why. I'll come in, we'll sit on the couch, you'll rest your head on my shoulder, and I'll stroke your back."

And what's wrong with two friends consoling each other after a traumatic experience? My heart began to pound as his fantasy played out in my mind.

"Wait, there's more. Then I'll smell your hair and maybe kiss the top of your head. Then you'll look up at me, and your lips will be begging to be kissed, and I won't be able to help myself, and then we're right back where we started."

He closed his eyes, as if imagining the scenario he was describing. That sounded pretty good to me.

You should write a romance novel. It would be a shame to waste language like that.

"Don't be a smartass—you know that's what would happen." He was all business again.

What if I promise not to kiss you? I can behave myself. Just friends. I held my breath.

"You may be able to hold yourself to that, but I don't think I can. I'm sorry."

That's bullshit.

"It's been more than a month since we were last together, and I'm not sure I can behave like a gentleman when I'm alone with you while you're wearing those sexy sweats."

What about ponytail girl? Jules said she's all over you. Ben didn't seem like the man-whore type, but our time apart felt like a century to me, so for a boy it must be forever.

"We're just friends. Nothing more. She's on the track team. We work out together." In my overactive imagination, Ben and the model had been doing way more than running wind sprints after school.

Oh, tall, blonde, and gorgeous isn't your type? I found that hard to believe.

"No, you're my type, I'm afraid. Baggy clothes, bad attitude and all."

Thanks . . . I think.

He still liked me, in that way. He still wanted to kiss me, to touch me.

"That didn't come out right. What I mean is, I find you more physically attractive than Aubrey—that's ponytail girl's name. She *is* very beautiful, but she just doesn't do it for me. Maybe I have weird taste."

Thanks again. You sure know how to make a girl feel special.

Maybe he would kiss me, just to show me. I held my breath, standing as close to him as I possibly could, praying he would be unable to resist.

"You know what I mean. You're beautiful, I haven't touched another girl, and that's all I'm going to say on the subject. Now I have to go." With a casual wave, as if the last thirty minutes of blood and fear hadn't happened, he jumped into his car and drove away down the gravel drive, leaving me aching and alone.

Chapter 19

As I stepped over the threshold of 7 Seashell Lane for the first time in more than four years, I was nearly knocked over by a wave of sense memories. The way the afternoon light dappled the Oriental rug in the entryway, the smell of wood smoke from hundreds of fires. Not feeling at all self-conscious, I sat down on the soft wool carpet and closed my eyes. In my mind I could see the dining room—creamy white wainscoting and cranberry walls. A bronze turkey glowed in the light of a dozen candles in pewter candlesticks scattered across the table. It was perfect. But was it real, had it really happened, or had I just conjured up some idealized Norman Rockwell scene? Flipping through the photo album of my memory as Mrs. Fisher stood silently in the corner, I realized that most of the pages were blank, and the images that did exist were painfully generic—blowing out birthday candles, a day at the beach, riding on a carousel. Perhaps I had unconsciously fabricated them all to fill in the Swiss cheese holes of my memory. Like the flawless scenes in the photographs that came in picture frames, displaying model families engaged in idyllic activities, maybe my memories were merely suggestions of a life I wanted but had never actually lived.

"Are you all right?" Mrs. Fisher's voice broke into my reverie and I stood up, shaking off my brief foray into my possible past. I nodded.

"Please feel free to walk around. I'll be in the kitchen, whenever you're ready." Lightly touching my cheek, Ben's mother left me alone.

At the top of the stairs, I turned right. The room at the end of the hallway was mine. That much I remembered. For nearly five minutes I stood there, my hand resting on the doorknob. Did I want to go home again? Each step I took into my past could bring me a step closer to finding that lost piece of myself that, once replaced, would allow me to speak. Or, I feared, I could tread too far down the wrong road, burying that lost piece even further, maybe irretrievably. But I realized I had already chosen my path, and so I turned the handle and stepped into my old life.

The pine bed, corduroy-covered armchair, and rolltop desk were all still there, and as I breathed in, I inhaled my childhood. Closing my eyes, I lay down on the rag rug where I now remembered I had played hour upon hour with Legos. It smelled like crayons and baby powder and beeswax furniture polish. My mother's voice echoed up the stairs. "Sasha, dinner's ready in five minutes. Put your blocks away." "Sasha, we have to leave now, or you'll be late for school." "Sasha, Jules is on the phone." When I opened my eyes, I almost expected to see her standing in front of me—her voice had been so clear in my head. Until that moment, I had forgotten what she sounded like. Suddenly I missed her terribly, this woman who for the last four years had been a hazy figure lurking at the edge of my conscious mind. Now I could hear her laughter, smell her perfume, feel the scratchy wool of her favorite winter sweater as I rested my head on her shoulder.

The pain of my loss was palpable, and I crawled onto the bed—my bed, now Ben's bed. That was weird. This was the bed I had shared with three baby dolls, where I read my mother's

Judy Blume books under the covers with a flashlight when I was supposed to be sleeping. Now I was curled up on the same patchwork quilt that had always been there, and when I flipped back a corner, there were my flannel sheets dappled with pinecones. Ben's family had slipped seamlessly into every corner of my life, right down to the linens. If it had been anyone else, I would have been incredibly resentful and kind of creeped out. But since my family could no longer live here, it seemed right that Ben and his family did.

I was as ready as I would ever be. My future was waiting for me in my old kitchen. Gently smoothing the quilt, making sure that everything was in its place, I stood staring at my reflection in the mirror over the dresser, considering my options. It was now or never, and surrounded by the remnants of my childhood, I felt safe as I was about to venture into an indeterminate future. Nothing bad could happen to me under this roof. Of that I was certain.

In the kitchen Mrs. Fisher sat on a stool, reading the newspaper. On the stove, the old copper teakettle began to whistle. Without thinking, I turned off the flame and sat down on another stool.

"So, how was it?"

"VERY STRANGE. SOME THINGS I REMEMBER WELL—THE SMELL OF THE FIREPLACE AND CRAYONS AND THE SOUND OF MY MOTHER'S VOICE—BUT OTHER THINGS, LIKE TRIPS TO THE BEACH . . . I'M NOT SURE WHETHER THOSE REALLY HAPPENED."

She was so easy to talk to, in spite of her gypsy fortune-teller vibe. I didn't worry about sounding stupid or crazy, and unlike with Dr. O., I didn't worry that Mrs. Fisher was analyzing every word I spoke for some deeper, perhaps Freudian meaning.

"That's a good start. You're experiencing Proustian memories —the kind Marcel Proust wrote about in *Remembrance of Things Past* when he smelled the madeleines and his childhood came rushing back to him. As the most basic and primeval of our senses, the sense of smell is the one most closely tied to human memory. A single odor is enough to evoke tremendously detailed recollections of one's past. The power of the human brain is quite extraordinary." She paused. "Enough of that. I'm a college professor to the core, and I find it hard not to lecture. My apologies."

"DON'T APOLOGIZE. IT'S REALLY INTERESTING, AND I THINK IT MIGHT MAKE THINGS EASIER IF I LEARNED HOW MY BRAIN ACTUALLY WORKS."

"Well, I think you're going to learn all kinds of things, and I'm here to help you. Now, are you ready to explore your subconscious with a little hypnosis?" It sounded perfectly simple and logical when she put it that way. She could have been asking me if I wanted to go to the mall and try on shoes.

"NO ONE HAS EVER BEEN ABLE TO HYPNOTIZE ME. MY PSYCHIATRIST SAYS SOME PEOPLE ARE NATURALLY IMMUNE." Dr. O. and I had been down this road to nowhere on more than one occasion.

"Resistant, maybe, but I've never met anyone who's totally immune."

Mrs. Fisher's smile was so warm and reassuring that I could already envision a pocket watch swinging seductively on a chain and me falling into a deep, and hopefully productive, trance. I suppressed a yawn.

"BUT DR. O'ROURKE IS SUPPOSED TO BE ONE OF THE BEST PSYCHIATRISTS IN NEW YORK, IN THE WHOLE COUNTRY, EVEN. SHE SPECIALIZES IN POSTTRAUMATIC STRESS."

Mrs. Fisher shrugged her shoulders but looked no less confident. "I suppose there's an exception to every rule, and of course I could be wrong, but I'm willing to take the chance. How about you? You want to try?"

"NOTHING TO LOSE."

Sitting in Ben's kitchen, my kitchen, I was desperate to move forward. Worst case, I would still be mute and Mrs. Fisher might be a little embarrassed. We could both handle that.

"That's my girl. Drink this, and let's see where it takes us."

Mrs. Fisher smiled encouragingly as she filled a mug. The cloudy green liquid smelled like grass clippings and dirt.

"WHAT IS IT?" I wrinkled my nose. My stomach rumbled, protesting what it knew was coming its way.

"It's a special blend of herbs, mostly *Magnolia dealbata*. Cloudforest magnolia. Native tribes in Mexico used it as a tranquilizer and anticonvulsant for centuries. But I mix it with a few other things to create the desired effect. Think of me as an archaeologist, and this decoction is a mind shovel. We're going to dig up all the treasures buried deep inside that beautiful, troubled head of yours."

"IS IT LEGAL? MY AUNT AND UNCLE ARE LAWYERS. IF THEY FOUND OUT I WAS TAKING DRUGS, THEY'D KILL BOTH OF US." I had visions of Shoreland Police Chief Dodd hauling Mrs. Fisher and me, both wearing bright orange jumpsuits and prison-issue sneakers without laces, off to the single jail cell in the basement of City Hall.

"Technically, some of it is probably not completely legal, but I do have a medical degree, so I'm permitted to prescribe drugs when necessary. And I think your situation definitely requires pharmacological intervention."

Charlotte would not be happy about this development. She and Stuart were beyond straitlaced: they never smoked, drank decaffeinated coffee, and considered NyQuil a recreational drug. If Charlotte knew Ben's mother was serving up a steaming cup of hallucinogenic herbal tea, she might not be so interested in getting Ben and me back together.

"IS IT LIKE REGULAR HYPNOSIS? CAN YOU MAKE ME DO WHATEVER YOU WANT?"

I really liked Mrs. Fisher—or should I say Dr. Fisher—but the prospect of losing control in the company of a relative stranger, no matter how kind and honorable she appeared, was slightly unnerving.

"Don't worry. I won't make you walk like a chicken." She pushed the steaming mug across the counter.

"WHAT'S GOING TO HAPPEN TO ME?"

"It should help you relax beyond anything you've ever experienced, beyond what you believe possible. Hopefully you'll open up once the barriers of your conscious mind are broken down. Your free-thinking, unconscious brain will be let out of its cage, so to speak."

"SO YOU'RE SURE I WON'T ACT LIKE AN ANIMAL? I DON'T WANT TO MAKE A FOOL OF MYSELF."

I was three sips from getting emotionally naked in front of Ben's mother, and I was starting to feel uncomfortably warm.

"Sweet girl, don't worry. I won't let anything bad happen, and I promise that whatever does happen, it will remain between you and me. Ben will never hear about it."

She crossed her heart and blew me a kiss. How did she know that was what I was worried about?

"WILL THIS STUFF MAKE ME TALK?"

Maybe today would be my day. What would I say to Ben when he walked through the door? *I've fallen in love with you?*

Will you marry me? Probably a tad much for my first words. Maybe just, *I've missed you.*

"You might, if your trauma doesn't extend to your unconscious mind. But different people react differently. I can't say for sure what will happen to you. We'll never know unless we try, however. *L'chaim.* Drink up." She tapped her cup, which was filled with coffee, against mine.

"OKAY, YOU'RE THE DOCTOR."

I raised the mug to my lips. It was like drinking my front lawn. I held my nose and chugged.

"Just relax and let it take effect. You might feel a little buzzed. Do you drink at all? Do you know what that feels like?"

"I'VE NEVER DRUNK ENOUGH TO GET BUZZED. WHAT HAPPENS?"

Jules was always telling me that drinking would relax me, and that I definitely needed to chill out. But beer tasted like shit, and I was too much of a coward to raid Stuart's liquor cabinet.

"For me it's kind of a dizzy feeling." Mrs. Fisher closed her eyes and wiggled her fingers in front of her face.

"THAT DOESN'T SOUND GOOD." How embarrassing would it be to open my mouth and have something come out besides words. Maybe I should ask for a bag, just in case.

"A relaxed, delicious, dizzy feeling, not room-spinning, nauseated dizzy. Tipsy. It's fine. You'll see."

We stood on opposite sides of the island, watching each other, waiting for something to happen. After a few minutes, I began to feel lightheaded and looked down to make sure my feet were still touching the floor. I held on tight to the marble countertop, just to make sure I didn't float away.

"Maybe you should sit down. I think it's working." Mrs. Fisher took my hand and led me into the living room, settling me in an oversized chair by the fireplace. "Close your eyes." Her voice hovered in the air next to my ear. "Breathe deeply— go back in time, to your earliest memory. What do you see?"

Impossibly tiny pink Converse sneakers. Impossibly tiny hands with sparkly blue nail polish. Tongue out with the effort.

"That's it. The rabbit goes around the tree and in the hole. Pull it tight. You did it, Sasha." My father kissed my head and swept me up onto his shoulders. "Let's go show Mommy."

"Giddyup, Daddy." My laughter tinkled like wind chimes as I gripped my father's ears and we galloped into the kitchen.

"Look, Mommy, how many three-year-olds do you know who can tie their shoelaces?"

"Not many. How about a cookie to celebrate?" The smell of brown sugar filled the air, and I could taste the chocolate melting on my tongue.

"Thank you, Mommy. Yummy."

I was licking the chocolate off my fingers and then, as suddenly as they had appeared, the images behind my eyes faded, like a movie screen going dark. I tried to open my eyes, but they were glued shut, and I shook my head in frustration.

Mrs. Fisher put her hand on my arm. "That's very good. Now you're a little older, what do you remember?"

"Mommy, where are you?"

Panic rising, heart hammering. It was Christmastime. We were at the toy store, making a list for Santa, so he would know exactly what I wanted. The shelves were filled with baby dolls, and I couldn't decide whether I liked Sophie or Samantha. I had to cuddle them both, to see which one wanted me for a mommy. But where was *my* mommy? Clutching Sophie—she was definitely the right baby—I tried to hold back the tears. I didn't want to frighten my baby, and Mommy would never forget about me, would never leave me behind, would she? Was I supposed to stay put or go to the cash register? Which one did Mommy tell me to do if I ever got lost? *Think Sasha, this is important.* Closing my eyes, trying to remember what I was supposed to do, whispering to Sophie, "It's okay, we'll find her."

"Sasha, are you ready to go? Is that the baby you like?" My mother knelt down and patted Sophie's bald plastic head, and I burst into tears. "What's the matter, muffin? What happened?"

"I couldn't see you, I thought I lost you, I thought you forgot about me." I huffed and puffed as I tried to catch my breath.

"I'm so sorry. I was standing right there, looking at a game for Liz, and I didn't realize you didn't know where I was. Poor baby. I would never leave you behind, ever. Mommy will always be here. Always." She held out her arms and I fell into them, still clutching my doll.

Suddenly it was thirteen-year-old me standing in the toy store, holding the doll in a death grip, screaming at my mother, who was nowhere in sight. "You said you would always be here, but you left me behind!"

My eyes flew open, and my hair was matted with sweat.

"Are you all right?" Mrs. Fisher put her arms around me, patting my back, rocking back and forth. "It's okay, I'm here. It's not really happening. Just a dream."

I mimed typing and she handed me my Hawkie Talkie.

"I WAS IN A TOY STORE WHEN I WAS SIX, AND I THOUGHT MY MOTHER HAD LEFT ME AND THEN SHE CAME BACK. AND ALL OF A SUDDEN I WAS THIRTEEN BUT STILL IN THE TOY STORE, HOLDING THE SAME DOLL, BUT MY MOTHER WAS GONE." Exhausted and out of breath, I felt like I'd just swum the English Channel.

"Memories can be messy. It's very easy to mix up actual events with fears and anxieties. Different time periods can blur together, especially if the emotions underlying the different events are the same. Your panic at being lost as a child is very reminiscent of the anxiety and abandonment issues you probably experienced when your parents died. Fear of abandonment is not an emotion exclusive to small children."

"WOW. YOU'RE GOOD AT THIS."

This woman had explained everything I was feeling in such a simple, straightforward way. Being able to relive events from my past and understand them in the context of my life now was so powerful.

"Do you feel better?"

"SO MUCH BETTER. AND IT'S LIKE BEING WITH MY PARENTS AGAIN. IT'S SO REAL. SINCE I NEVER GOT TO SAY GOODBYE TO THEM, IT'S LIKE HAVING A VISIT. THANK YOU SO MUCH."

Even though it was scary and emotionally wrenching, it felt good to reconnect and realize that my family was still very much alive in my memories, however hidden they were.

"I'm glad, but you look like a limp dishrag, so I think that's enough for today. Now that we know what works, I think we're on our way."

"DID I SAY ANYTHING WHILE I WAS UNDER? HOW LONG HAVE I BEEN OUT?"

It was dark outside, so it had been a couple of hours at least. Maybe Ben would come home soon. I knew I looked like hell, but I was so desperate to see him again that I didn't care.

"No words, but you did make sounds, like a newborn kitten —you were way down inside yourself. Remember that lava has to travel from middle earth to the surface before it can erupt. It's a long trip."

"SO HOW LONG UNTIL I EXPLODE?"

"Hard to say, but I'm confident it will happen. Would you like a cup of regular tea? You look like you could use it, and you can tell me more about what you remembered." We walked arm in arm back to the kitchen. "How about a cookie to celebrate your accomplishment?"

I gasped. "THAT'S ALMOST EXACTLY WHAT MY MOTHER SAID."

"Great minds work alike."

For a second I wondered if my mother had been reincarnated in the body of Ben's mother, but that was just nuts, wasn't it?

"IT WAS THE WEIRDEST THING, THOUGH; I WAS SEEING THINGS THROUGH MY OWN EYES, BUT THEN I WAS WATCHING MYSELF FROM A DISTANCE, LIKE MY LIFE WAS A MOVIE. HOW DID THAT HAPPEN?"

"The brain works like that. On the one hand you're reliving what happened, but you're also like a third party observer, because you're seeing something that already happened. It's strange, but if you think about it, when you dream at night, don't you sometimes watch yourself as if from the outside?" Reverting to her role as teacher, Mrs. Fisher was a font of fascinating information.

"I GUESS THAT'S TRUE. I NEVER REALLY THOUGHT ABOUT IT."

I sipped the hot, sweet tea, eager to try it again. As unsettling as hypnosis was, it was exciting.

The back door slammed. "Hey, Annie, I'm home." Into the kitchen strolled middle-aged Ben, tall and slender with the same wild hair, but tinged with silver. This was clearly his father. Ben would age well. Yet another check in the plus column. "I'm sorry. I didn't realize you had company. I'm Michael Fisher, Ben's dad."

"Hi, babe." Mrs. Fisher reached up and kissed her husband on the cheek. "This is Sasha Black, Ben's friend . . . and the young lady who grew up in this house."

I stood and reached out to shake hands. But instead Ben's father put his arms around me in a bear hug. "I knew that. I feel like I know you already. Ben has told me so much about you." I hoped not everything.

"NICE TO MEET YOU, DR. FISHER."

Tears lined up under my eyelids, waiting for their marching orders. There was something so emotional about being in my old house with two people about the age my parents would have been if they were still alive, who clearly loved each other, and for whatever reason, seemed to care about me.

"Please call me Michael. Dr. Fisher makes me feel like I'm in class." Michael pulled up a stool and sat down next to me.

"And you must call me Annie. All this Dr. and Mrs. stuff is way too formal."

Had I landed in some alternate universe? Here I was sitting in the kitchen with the parents of the boy I loved, but who didn't want to see me until I sorted myself out, which I was trying to do with the help of said boy's mother. It was all perfectly comfortable and easy. Maybe it was the house that made me feel that sense of safety and belonging, but maybe it was these extraordinary people. I didn't ever want to leave, and that made me feel disloyal to Charlotte and Stuart.

"So what have you two ladies been up to this afternoon?" He ran his fingers through his hair and gazed adoringly at his wife.

"We've been taking a little stroll down memory lane, courtesy of my special herbal tea." Annie gestured to one of the many little jars on the shelf next to the stove.

"Ah, I thought it smelled like the inside of a lawn mower in here. Tastes like shit, but it's good stuff. How'd it work?" Michael looked at me expectantly.

"IT DEFINITELY WORKED."

"Almost too well, I think." Annie gave me a peck on the cheek. "A little upsetting to go back when the door's been closed for so long. I think next time will be easier, don't you, Sasha?"

I nodded. She seemed to know exactly how I was feeling without me having to say anything. Was that perceptiveness what they called emotional intelligence? Or perhaps I had forgotten what it was like to have a mother figure in my life. As amazing as Charlotte had been the last four years, she wasn't long on maternal instinct, and I realized I had missed having someone who could understand me without my having to explain myself. Maybe this woman had absorbed my mother's essence from sleeping in her bed, eating off her dishes, inhabiting her space.

The back door opened, and there he was. For once, I hadn't been thinking about him. "Hi, I'm home. Oh, sorry. Today's Wednesday, isn't it?"

Ben looked at his mother, his father, the stove—everywhere but at me. My fantasy that he would smother me with kisses, unable to control himself, evaporated. Instead it was the classic post-breakup awkward moment. What do you say to someone who a week earlier had gotten his face bashed in trying to rescue you from sexual assault, and before that had almost been sexually assaulted by you? There was no Hallmark card for that. For a moment no one spoke.

"Hey, Sasha, what's up?"

He acted surprised, but he had to have known I was here. Before he even came through the door, he could hear my thoughts. If he'd really wanted to avoid me, he could have.

"YOUR NOSE LOOKS GOOD. YOU LOOK LIKE YOU AGAIN." I typed. Thinking at him while his parents were in the room seemed rude.

Tapping the end of his nose, which actually looked a little bigger than it had before, he said, "I'm a quick healer."

Mrs. Fisher rolled her eyes and said, "A bag of frozen peas is no substitute for a visit to the emergency room, but he finally let me line things up. So it's not perfect, but at least his nose is back in the middle of his face."

"It would've been fine anyway, Mom." Ben rolled his eyes at his mother, clearly still embarrassed that he'd been on the wrong end of a well-placed left hook.

"I'm sure, darling. A bumpy, crooked nose gives you character. Don't you agree, Sasha?"

Ben held up his hand. "Enough. Just leave me alone." This was a side of Ben I'd never seen. Usually, he was the adult in the room, but now he was all child, and I kind of liked it.

"YOUR PARENTS ARE AMAZING. THANK YOU FOR LETTING ME GET TO KNOW THEM."

"They're pretty cool, most of the time." Ben glared at his mother. "I hope they can help you."

"IT'S GOOD TO SEE YOU." I could be mature and gracious and rational, or at least pretend to be all those things.

"You too," he mumbled. He stood on the far side of the room, shifting uncomfortably from one foot to the other, still avoiding my face. I stared directly at him. My eyes were drawn to his like magnets.

This was painful. I put down my talking box. *I was in my room. Your room, I mean. I hope that was okay.* I left out the fact that I lay down on his/my bed.

"That's fine. Anything that might help you get better. I do want you to get better, Sasha."

He came over to me, put his hand on my arm for an instant, and then ran out, his feet pounding up the stairs, the door to his bedroom slamming. Like a phantom pain, the sensation of his fingers on my skin remained even after he'd gone.

Dr. Fisher cleared his throat. "I think I'm going to go for a run before dinner. Sasha, it was a pleasure to meet you. Please come back soon. This will always be your home." Placing his hands gently on my shoulders, he kissed my forehead. "Everything's going to work out just fine. Patience," he whispered in my ear and left the room.

◆

A week later, I returned to 7 Seashell Lane for round two. Excited and nervous, I could almost believe that my day was at hand. Didn't I deserve a little good karma after all I'd been through? I went around the back and walked into the kitchen, just like I had done my whole life. Ben's mother was standing in front of the stove, copper teakettle in hand.

"Perfect timing, Sasha. You look ready. Shall we?" she asked as she poured boiling water into an oversized mug. The kitchen immediately began to smell like a garden.

Not even realizing I was doing it, I scanned the adjoining rooms, looking for Ben, and then typed into my machine. "YES, I'M VERY READY."

"Ben's not here today. I'm really sorry about last week. He could've behaved a bit better, I know, but under all his middle-aged mannerisms, he's still a seventeen-year-old boy. You two will work it out. I have a good sense of these things, and I think I know my son pretty well." Annie handed me the tea, picked up her own mug and we tapped them together. "Cheers, darling."

I nodded and guzzled the wretched potion. There was no point in being timid. I would have drunk gasoline if it meant getting Ben back any sooner. As the vague sense of vertigo began to take hold, I tottered into the living room and curled up in the memory chair, closing my eyes, waiting for Annie to set the scene, launch me into my past with her soothing patter.

"It's winter, almost Christmas, you're going to a concert at a church. Can you see it? What are you wearing? Is it snowing?" Mrs. Fisher's soft, rhythmic voice lulled me back into my dream state within seconds.

Like an old movie coming into focus, the Douglas fir we had just decorated that afternoon, white lights flashing on and off, kissed the ceiling in the corner of the living room. Gifts were piled high underneath. It smelled like winter. Christmas music was playing on the radio.

"Liz, Sasha, let's all wear our sweaters. It'll be fun." My father held up one of the four matching Icelandic sweaters he had bought on the Internet in a fit of holiday enthusiasm.

"It's bad enough you're making me go. There's no way I'm dressing up like some freaky family of folksingers. Everyone'll think we're one of the acts." Liz stomped out of the room and up the stairs, slamming her bedroom door.

"Sash, how about you? Please?" My father batted his eyes, half-joking, half-pleading.

"No way, what if I see someone I know?"

Until Liz had pointed out the dweeb factor, it hadn't occurred to me that wearing matching sweaters was a bad thing. But in recent months she had been introducing me to the world of perpetual mortification in any activity involving our parents. On the rare occasion that we saw a movie together, she wouldn't even sit with us, just in case she saw someone from school.

"Oh, Sasha, I'm losing you, too, aren't I?" My father stood on tiptoe, adjusting the string of lights near the top of the tree.

"Jay, what did you expect? Let them wear what they want. Would *you* have dressed in matching leisure suits with *your* father? Liz is right—we *would* look like some queer Partridge Family redux." My mother patted my father's back. "But if it makes you happy, I'll wear the sweater. I loved the Partridge Family, and at my age, nobody's looking at me anyway."

"It won't be the same, but I suppose you're right. Where did the time go? Why can't they just stay little a little longer? You know, when we didn't embarrass them simply by the fact of our existence. I want to be Daddy, not that loser whose only purpose in life is to open his wallet and hand over the car keys." Moving the lights back and forth across the same three branches, my father continued to mourn the passing of our childhood. "I'm not ready for it to be over. If they're getting older, then that means we are, too."

"Face it, Jay, we *are* old. And this is all just a natural part of the process. If they didn't feel this way, you'd be worrying that in thirty years they'd still be living in the basement, working in the school cafeteria, having a meaningful relationship with a cat. Is that what you want?" My mother's voice was earnest. "Stop fiddling with the lights. They're fine."

"Mom's right. They're just some dumb sweaters. I promise, I'm always going to be your little girl, even if I won't do the Von Trapp family singers thing."

I hugged my father and then my mother. In the part of my mind that was able to observe this rerun of my past, I thought about how ridiculous I had been. If only I could go back, I would put on a thousand stupid sweaters just to please my dad. Such a small thing would have made him so happy. How could I have been so selfish?

"Come on, Liz, we have to leave or we're going to be late," my mother called up the stairs. "I have the tickets in my bag. Liz, are you coming? We're stopping for Mexican food on the way home."

That did it. Footsteps in the hall and down the stairs, and Liz raced into the living room.

"I don't have to wear the sweater, though, right? We're going out for Mexican anyway?" Liz tried to look annoyed, but even she had to smile at my parents in their matching moose pullovers, and at the fact that for a chicken burrito, Liz would do practically anything.

"Wear whatever you want, darling daughter. Go naked if you like. I get it. You're all grown up, your mother and I are practically ready to be put out to pasture . . . we're living on borrowed time."

Although my father hadn't meant it that way, it was true—less than an hour later, they were all dead. This was hard to watch, but the movie of my memory just kept playing.

"Sarcastic much? Don't be so melodramatic, Dad. Sometimes an ugly sweater is just an ugly sweater. Okay?" Liz turned to look at me in my fishermen's sweater and blue jeans. "So they couldn't break you, huh?"

I didn't want Liz to think she was such a strong influence on me, so I said, "The moose sweater's itchy, and hot."

"Yeah," she teased, "that wool sweater you're wearing will definitely keep you cool. I get it."

Liz smiled and gently smacked the side of my head. It was the last time she ever touched me. I was not enjoying this scene from my past, but I couldn't change reels, even though I tried hard to turn it off.

The phone rang. "Hello," my mother said. "Oh, Charlotte, I'm so glad you got my message. So can you come with us? They're singing the 'Hallelujah Chorus.'"

After a long pause, "That's too bad. You and Stuart work way too hard. I hope you won't have to work on Christmas Eve." Another brief pause, and then my mother laughed at something Charlotte must have said. "Love to you guys. I'll talk to you tomorrow. Call me when you have a free minute in the office. Bye."

My mother hung up the phone and turned to my father. "I am so glad I decided not to go to law school. They're on call twenty-four hours a day. It's like being a doctor, but without the free samples."

"We'll just have to do some extra singing when they come over for Christmas Eve dinner. Let's go. Girls, grab your coats." My father flicked a switch and the Christmas tree went dark.

"Everyone buckled up?" My mother had been asking us that question every time we got in the car together since we were old enough to buckle ourselves.

A light snow was falling, and it looked like we were driving through a just-shaken snow globe. The trees by the side of the road looked like they were dusted with sugar, and the lighted windows of houses in the distance made them look like the miniature villages sold in craft shops. I closed my eyes and thought about Christmas vacation and my birthday, only a few days away. How many of those gifts under the tree were mine? Not that I was especially greedy, but I loved surprises, and there was nothing better than tearing the paper off a package and opening a box to find the perfect special something chosen just for me. It made me feel like my parents knew me and understood me, listened to my hopefully subtle hints when I mentioned a pair of boots I had seen or a book I wanted to read.

"The Twelve Days of Christmas" was playing on the radio, and we were all singing along. Our voices blended well, and we made quite a sweet-sounding quartet, even without the matching sweaters. " . . . five golden rings, four calling birds, three French hens . . ."

"Jay, watch out, that car is coming right at us!" My mother's voice was shrill with fear. The bright white light of someone's halogen headlights filled our car, casting a ghostly pall over everything.

"I can't see," my father shouted as he braked and swerved away from the oncoming car.

A chorus of shrieks replaced our four-part harmony. The squealing of brakes clawed at my brain, and I put my hands over my ears. Then a booming sound as we hit the tree, and the scratchy crunch of metal on metal, glass raining down on me as the windows shattered. And then the air was still, except for the dripping as the car bled to death around me. As bright as it had been seconds earlier, it was pitch black now. *So this is what death feels like*, I remembered thinking. Where were the tunnel, the white light and the angels? Gasoline fumes enveloped me, and I knew I was still breathing. *But not for much longer*, I thought calmly. The stench of blood was so strong I could taste it, like a penny in my mouth. Was it mine? Rather than pain, death was an odor, and I tried holding my breath so I didn't have to smell it. But the instinct to breathe was stronger than my urge to shut out the world, and I inhaled the stinking cacophony. A few minutes passed. I wasn't dead. Now what? Wedged in my seat, I couldn't move, so I waited, skin clammy from the snowflakes melting on my face, too weak even to open my eyes or call for help.

I must have lost consciousness, because I woke up to a light shining through my eyelids. Were the halogens back? No, too small for that. It must have been a flashlight beam, but I still couldn't open my eyes or make a sound. *We're being rescued*, I thought. Like sitting through a movie where I already knew the ending, I continued watching my dream play out, waiting for the tragic final scene. But now, here it was: in addition to the light, there was a smell. Unlike the bitter, acrid smells of the crash, this scent was a spring day, a field of flowers, a wedding bouquet. Now I must be dead. This must be how heaven smells. And then, just as I was getting to the important part, the part that could make the difference, my movie faded to black.

When my eyes flickered open, Annie's face was just inches from mine, and her cheeks were wet with tears. "That must have been awful. You were screaming and crying. What did you see?"

I tried to talk, but nothing happened. Grabbing my Hawkie Talkie, I frantically punched at the keys. "I SCREAMED? I MADE ACTUAL NOISES?"

"Very loud screams. The kind where the neighbors might call the police." Annie smiled and stroked my hair. "Definite progress."

"I SAW THE NIGHT OF THE ACCIDENT. I REMEM-BERED THE CRASH. THERE WERE HEADLIGHTS AND ANOTHER CAR HAD CROSSED ONTO OUR SIDE OF THE ROAD, AND MY DAD WAS TRYING TO AVOID AN ACCIDENT WHEN WE HIT THE TREE."

"How terrifying that must have been. Did you see the other car?" Annie grabbed a pad of paper, ready to take notes in case my hypnotic memories faded away.

"JUST BRIGHT HALOGEN HEADLIGHTS. AND THEN, AFTER WE HIT THE TREE SOMEONE WAS SHINING A LIGHT IN OUR CAR, BUT MY EYES WERE CLOSED AND I COULDN'T OPEN THEM. THERE WAS A SMELL, A WONDERFUL FLOWERY SMELL MIXED IN WITH THE SMELL OF BLOOD AND GASOLINE. IT MUST HAVE COME FROM THE PERSON WHO WAS LOOKING IN THE WINDOW."

Chapter 20

Instead of Mrs. Fisher standing in the doorway as I walked up the front path, it was Ben. My instinct to flee fought with an almost uncontrollable urge to run into his arms. Unable to decide, I continued walking towards him, more slowly, stalling for time.

Where's your mom?

Ben was never home on Wednesday afternoons when I visited 7 Seashell Lane. Except for our locker room skirmish and his possible mistake in the kitchen a couple of weeks earlier, he had made good on his promise to avoid me until I had properly inventoried my warehouse full of problems. What had changed?

"An hour ago my father called to say he scored tickets to some show my mother has been dying to see, so she raced off to catch a train to the City. She called me to come home and wait for you. She said she texted, but you didn't text back."

He came down the steps to meet me. I could feel the color rising in my face. Not only could he read my mind, but he could certainly see what I was thinking and feeling just by my blush.

I always forget to turn my phone on. I guess I'll come back next week then, or I can come another day. Just have your mom let me know what's best for her.

This wasn't so hard—a civil, neutral conversation. With effort I held it together, and I tried not to imagine him kissing me, whispering in my ear, caressing me. My body burned with the effort. *Take it easy, Sasha,* I told myself. *Just get the hell out of here before you embarrass yourself.*

"You want to come in? As long as you're here."

What was this about? Push me, pull me.

I should probably go home.

Normally I would have given a limb to have Ben invite me in, but I was slowly learning to live without him in my everyday life, and I knew that spending the afternoon with him would undo all the progress I had made. Ten minutes alone with him and I would be right back on page one—desperately in love and totally bereft. Not fair of him to screw with my emotions, especially since he knew exactly what I was feeling.

"Just come in. I want to show you something. It won't take long."

Before I could figure out some clever comeback, he took me by the hand and led me up the stairs to his room. Mrs. Fisher had said I could spend more time there if I thought it would help me remember, but I hadn't taken her up on her generous offer. It only made me miss Ben, and I couldn't trust myself not to rummage through his drawers, sniffing his T-shirts, maybe even stealing one to sleep in. It was a short stroll from jilted girlfriend to drooling stalker.

Okay. What do you want to show me? I sat on the edge of my old bed and waited, trying to control my breathing, unsuccessfully trying to look nonchalant.

"Um, I want to try something, if you're okay with it."

He stood in front of me, holding my hands in his, just looking at me. It was unnerving—I felt like he was looking right through me. I wished I'd worn mascara, lip gloss—some girl armor to protect me from his X-ray vision. Damn the sweats.

Was my breath okay? Without saying a word, he gently pushed me back onto the bed and stretched out next to me. Brushing the hair out of my eyes, he kissed my forehead, my nose, and finally my lips.

What the hell are you doing? I thought you didn't want to be fuck buddies.

Boys were too confusing. When did the rules change, and why didn't I get the memo? All these weeks I had been fantasizing about just such a moment, but now that I was trying desperately to stand on my own two feet, he was determined to get me on my back. As much as I wanted him to kiss me some more, I felt like he was manipulating me, and I didn't like it. I may not have had much self-respect, but I did have enough to make me feel like I was being railroaded. Talk about an abuse of power.

"I'm not planning on going all the way. Your virginity is safe."

He kissed me, his tongue searing my mouth with delicious fire. I had almost forgotten how incredible it felt.

You've got that right. I made a show of crossing my legs. *I'm not some old toy you can just take off the shelf and play with once in a while. What about my feelings?* I tried, not too hard, to sit up, but he wouldn't let me. *I was just starting to get over you, and I'm making real progress on my own. Just ask your mother. Stop messing with my head.*

"Please don't bring up my mother right now. Just go with it. I'm not just using you for my own selfish purposes—I swear— as much as I'm enjoying this. I have a really good reason for what I'm doing. Trust me."

How many scheming boys had said just those words to how many stupid girls? My stomach turned over as he kissed my neck and nibbled on my earlobe. I felt like I was going to spontaneously combust inside my sweats. This was way better than Mexican hallucination tea.

It had better be a very good reason. Jules's mother says you should never trust boys who say trust me.

I was all bluster. What little determination I possessed had dissolved with that very first kiss. Talk about a pushover. Before I could wrestle with my self-esteem, my sense of empowerment, or my independence, most of my clothes were in a pile on the floor, alongside Ben's shirt.

"You're thinking too much," Ben whispered in my ear. "Just relax and let me make you feel good." His fingertips lightly brushed my arm. "Do you like it when I touch you like that?"

No, I hate it. You know how much I hate you right now? You are such a shit. His hands and lips were everywhere—my arms and legs tingled, and I couldn't get enough air. If someone walked in on us, I would die on the spot. *You're sure there's no chance your parents could come home?*

"Focus, Sasha, and stop talking about my parents. We're all alone. Concentrate on what you're feeling. Let your body take you there."

Take me where? I've never done this before.

Ten minutes earlier I'd been steeling myself for another cup of steaming mulch and a tumultuous trip down memory lane, and now . . .

"Really? Your clenched fists and deer-in-the-headlights look don't give you away at all." He flashed his perfect teeth.

Do you think that making fun of me is going to help? I'm not scared. I just don't understand why you're doing this. What changed? I'm totally confused.

"Stop thinking, and kiss me back. You spend way too much time thinking." His body surrounded mine, and I was lost. "Yes, that's it, Sasha. Don't think, just feel."

It was no use. I couldn't fight the sensation as it reverberated through every cell in my body. It swallowed me like a wave, and I was in another place, until I heard the scream. *What was that? Who's here?* I knew we would get caught. I had never been so humiliated in my entire life.

Kissing my damp forehead, Ben said, "That was you, numbnuts. Four years of psychotherapy—fifty thousand dollars. Five minutes with me—priceless. So what do you have to say for yourself?"

That was me? "Thank you?" It came out as a croak, but it was my voice. I put my hands to my throat. *How did that happen? And how did you know that would happen?*

"I didn't know for sure, but the one Dr. O'Rourke book you didn't read was all about the power of sex to build a detour around a person's psychological train wreck. Apparently she's right about that."

"I don't know what to say."

The realization that I was coming out the other side was too much, and I burst into tears. My voice had finally swum to the surface.

"It doesn't matter what you say. It's all good, Sash." Ben was grinning like the Cheshire cat.

"Does this mean you're not going to leave me again?" Was he really back, for good?

"I'm not going anywhere, although if you'll just excuse me for a minute . . ." Ben stood up. "Your enthusiasm was, um, contagious, and I need to go clean up."

There was a wet spot on his jeans. Awkward, but it meant that this was more than just sex therapy.

"Sorry about that."

"Don't ever apologize for making me feel like that. Stay put. I'm going to take a quick shower." As he disappeared into the bathroom, I reached for my sweats. "Don't put your clothes back on," he called through the door.

Five minutes later he came out wrapped in a towel. "Close your eyes."

I heard his towel drop to the floor and squinted through my closed eyelids. Broad shoulders tapering to a narrow waist, he looked like one of my art book marble statues, and I couldn't decide whether I wanted to sketch him or jump him. He turned around, and he was as beautiful from the front as the back. My first glimpse of a naked man, and I didn't turn to stone. Things were definitely looking up.

"No fair peeking," he said, but he was still smiling. He slipped into sweats and climbed back onto the bed. I crawled into his waiting arms. "Are you all right?"

"I'm not sure." I kept clearing my throat, trying to ease the raspiness. "My voice sounds funny."

"You haven't used your vocal cords in more than four years. It's going to take a while for them to get back to normal. I like it this way. It's sexy."

I made a face. "I sound like those chain-smoking old men who hang out at the diner by the train station."

"But a very sexy chain-smoking old man. Are you okay *other* than your voice? How does the rest of your body feel?" He rested his hand on my bare stomach.

"Oh, *that*. Yeah, that was more than okay. I've never done that before."

"I figured that, but I think you needed it. I know I did." He kissed my nose and buried his face in my hair.

"What if your grand plan didn't work?" The way I felt when he touched me, the talking was pretty much a bonus.

"We would have had fun trying, even if it didn't bring your voice back. And I couldn't stay away from you anymore.

I know now that what you said that night at the restaurant was just talk. You would never give up, no matter how long it took."

"I wouldn't."

"My mother says you've been working so hard these past weeks, trying to get better, in part for me." His voice trailed off at the end. He really did care about me—maybe as much as I cared for him.

"I'm never going to give up. Being with you, I just feel so incredibly normal, and happy. It hadn't occurred to me that telling you how wonderful you are would scare you away." It had never entered my mind that Ben would ever be afraid of anything. Even when facing the four knuckle-draggers whose necks were wider than their heads, he hadn't blinked.

"When you said those things to me in the restaurant, I panicked. Stupid, but I flashed forward twenty years, and I saw you resenting me for holding you back."

"But why didn't you just ask me?" If he was so tuned in to my inner monologue, why didn't he know what I meant anyway? I guess even mind readers can get their signals crossed sometimes.

"Because I'm a moron. Can you forgive me for hurting you?" He kissed me again and again. "You've already suffered a lifetime's worth of pain, and I heaped on even more."

"Forgiven." I couldn't stop smiling. "This can't be happening. The two things I've missed most—you and my voice—and I get both back in the same day. Are you sure I'm not dreaming?"

"It's very real. And it's a very good day." Ben's cell phone rang and I reluctantly let him get up from the bed. "Yes, Mom, Sasha's fine. She's right here . . . No, I asked her to hang out for a little while . . ." Ben handed me the phone and whispered,

"Talk to her. She'll be so surprised. But I don't think you should tell her how we did it."

You think? Hi, Mrs. Fisher, Ben and I just slid into third base, and I got my voice back.

Did he really believe I could or would explain to his mother what we had been doing? Annie Fisher was easy to talk to, but there was a line. Taking the phone, I was excited to share my accomplishment. Mrs. Fisher had started me on the trek up the mountain to recovery, and Ben had helped me reach the summit, so to speak. Then I had to call Charlotte and Stuart. They would probably pass out when they heard my voice.

But when I tried to speak to Mrs. Fisher, no sound came out. Back to the beginning—once again, I was a fish out of water. A few sentences tossed out so easily, and then nothing. Bile rose in my throat, and I dropped the phone, barely making it to the bathroom.

"No, Mom, everything's okay, but I have to go. There's someone at the door. Enjoy the theater. Bye." Ben's words tumbled out as he rushed to get off the phone.

He ran into the bathroom, finding me in the fetal position on the tile floor. "Are you okay? What happened?"

When I tried to talk to your mother, nothing happened. I've lost it again.

I covered my face with my hands, wishing I could disappear. Just as I was emerging from my cave, a giant boulder had crashed down, once again trapping me inside.

"Are you sure? How can that be? I guess we'll just have to fool around some more. Make it stick." Ben cradled me in his lap as he sat with his back against the bathtub, not sounding especially concerned about my latest setback.

"That's beyond not funny." Didn't he see that this was a catastrophe? Of all people, I figured Ben would understand.

"You just said that out loud. Your voice is back. You're a little rusty, that's all. But maybe we should get naked again, just to make sure." He buried his face in my neck, and I moaned as his lips danced over my skin. "That's the best sound in the whole world. Do it again," he ordered. Maybe he was right; I just needed a little more of his special treatment.

"Is this what they call makeup sex?" Knowledge imparted from *Cosmo*'s monthly sex column. Now that I knew my speech wasn't an aberration, I felt better, but something wasn't right.

"Technically no, since it's impossible to have makeup sex if we're not actually having sex, but I like where you're headed with this." He playfully pinned me to the bathroom floor, kissing his way from my neck down to my stomach. "You want to start a fight?"

"Stop." As difficult as it was, I pushed him off me and sat up. "I need to know what's going on."

"Fine, as long as we can pick up where we left off after. I need you, Sash. I want you so much."

He looked straight through my eyes into my mind, and for a few seconds, I didn't care if I ever said another word or even left his bedroom for the rest of my life.

"Maybe I can only talk to you. Is that possible?"

But that was ridiculous. If my voice was back, it was back, wasn't it? What difference did it make who was listening? Ben jumped up and retrieved his laptop from the desk. He sat down next to me on the tile floor and Googled "hysterical mutism."

Ben scanned the page. "According to Wikipedia, which is of course the ultimate medical authority, *selective* mutism is a physical manifestation of an anxiety disorder, most prevalent in children. Those suffering with this condition can speak only in the presence of certain people, such as close family members with whom the individual feels completely safe and comfortable. When the patient is in the presence of others, he or she may be rendered completely mute. For example, a child may be able to speak only to her mother, but no one else. This disorder may respond to intensive behavior modification therapy. Medication isn't favored, as the side effects in children and adolescents include depression and suicidal thoughts. There you go."

"So now I'm only partially insane." My head began to throb.

"I still think you're totally nuts, but the fact that you can speak to me means you're headed down the right path. You just need patience . . . and lots more fooling around." He kissed my stomach again. "More scream therapy."

"Is that your professional opinion, Dr. Fisher?" I giggled as his tongue circled my belly button.

"Don't question my methods, young lady. I managed a partial cure in under five minutes," he said in an exaggerated German accent. "Give me an hour, I could have you singing in a Broadway musical."

"A little bit cocky, aren't you?"

Could he do that for me? I was beginning to believe he could do anything.

"Is that a challenge? Because I'm ready." He started to slip out of his sweats.

"What are you doing?"

Maybe a total recovery would require more than just a little messing around. Was today the day? As much as I'd fantasized about going all the way with Ben, now that the possibility was literally at my fingertips, I freaked. But I could imagine worse cures. Virginity lost in the name of medical science . . .

"I'm just kidding. Breathe. As much as I want to see how far Dr. O.'s research can take us, I know you're not ready. You have to crawl before you can walk. Just promise me I'm your only therapist."

"I promise. Promise me you won't take on any other patients." Talking, flirting, out loud. My voice was still rough, but I felt lighter than air. *I love you, Ben.*

"Are you sure that's not just hormones talking? I mean, that *was* your first happy ending." He rested his hand gently between my legs.

"I know the difference between love and sex." The sensation of his hand through the thin fabric was electric, and I pushed against his palm.

"I think you do. And I do, too. I love you, Sasha." It was the perfect starry-eyed movie moment—except for the fact that we were lying on the bathroom floor.

Chapter 21

"JULES, THERE'S SOMETHING I HAVE TO TELL YOU."

I described Ben's creative physical therapy and its miraculous, though limited, results. Whenever I wasn't with Ben, and therefore mute, I sometimes found myself thinking it had all been some elaborate dream sequence. Sharing my experience with Jules made it real.

"So the shin bone's connected to the knee bone, and the larynx is connected to the honey pot," she sang.

"CHARMING." That wasn't exactly what I'd hoped she'd say when I told her.

"As much as I love you, and as much as I want to hear your sweet voice again, there is absolutely no way I'm going to give you any lady love to jump start your voice box. You know that, don't you?" Jules stuck out her tongue.

"NO WORRIES. I HAVE NO INTEREST IN CROSSING THE PICKET LINE, EITHER." I made a face back at her.

"Who would have thought a little heavy breathing could be so effective? Why would anyone ever go to talk therapy? I mean, really, there's no contest," Jules said, moaning to make her point.

"BEN FIGURED IT OUT AFTER READING DR. O.'S BOOK, *CLIMAX*."

"It would never have occurred to me that getting your rocks off could cure mental illness. I guess that's why she gets paid the big bucks. I wonder what else it can fix?"

"I'LL LET YOU KNOW AFTER BEN AND I DO MORE RESEARCH. HAVE YOU EVER . . . ?"

It was the most extraordinary feeling on earth. Had Jules ever had one? She might not have told me, seeing as until recently it seemed like a remote possibility for me, and she might not want me to feel like I was missing out on yet another major benefit of life with the normals.

"You're all full of yourself now that you've experienced Dr. O.'s Big O. Actually, I haven't." She paused. "Don't look so shocked. Think about it. How many guys our age are concerned with much beyond getting their own oil changed? I mean, really."

"BEN'S LIKE THAT WITH EVERYTHING. HE CARRIES MY BOOKS, OPENS DOORS FOR ME, TAKES CARE OF ME." Maybe he really was a unicorn.

"He's a perfect gentleman, Sash. May you always come first in this relationship." She poked me in the ribs.

"I GET IT." Jules was queen of the bad pun.

"So, are you going to knock boots anytime soon?"

"KNOCK BOOTS? WHO TALKS LIKE THAT? I'M ASSUMING YOU MEAN DOING THE DEED?"

"Well, duh, Miss Screaming Orgasm. Don't you like that? As euphemisms go, it's got some style. So, are you?"

"NOT ANYTIME SOON. IT'S A BIG STEP FROM A HAND JOB TO GOING ALL THE WAY, DON'T YOU THINK?"

As much as I could imagine spending the rest of my life with Ben, making love was serious business. Letting someone inside your body as well as your mind was the ultimate act of trust. Was I ready for that? I was only seventeen, and a young seventeen at that. And not to be forgotten, the possibility of pregnancy, no matter how careful we were, was terrifying. Imagining myself as someone's mother was like picturing myself as president of the United States. And truthfully, how much more incredible could anything feel than what I'd just experienced? Like Ben had said, slower was better.

"My mother would be so proud of you, except for the letting him stick his hands down your pants part." Jules could be so crude sometimes. I think she talked like that just to watch me squirm. "Another successful graduate of the Lucy Harper School of Sexual and Moral Independence."

"YOU'RE NOT GOING TO TELL HER, ARE YOU?"

I hadn't planned on sharing news of my voice with Charlotte—it would hurt her feelings that I felt safe enough with Ben to talk, but not with her, even though it was subconscious and out of my control. And there was no way I was going to tell her about my primal scream therapy, although I probably would need to tell her that Ben and I were back together. But if Jules planned on blabbing to her mother, I would have to come clean about everything before it got back to Charlotte and Stuart.

"Of course not. That would only make her launch an investigation into *my* social life. Not that there's anything much going on, but I prefer to stay off her radar. If she thinks I'm doing more than holding hands, she'll ship me off to a convent until I turn thirty."

That had to be an exaggeration, but Jules looked serious.

"THANK YOU. IT'S PRIVATE AND I DON'T WANT ANYONE TO KNOW, EXCEPT YOU. I'M NOT EVEN TELLING CHARLOTTE AND STUART."

"I'm proud to be part of the inner circle. So tell me exactly what it felt like. Did you have to do anything to him? There's no free lunch." Jules nodded knowingly, although I wasn't sure at this point how well informed she really was on this topic.

"NOTHING. HE TOLD ME JUST TO RELAX AND ENJOY IT. AND I DID. HE SEEMED TO ENJOY HIM-SELF." I didn't want to tell her about the wet spot—I hoped she could read between the lines.

"So he got off on all your moaning and screaming. Just wait. It's definitely a two-way street."

"I WANT IT TO BE. IT WOULD BE SELFISH TO MAKE IT ALL ABOUT ME ALL THE TIME."

As amazing as it felt to be catered to like that, it must be a rush to make another person feel that good, to lose control like I had—kind of powerful. I wanted to know what it felt like to make Ben so excited he completely let go. Did boys make noise like girls? I wondered.

"There's nothing wrong with being the center of attention. Just be careful. It's a short step from petting to poking. You're definitely not ready for that, no matter how many car doors Ben opens for you."

Even though I was now slightly more experienced than Jules—speaking only in terms of quality, not quantity—she was still in charge, still the mother hen, warning me off the dangers that lurked behind the green eyes and good manners.

I rushed to Ben's defense. "I KNOW THAT. I'M IN NO RUSH TO GO ALL THE WAY. HE'S NOT EITHER."

"That's what boys say, and then you let your guard down, and before you know it, you're holding a screaming newborn on some MTV special and whining about being a single mother."

"HE'S NOT LIKE THAT." I think Jules had been spend-ing too much time with her mother lately. She didn't used to be so wary of guys. Not every high school boy was a sexual predator in training. "DID SOMETHING HAPPEN? DID SOMEONE DO SOMETHING TO MAKE YOU SO SUSPICIOUS?"

"No, no one's ever done anything to me . . . unfortunately. Don't look so shocked. I'm just kidding, and I have to admit, I'm a little jealous. He loves you, Sash, like nobody's business. You're so lucky."

"I AM LUCKY. WHO WOULD HAVE THOUGHT I'D BE SAYING THAT AFTER EVERYTHING THAT'S HAPPENED?"

"You deserve some good stuff. I'm sorry I'm being petty. You're my best friend, and you've been living in hell for a long time. Welcome back. It's your turn."

Chapter 22

"That woman over there keeps staring at you. Do you know her?" Ben gestured with his chin toward the front of the restaurant.

I turned around and there was Dr. O., deep in conversation with a man who looked like Sigmund Freud, round glasses and all. Was this man her husband? Her life outside her occupation as a shrink had never crossed my mind.

You don't recognize the author of your favorite sex book? Isn't her picture on the cover?

Even though I could speak out loud to Ben, I often just thought at him out of habit, and he didn't mind, although it must have looked funny to anyone who was paying attention— like he was totally monopolizing the conversation as I stared at him with stars in my eyes.

"I was too busy soaking up her knowledge. But now that you mention it, she does look kind of familiar—but her hair's different, and she's way older," he said, trying not to look like he was staring at Dr. O.

So what's she thinking about?

I had never asked him to share other people's secret thoughts before. What a waste of an amazing resource. But maybe there was a mind readers' code of ethics that would prohibit him from disclosing such private information.

"You really want to know? Let me concentrate. There's so much going on in here."

Saturday night in a crowded restaurant—there must have been a hundred voices echoing in Ben's head. He shut his eyes and turned in Dr. O.'s direction. With his eyes closed, I was free to study his face. He really did look like a piece of classical sculpture, even with his post–locker room nose.

"You're distracting me. But thank you. I think you're beautiful too."

Sorry.

"She's wondering if she should come over here. She doesn't know that you know she's here. She's curious about me. She likes my hair. It reminds her of a boy she dated in high school." He opened his eyes and placed his hands on the table, palms up.

That's it? I had been hoping for something juicier.

"Pretty much. Oh yeah, the scallops are chewy, and she's wondering if Bill is going to want to sleep with her tonight. It's their third date."

TMI. I should have quit while I was ahead. I stuck out my tongue. Thinking about Dr. O. having a sex life was like imagining one's grandmother getting busy.

"That's why I try to filter. Hearing other people think about sex is not as exciting as it sounds—present company excepted."

So you want to meet her? I guess she is kind of a rock star, at least in the world of the damaged and confused. Just don't tell her I can talk when I'm alone with you. She'll want me to come in more often, and I really would rather work this out with your mom instead. And don't you dare tell her about your application of her theories.

"I definitely want to meet her. She's my idol. I promise I'll be discreet. A gentleman never discusses his conquests, even if she's kind of the one who suggested it. Would it be too much if I asked for her autograph?" Ben reached in his pocket and took out a pen.

Maybe a little. All right. Let's get it over with, Captain Romance.

For some reason it felt funny connecting these two threads in my life, even though I couldn't imagine Dr. O. not being totally captivated by him. We squeezed between the maze of tables until we were standing next to Dr. O. and her date, who still looked like Sigmund Freud up close, but with a Miami Beach tan and a thick gold necklace glinting in a nest of gray hair sprouting from his open collar.

"Dr. O'Rourke. Sasha spotted you, and she wanted me to meet you. I'm Ben Fisher." He shook hands with both of them.

"A pleasure to meet you, Ben. This is my friend, Dr. Parsons. You're glowing, Sasha. So the two of you worked things out?" I nodded. "I'm so pleased for you both. Ben, Sasha told me you were living in Florence not too long ago. One of my favorite cities—I travel a great deal for work. In fact, I just got back from Prague."

We stood for what seemed like days, Ben chatting away about Europe, while I smiled and counted the seconds until we could politely make our escape. Making small talk was painful; listening to small talk was cruel and unusual punishment. Ben squeezed my hand—how convenient to have a boyfriend who knows exactly what you're thinking.

"I've read a few of your books. You've done such good work for so many people, helped them come farther than they imagined possible." He squeezed my hand again, and I stepped on his foot.

You and Jules should get together and trade shitty puns.

"I'm just glad I've been able to help, and I wish that I could have done more for Sasha, but she's on her way now, in large part, I think, thanks to you. You've allowed her to concentrate more on her future and less on her past, and I think in that strategy may lie Sasha's personal victory," Dr. O. said, beaming at Ben.

Why were they talking about me as if I weren't even there? Once again I felt like a child in a room full of adults.

"That's very kind of you to say, Dr. O'Rourke. It's such an honor to have met you. Dr. Parsons, nice to meet you, as well. Enjoy the rest of your dinner."

Ben was like the mayor. His manners were flawless. He could have been Cary Grant or Gregory Peck reincarnated. Nobody in high school talked like that. Most Americans didn't talk like that.

"I'm so glad we ran into each other. There is no greater joy in my life than to see my patients living full, happy lives. Sasha, I'm so proud of you."

Dr. O. stood up and put her arms around me. She was all choked up. Maybe it was Ben, or maybe it was the wine, because she wasn't usually a teary-eyed hugger. My cheek rested briefly on her shoulder as she embraced me. Suddenly seized by a wave of nausea, I pulled away and ran to the back of the restaurant, nearly knocking over a waiter carrying a loaded tray, down a hallway I prayed led to the restroom.

As I fled, I heard Ben say, "Bad scallops, maybe? If you'll excuse me."

In the safety of the locked bathroom, I squatted in the corner, head between my knees. Stars danced before my eyes. *Just breathe. Don't pass out on this filthy floor.* Tiny jackhammers drilled mercilessly behind my eyes. What just happened?

Frantic knocking on the door and voices—Ben and Dr. O. together. "Sasha, are you okay? Are you ill?"

I splashed cold water on my face and opened the door, nodding. *We need to go home, right now.*

"Thank you for all your help, Dr. O'Rourke. I'm just going to take her home. She must be coming down with something. So sorry to disturb your dinner. Come on, Sasha, let's get you out of here."

Ben took my hand and led me through the restaurant, every eye in the place following the tall, handsome boy leading the blotchy, clearly unhinged girl. At the front, Ben handed a fistful of cash to the hostess, apologized for any inconvenience, and shepherded me into the calm of the parking lot. We sat in the car for several minutes, staring out the windows, not speaking, just listening to each other breathing.

"So what just happened? You're not sick. I would feel it if you were physically ill. You just freaked out, and I have no idea why. Your thoughts are a mess—something about a smell?"

"Can we just go? Please?" I whispered.

I opened and closed my fists, willing myself not to start hyperventilating again. The hammers pounded less fiercely, and for that I was grateful.

Ben cupped my face in his hands, searching my eyes. "Not until you tell me what's going on."

More than anything, I wanted to tell him, wanted to share my fears. But I hated feeling like the mental patient, always on the edge, a single whiff enough to send me careening off the cliff into a ravine of psychosis.

"You know my old nightmare, the one about the accident—the noise, the smells, the snow? Besides the odor of burning wires and gasoline, there was a sweet smell, like perfume."

"And you smelled that perfume in the restaurant, and that's what set you off? That makes sense—smelling your mother's perfume could stir up all kinds of emotions. You poor thing." He kissed me gently and started the car. "It'll be easier next time."

"I smelled it on Dr. O.'s sweater, and it's not my mother's perfume or any perfume I've ever smelled before, or since."

I watched him behind the wheel, never forgetting to signal, never going over the speed limit. He drove with the precision of someone taking his driver's license test.

"So what are you saying?" We were safely stopped at a red light, and he looked over at me. "Dr. O. was at the scene of the accident? Next to your car?"

"It does sound crazy when you say it like that. But maybe she caused the accident and was checking to see if anyone was still alive before she left the scene." Utterly ridiculous, but incredibly real to me.

Ben shook his head. "I find that hard to believe. She leaves the scene of a devastating crash, and then becomes your therapist who's supposed to help you recover your memories of the accident *she* caused? You've been watching way too much TV."

"I hardly watch any TV, and that's exactly what I'm thinking." It had sounded more plausible in the bathroom stall. "Maybe that's why I'm one of her few failures. She's supposed to be this ridiculously successful shrink, and she couldn't even manage to hypnotize me. Doesn't make much sense, does it?"

"Well, Perry Mason, it's a nice theory—very neat and tidy. But don't you think it's weird that the woman who killed your family would then take you on as a patient?"

The light changed and, looking both ways, Ben drove toward home, his eyes never leaving the road even as he tried to reason with me.

"If I remembered what happened, she would be in deep trouble, and the only way to be sure my memories stay buried is if she were my therapist. Or maybe she wanted to try and make up for what she did to me, somehow make it right." I shrugged my shoulders.

"Sounds a little too movie-of-the-week for me. Maybe you dreamed about that perfume *after* you met the doctor." Ben pulled into my driveway and turned off the engine.

"Definitely not. I remember it so vividly, because it was such an unusual smell, and it was *always* part of my dream, which started before I first saw Dr. O'Rourke. I smelled it again when your mother hypnotized me the last time."

I had been so sure, but could Ben be right? Could my mind be playing tricks? In the days and weeks following the accident, time had stopped for me. Could I be remembering it out of order now, in my desperate need to make everything fit neatly back together?

"Let's suppose by some insane possibility she did cause the accident. She wouldn't leave you and your family to die. She's a doctor, for fuck's sake. She took an oath."

"Maybe she was drunk or something. She was drinking wine at the restaurant. Like in a Greek tragedy, maybe alcoholism is her fatal flaw, and she realized it after she caused the accident. She panicked and left us there. And now she's trying to undo her wrong by making me well again." The more I thought about it, the more I liked this scenario. It was poetic and heartrending.

"Okay, Sophocles, so what you're saying is that she didn't help you, because she didn't want to get arrested for drunk driving? That she left you to die with your family, since you were the only witness?" Ben put his hand on my forehead, as if feeling for fever.

I nodded.

"And then she made sure Charlotte picked her to be your psychiatrist so she could work her head-shrinking magic on you to guarantee that you could never identify her as the killer, while at the same time healing your battered spirit. It would make a great screenplay."

"You think I've lost it, don't you?"

Maybe I would have to explore this avenue of investigation with Jules. She might be more open-minded. Charlotte and Stuart would be like Ben, certain that my train had finally jumped the tracks.

"A little. Are you sure you didn't hit your head in the bathroom at the restaurant?" He reached over and rubbed my scalp, looking for a bump.

"No, I didn't hit my head. But I do have a headache."

Why couldn't I just leave my past behind already? I wasn't cut out to be a therapist or a detective.

"What happens if she realizes you're on to her? Maybe she'll try to bump you off. You're lucky she's Irish and not Italian." Ben flicked his thumbnail against his front teeth.

"Am I supposed to know what that means?"

"You've never seen any gangster movies, like *The Godfather*?"

"Never." I sighed. "I told you, I don't watch much television."

"You have so much to learn. Speaking of learning, are your aunt and uncle home tonight?" Ben leaned across me to unbuckle my seatbelt.

"I can do that myself, you know. I may be crazy, but I'm not paralyzed."

Sometimes I felt like Ben's feelings for me were mixed up with his uncontrollable desire to fix things, and I was the ultimate remodeling project. He wanted to make me better, when I just wanted him to want me.

"It gives me an excuse to touch you. That's all." His fingers lingered on my arm.

"You don't need an excuse." I would be perfectly happy if he never let go of me.

"In that case . . . let me ask you again, is anyone home? Because we can play in the car, if we have to, but the couch, or your bed, would be way better." He tapped his fingers on my arm, waiting for my answer.

"They went to some jazz club in the City."

The anticipation of his lips on mine, his hands on my body, made me weak in the knees. How was I going to walk into the house?

"Good news, and if you can't walk, I'll just have to carry you over the threshold. We can play wedding night." Ben climbed out and came around to my side of the car.

"I think you *will* have to carry me. I'm feeling a little shaky. That thing at the restaurant kind of threw me."

My palms started to sweat. Wedding night?

"No problem." He lifted me up, holding me against his chest and kicking the car door shut. "Don't start hyperventilating again, Sasha. I was just kidding. As much as I want you, and I do, tonight's *not* the night. So relax. It's your call . . . it always will be."

But could you do that other thing again? I really liked that. Too embarrassed to say that out loud, I reverted to my old ways.

"What other thing?" He paused outside the door to my room. "I'm not sure what you mean."

You know. That thing . . .

"I want you to tell me what you want." He put me down on my bed in a patch of moonlight.

I shook my head.

"Use your words, Sasha." He was going to make me work for it.

I closed my eyes so I didn't have to look at him. "Fine, be that way. I want you to touch me the way you did when I was at your house. I want you to make me scream again. Is that what you want to hear?" As mortifying as it was to say it out loud, it was definitely worth it.

"That's exactly what I want." He lay down on top of me, his legs hanging off the end of the bed. "Am I crushing you?" His elbows rested on the bed as he planted tiny kisses all over my face.

"No, you could never hurt me, but that tickles." I twitched my nose.

"Just you wait." In one motion, Ben slipped out of his shirt and started to unbutton mine. "This is okay, right?"

"What if I said no?"

"I might not take no for an answer." Ben swallowed hard. "Oh, that was bad. Did that make you think of those football assholes? I'm such an idiot. I was just playing—you know that. I would never force you to do anything."

I'm fine. I wasn't thinking about them at all. I like when you tease me like that. It's really hot, actually. I ran my hand down his chest, and he shuddered. *So we're okay?* He nodded. *Then back to work.*

He kissed his way from my lips down to the top of my jeans, unbuttoned them, and pulled down the zipper. Although I was incredibly ticklish, I tried to hold it together.

Ben looked up. "You can laugh. I don't mind."

Pressing his lips against my stomach, he kissed a trail down to my panties. Instead of laughing, I moaned. Mind reading wasn't his only gift.

A car door slammed once, then twice, and I let out a yelp. "Shit, that can't be them." Time flew when we were together, but it couldn't have passed that quickly. I looked at the bedside clock. "It's only nine-thirty."

"It's fine. Just put your shirt back on . . . and breathe." Ben tucked in his own shirt and stood in front of the mirror, trying to tame his wild curls. "Do you need a little help with that?"

Alarm bells going off in my head, my fingers fumbled with the buttons. Calm and collected, as usual, Ben quickly did up my shirt and ran his fingers through my hair. "You've got a wicked case of bed head. Maybe you should put your hair up."

"Good idea. We have a little problem beyond my hair, though. I decided not to tell them about my voice, and I kind of hadn't gotten around to telling them that we were back together, either. Charlotte's going to go apeshit." Procrastination was a bad habit of mine, and I needed to do something about it, soon.

"Probably an understatement. Here I am in your bedroom, and it's obvious we haven't been playing chess. So I guess you can tell them now, at least about the back together part. The sometimes-talking part can wait. You don't want to shock them with too much news all at once."

We stood toe to toe, smoothing each other's clothes. The front door slammed and I could hear voices and laughter. At least they were in a good mood.

"Come on," Ben whispered. "The best defense is a good offense." He took me by the hand and led me into the kitchen.

"Oh!" Charlotte jumped. "Ben, you startled me. What are you doing here?"

Stuart, more astute than my aunt, quickly sized up the situation. "Hi there, Ben. Long time no see. How've you been?"

"Very good, sir. And you?" With his military academy posture and Ivy League diction, Ben looked and sounded guilty of *something*.

"It's good to have you back. Charlotte, Sasha and Ben have evidently patched things up. Congratulations, kids."

I picked up my voice box. "WE JUST GOT BACK FROM DINNER. I DIDN'T THINK YOU'D BE HOME UNTIL MUCH LATER."

"Apparently." Stuart unsuccessfully tried to stifle his smirk and raised his eyebrows at me.

"When did you two start seeing each other again? Sasha, why didn't you tell me? Ben, do you realize how upset we were when you left Sasha? That was a terrible thing to do."

We? While I was happy that Charlotte cared, sometimes it sounded like it was all about Charlotte.

"I'M SORRY I DIDN'T TELL YOU. I WANTED TO SEE IF IT WAS GOING TO STICK BEFORE I SAID ANYTHING. IT WAS JUST BECAUSE I DIDN'T WANT TO UPSET YOU." Perfect explanation—diplomatic, logical, Charlotte-centered.

"Oh, sweetheart, you can tell me anything. You shouldn't have to go through all of this alone. Give me a hug," Charlotte said as she held out her arms.

No matter how clumsy she sometimes was at the parenting thing, it was obvious she loved me and had only the best intentions. I needed to cut her some slack.

"Mr. and Mrs. Thompson, I'm really sorry about what happened between Sasha and me. I just felt she wasn't focusing on her recovery as much as she should, and I didn't want to be a distraction. But I realize now that I couldn't stand being away from her, and maybe I can help her get better if I work really hard on our relationship."

"You're good," Stuart whispered to Ben. "You should go into politics with patter like that. Brilliant."

"I really mean it. It's not just talk." Ben looked earnestly at my uncle and clasped my hand tightly.

Charlotte yawned and looked at her watch, apparently satisfied with all the explanations. "All's well that ends well. Now I have to go to bed. We skipped the jazz club because after two cosmos all I wanted to do was go to sleep early, so that's exactly what I'm going to do. Goodnight, children, and Ben, welcome back to the fold. Don't you dare hurt my baby again." There was no bitterness in her voice as she kissed Ben on the cheek. "Come on, Stuart, you promised me a massage." She slowly climbed the stairs and disappeared into her bedroom.

"Duty calls. Goodnight, then. Sorry to interrupt your reconciliation. Feel free to get back to whatever it was you two were doing." With a naughty wink, Stuart took a bottle of champagne out of the refrigerator and two glasses from the cupboard. "Why waste a good massage? Don't come a-knockin'."

A door slammed upstairs, and then we heard the pop of a champagne cork and Charlotte's unmistakable giggle.

"I like your uncle."

"He's a great guy. I'm really lucky."

Stuart was the perfect tempering influence. He managed to keep Charlotte's more hysterical tendencies at bay, and although he'd never wanted kids of his own, he truly was a natural and gifted parent. Whatever the situation, he said and did exactly the right thing. No drama, just consistent, loving logic.

"I guess I should go home now?" Clearly Ben was hoping we could pick up right where we left off, but I felt funny messing around downstairs while my aunt and uncle were going at it upstairs.

"Raincheck?" Kissing him chastely, my lips resting on his cheek for a few extra seconds . . . why was I sending him home again?

"I guess it *would* be a little weird, huh?" he asked. I held up my thumb and forefinger. "Will you at least walk me out to my car?"

In the dark driveway, Ben picked me up and sat me on the hood. I wrapped my legs around him, his hips pressing hard against me, and I could feel how much he wanted to stay.

"Are you sure we can't go back inside?" he asked. His voice was husky.

"I'm sure," I said, panting, although if he'd insisted, I would've relented.

My body and my head were waging a death match as to which one was going to be in charge. But as usual, gentleman and voice of reason, Ben said no more, refusing to take advantage of my ambivalence. He softly kissed my swollen lips and held me tight, not forcing the issue.

After a few minutes of making out, he said, "I'm never going to fall asleep tonight, Sasha. This is bad."

Dream about me, about next time. Can I touch you, like you touched me? I don't want to scare you away again.

There was bold, and then there was pushy to the point of offensive. I had made that mistake once already. Had I just crossed the slut line again?

He groaned. "Not scared, but you shouldn't have said that. I'll never make it until next time." Picking me up, he carried me back to the front door. "I have to go home now, and take the first in a series of cold showers. I love you, sweet girl."

"I love you, too, and thank you for everything, for taking such good care of me tonight, and not totally mocking my Dr. O. theory."

"No offense, but for the last hour, Dr. O. and her perfume haven't exactly been on my mind." He kissed my neck, lingering for a few seconds, the sound of his excited breathing hindering my resolve to behave.

"Mine either. But thanks anyway, and please stop doing that. I feel faint."

I took long slow breaths of the cool, damp night air, trying to keep the dizziness from overwhelming me. As amazing as it felt, I needed to calm down.

"Sorry. Can't help it. Even though I think you're off the wall with this, I'll help you however I can. The sooner we get your head squared away, the sooner we can focus on the rest of you." He put both hands around my waist and squeezed.

"Goodnight, Ben. Sleep tight."

I rested my head against his chest. His heart was beating like he'd just run a race.

"Unlikely. Fantasize about us. If I can't sleep, I'll just sit in my car and listen to your thoughts—my own private porn tape."

"You're kind of pervy for a gentleman."

"Isn't that what you like best about me?"

As he said this, he blew gently in my ear. I felt it in my toes. At that moment, I would have done anything he asked.

"That, and your hair." I grabbed a handful and yanked playfully. "Now go home before I change my mind—*your* virtue could be in danger if you stay."

"If only . . . goodnight."

He peeled himself off of me and drove away, leaving me alone in the dark—in love, in lust, and in limbo. Was it possible to maintain this kind of closeness with him—fooling around but stopping before we took the final step? I hoped so, but the way I felt, I was beginning to doubt it. Maybe Dr. Reuben had some insight into this dilemma. I went upstairs to consult my sex manual.

Chapter 23

Ben had insisted on accompanying us on our research expedition to the mall. "I'm the only other person who smelled Dr. O.'s perfume. Jules doesn't have the faintest idea what you're looking for. Don't you think another pair of nostrils could be helpful? I mean, there must be thousands of perfumes. Your nose will be worn out after a few sniffs."

"I suppose you're right. But no making fun of me," I warned him.

"No more than usual." He pulled into Jules's driveway and honked the horn every five seconds until she came running out. "I don't think she likes me."

"She likes you well enough. All that honking will only help, I'm sure."

Jules opened the car door and slid into the back seat. "Sorry, I didn't hear you. Why didn't you honk?"

"Horn got stuck. Sorry."

Why was he acting like a stupid teenager now? "BEN, DON'T TEASE."

We were barely at the corner when Jules said, "Sasha told me what you did for her. Don't blush. I'm impressed. She said you were very, um, how shall I say . . . dexterous."

Jules cleared her throat loudly. I reached back and slapped her knee.

"You can call me Dr. Fisher, amateur therapist." Ben blew on his knuckles.

"You think it would work for me?" she asked.

Jules was having too much fun. If she weren't my oldest and best friend, I would have sworn she was making a play for him. Either that or she hated him—it was hard to tell which.

"STOP IT, JULES. YOU'RE EMBARRASSING HIM . . . AND ME."

"I could see *you* playing for the girls' team, Jules, but I don't see Sasha as a switch hitter, no matter how much she wants to talk to you." Ben glanced at Jules in the rear view mirror and laughed.

"Ooh, the kitten has claws. Maybe I'll let you stay, after all." Jules scratched at the back of Ben's seat.

"STOP FLIRTING YOU TWO. WE HAVE A JOB TO DO."

"Yeah, about that. Why am I here? I wasn't with you at the restaurant, so I didn't get to sniff the good doctor's sweater. What use am I?"

"That's exactly what I said, but Sasha thinks I'm a little too skeptical about her theory that Dr. O. is a hit-and-run driver with a guilty conscience and a nasty white wine habit. Apparently you're much more receptive to her ideas, however nutty they are. Maybe it's that artistic thing you've got going on." Ben kept peeking in the mirror to gauge Jules's reactions to his taunts.

"So I'm just here for moral support. That works for me. I'm not about to let you steal my best friend from me, Dr. Fisher, even though you've given her the ultimate gift . . . and, no, I'm not talking about your voice, Sasha." Jules moaned quietly, just in case we'd missed her point. "I have to admit, I'm a little jealous. Your first ride on the merry-go-round, Sash, and you get the brass ring."

Ignoring Jules, Ben crooned along with the radio. "Fly me to the moon . . ."

I loved his voice and the old-fashioned music he favored. Yet another unique and charming trait, although apparently not to everyone.

"Fine, I'll change it. You struck me as someone who would appreciate a little Sinatra," Ben said as he started pressing buttons on the dashboard, stopping at some Top 40 station. "I didn't think you'd have such generic taste, Jules."

"What are you talking about? Sasha, what is he talking about? I didn't say a word." Jules was totally perplexed. "But as long as you mention it, do you think we could listen to something from this century? I'm not as turned on by this retro crap as my best friend seems to be."

Looking sideways, I clapped my hand over my mouth. *Oh, shit. Did you just read her mind? I never told her about your special talent . . . well, your other special talent.*

Ben slapped his forehead. "Shit," he said under his breath.

"WE'RE HERE." Not a moment too soon we had arrived at the mall.

Jules pulled me aside and we walked a few steps ahead of Ben as we crossed the parking lot. "What's with him? Is he crazy?"

I just shrugged. What could I say?

"The funny thing is I was thinking that Sinatra was a total snooze and why couldn't we listen to something less Paleolithic. But how could he know that?"

"WEIRD."

Would she figure it out for herself? Or would she hopefully forget about the whole thing when she got distracted by some shiny object in the cosmetics department?

"All right, ladies: deep, cleansing breaths. Where do we begin?"

Ben inhaled slowly and ushered us into the hall of mirrors that was the makeup department. There had to be a thousand different perfumes on display, along with cosmetics and powders and soaps. Trying to isolate a single scent among this jumble of fragrances would be difficult.

"Sash, are you crazy? There's no way you're going to be able to pick out one perfume when they're all mixed together."

Jules had barely spoken when a young woman in a cocktail napkin that passed for a skirt teetered over in stilettos, offering us a spray of a new scent, Kinky, in a black glass bottle wrapped in tiny silver chains.

Ben winked at me. "Is that for men or women?"

"We have a scent for each, sir. Would you like to try it?" She was practically purring as she stood next to him, her impressive breasts not so accidentally brushing his arm.

"What if I hate it?" Ben looked like he was about to lose it. "I'll be stuck with it all day."

We have work to do. Stop flirting with Bambi. By the way, what do fake boobs feel like?

Ben's obvious indifference to her charms made the situation amusing. She *was* smoking hot, and she was definitely making a play for him, but he wasn't buying, no matter how hard she sold it.

"Why don't you see if you like it on me first?" She slid her pale, slender wrist under Ben's nose. "Does it do anything for you? Kind of sexy, isn't it?" Definitely not talking about the perfume.

"You know, I really think I'm more of a Brut guy. I'm not sure I'm ready to get Kinky."

I took his hand and led him away. *Are you having fun?*

"I'm having the best time. Jules, are you having fun yet?"

Jules just stared at him curiously. Apparently the lipstick and perfume had failed to take her mind off what had happened in the car. In an effort to get back to business, I tried to describe what I was looking for.

"IT SMELLED LIKE FLOWERS, FRENCH SOMEHOW."

"That definitely narrows things down, Sash. French, flower? Hardly any perfumes fit into that category." Jules took a deep breath and shook her head. "You realize we're looking for a needle in a haystack, assuming you even remember the smell after sniffing all this crap." She sneezed.

"I'LL REMEMBER THAT SMELL UNTIL THE DAY I DIE. IF IT'S IN THIS STORE, I'LL FIND IT."

But what if it wasn't in this store? Or any other store?

"So let's be logical." Ben walked over to one of the glass counters where an older woman in a low-cut blouse stared into space, clearly wishing she were anyplace else. "Ma'am, do you think you can help us? We're looking for a certain perfume. We don't know what it's called, but we know what it smells like."

She looked relieved to have something to do. "It won't be easy, but we can certainly try. Can you describe the scent? Most perfumes fall into one of several categories: floral, citrus, musky, vanilla, tropical. If you could focus the search a bit, that would be helpful."

"It's definitely floral, and it smelled French. Does that make sense?"

"Sure, it's a place to start. Instead of a thousand perfumes, we can look at a few hundred." Was she being encouraging or sarcastic? It was impossible to tell.

One hour and fifty bottles later, we had nothing, other than stuffy noses and throbbing sinus headaches. Nothing smelled even remotely close to Dr. O'Rourke's perfume. Ben agreed with me. Whatever she had been wearing was no run-of-the-mill department store fragrance. This wasn't going to be so easy. But if it were simple, then it probably wouldn't be my life.

"I'm sorry I couldn't help you. Perhaps the scent you're looking for is a custom blend, in which case, you'd have to ask the person who wears it. But most people who go to the trouble and expense of commissioning their own fragrance don't like to share. Also, there are many perfumes sold in Europe that aren't imported to the United States and can only be purchased overseas. Good luck with your search." The saleswoman turned to another customer.

"Now what, Scooby Doo?" Jules seemed to have recovered her good humor, which in Ben's company meant sarcasm.

"I don't know, Shaggy. Back to the Mystery Mobile for a Scooby Snack? What do you think, Velma?" Ben threw his arm over my shoulder. Even in defeat, he made me smile.

"WHY DO I HAVE TO BE VELMA? I WANT TO BE DAPHNE. SHE'S THE PRETTY ONE, ISN'T SHE?" I hadn't watched that cartoon for years, but I did remember that Velma was the homely one.

"Yeah, but Daphne's stupid. I'd rather be with the smart, plain girl than the beautiful idiot. Beauty fades, but brains last forever," Ben said.

"So what are you saying? Sasha's a Velma?" Was Jules trying to make trouble or just following the game to its logical conclusion?

"JULES, DON'T START." Ben had told me many times he thought I was beautiful, and that was good enough for me.

"What I'm saying is that if I had to choose between brains and beauty, which I don't, because Sasha is way hot and incredibly smart, but if I had to choose, I would always pick brains. Smart is much sexier than cute. Just my opinion. Does that make you insecure, Jules? Because you know I think you're really pretty."

Jules and Ben continued to do this almost fighting, almost flirting thing, all the way back to the car. I still couldn't tell whether they liked or despised each other.

"WHAT'S GOING ON WITH YOU TWO? JULES, ARE YOU CRUSHING ON MY BOYFRIEND? BEN? IT'S TOO CREEPY. COULD YOU GUYS JUST BE NORMAL WITH EACH OTHER?"

We got in the car and Jules promptly started kicking the back of Ben's seat.

"Nothing, Sash. We're just playing. Your beau is cute, but he's way too old for me. I'm into Coldplay, not Cole Porter. But that 1950s thing is perfect for you, Sasha, and he does have a killer body. I have to give him that."

"You're making me blush, Jules. Should we call a truce? We're making Sasha uncomfortable." He turned around and the two shook hands. "No more insults?"

"Agreed." But Jules held up her other hand, fingers crossed.

"NOW THAT WE HAVE YOUR RELATIONSHIP SQUARED AWAY, WHAT DO WE DO ABOUT THE PERFUME?"

This expedition may have been a lark for the two of them, but to me this was a serious business. That smell was the key to getting my voice back.

"I have a wild plan. Why don't you just ask Dr. O. where she got it? If she had it custom made, you'll know she's the one." Ben glanced over at me as he drove. "Or is that too confrontational for you?"

"Curly has a good idea. Why not just face her head on? If she's guilty, she'll either collapse at your feet, begging for absolution, or she'll kill you to cover her tracks. Whatever happens, at least you'll know."

Considering Jules was the one who had started this whole investigation, climbing trees dressed in camouflage and watching old Hardy Boys episodes on DVD, she seemed awfully blasé about it now. She did have a short attention span, and I guess my progress in solving the crime hadn't moved swiftly enough to hold her interest.

"I could go for something, too. Let's stop and get something to eat," Ben said.

"What the . . . ? How did you know I was hungry? What's going on?" Jules looked from Ben to me and back again.

"Um." Ben cleared his throat a couple of times.

What's wrong with you? You never make that mistake, ever.

Ben shrugged his shoulders, and Jules leaned forward between the two front seats.

"HE MUST HAVE HEARD YOUR STOMACH GROWL." It was a lame attempt to explain away Ben's behavior, since I could see that he didn't want to tell Jules about his unusual gift.

"No, my stomach didn't growl. What aren't you telling me? Is this some kind of freaky Jedi mind trick?" Jules narrowed her eyes.

I looked at Ben and nodded. Maybe it was time.

"I can read minds, Jules. That's how I knew you were hungry," Ben said softly as he pulled into the diner parking lot.

Jules punched him in the arm, hard. "Are you kidding me? You actually want me to believe you've got ESP? Sash, your boyfriend is a total whack job. You know that, don't you?"

"IT'S TRUE. BEN KNOWS EXACTLY WHAT I'M THINKING, WHAT YOU'RE THINKING, WHAT EVERYBODY'S THINKING."

"Nobody can read other people's thoughts. Why are you two mindfucking me? It's mean." Jules rarely got angry.

"Nobody's mindfucking you. It's true. Go ahead. Think about something," Ben urged as we sat in the parked car.

After a few seconds, Ben smiled and said, "I'm not going to repeat what you were thinking, Jules, because I was raised not to use language like that, but I can assure you that my parents are legally married and I was not conceived out of wedlock."

"Lucky guess. I'm not convinced," she growled.

"JULES, YOU'RE BEING RIDICULOUS. THINK ABOUT IT. WHO WOULD MAKE UP SOMETHING LIKE THAT? ISN'T IT LOGICAL? WHAT GUY WOULD WANT ME IF HE HAD TO LISTEN TO A ROBOT VOICE ALL THE TIME?"

Having gotten used to Ben's gift, I couldn't understand why Jules was having such a hard time wrapping her head around it.

"Okay, Jules, think of a word, a very strange word, a total non sequitur, and that will be proof." Ben turned and stared deep into Jules's eyes. "Would it help if I wore a turban or carried a crystal ball? I know you're an actress, and it's all about the props with you guys."

Jules squinted back at him, gnawing at her lower lip. "Okay, smartass, what word am I thinking about?"

"Really, Jules? I should be insulted, but I'll cut you some slack. You were thinking of the word 'charlatan.'" Jules gasped and Ben held out his hand. "Now that you know, you must swear on your life not to tell anyone. Not that most people would believe it, but I would rather not be seen as a walking parlor trick."

Jules pumped his hand vigorously and crossed her heart twice. "To the grave. This is too cool. You really know what everybody's thinking?"

"When they're in relatively close proximity."

"So you know all the things I've been thinking about you?" Jules asked, looking embarrassed and contrite.

"Everything . . . from the jealousy to how you want to see me naked."

Ben was clearly enjoying having the upper hand. Jules's usually fair skin was the color of a ripe tomato.

Don't overdo it. You've made your point. Be nice to her. She's my best friend.

"What about me?" Ben asked.

You're my best boyfriend. Totally different category.

"No, you can't do that," Jules interrupted. "You can't do that mind-reading thing with Sasha when I'm around. Sorry, Sash, but you have to use the box. I don't like feeling left out."

"FAIR ENOUGH. SORRY. I WAS JUST TELLING BEN TO STOP HASSLING YOU."

"That's okay, then. Ben, you heard what Sasha said. You have to be nice to me, and no more listening in on my thoughts."

"Fine, I'll try to tune you out, but it won't be easy—you're really loud, even when you're thinking. Come on, ladies, I think this revelation calls for hot fudge sundaes. My treat."

Chapter 24

"Welcome, Sasha. Are you feeling better? Food poisoning can be a nasty business."

"I'M FINE."

My panic attack in the restaurant had gone unnoticed; in her mind I was simply the victim of iffy seafood. I was certain she would get suspicious once she thought about it, but after so many years, she was probably feeling invincible.

"It was so nice to finally meet Ben. He is a delightful young man, and very attractive, I must say. He seems to care about you very much. You're a lucky girl."

She settled in her usual spot and picked up her pen and legal pad. Still debating how I was going to handle this visit, I was on edge.

"I AM."

Too keyed up to make conversation, I answered in monosyllables. Unlike Jules, I was a terrible actress. Dr. O. was bound to sense something was up if I didn't pull it together.

"IS DR. PARSONS YOUR BOYFRIEND?" I would start slowly, ease my way into it.

"No, just a friend. Like you, I'm a single girl." There was nothing girlish about her. "I was married for more than twenty years, but I got divorced about four years ago."

Right around the time of the crash. More support for my theory, although I'm sure Ben would see it as a coincidence you could drive a moving van through. A million things happened four years ago—not just my accident. But still . . .

"DO YOU HAVE ANY CHILDREN?" As long as she was feeling chatty, maybe I could extract some useful information from my prime suspect.

"No children, I'm afraid. My greatest regret in life." She smiled sadly and looked down at her ringless left hand. "Wait a minute. *I'm* the therapist. I'm the one who's supposed to be asking the questions." Clapping her hands together, as if to dismiss all the bad thoughts and redirect our session, she took a deep breath. "So, Sasha, what's going on with *you*? Any memories swimming to the surface?"

"NO."

"None at all? I had hoped that your visits to the crash site might have triggered something."

Dr. O. looked disappointed. She drummed her fingers on her ever-present yellow legal pad. Her frustration didn't bolster my theory that she was the bad guy. Still too chicken to ask the simple question, I started down another line of inquiry.

"HOW WAS PRAGUE?"

Maybe she would let something slip. Was my sudden interest in her life outside the office enough to set off any warning bells? Would it occur to her that I had figured it out? Or, more likely, would she believe that I had finally grown up and now had the maturity to show interest in someone other than myself?

"One of my favorite cities, although I love every place I've traveled. Vienna is extraordinary—Freud and Sacher torte, what a combination. And of course Florence, Rome, and

Venice. Istanbul is incredible. Someday you *must* do some traveling. Maybe Ben will take you. He would be an enchanting guide, don't you think? So sophisticated."

"HE'S A CATCH. WHERE ELSE HAVE YOU TRAVELED?"

Dr. O. seemed pleased to be taking this trip down memory lane, and for the rest of our session she told me all about her incredible adventures. It was more interesting than looking at photos from someone's summer vacation . . . slightly. Suppressing an almost uncontrollable desire to yawn while trying to memorize the dozens of places she'd visited, I made it through the hour.

In a minute, Dr. O. would say, "I'm afraid our time is up," and I would have squandered my opportunity until next month. Should I do it? Should I man up and just ask her about the perfume? If it was a completely innocuous question, as Ben insisted, it shouldn't matter. Like he said, he didn't pick up on any guilty thoughts when he met her that night, and wouldn't she think about the accident every time she laid eyes on me? I couldn't argue with that logic, but I was sure there had to be some explanation. Maybe she was able to compartmentalize her thoughts so completely that she didn't think about that night unless she wanted to. That made sense. How else could she survive her guilty conscience—it would have smothered her by now, unless she was some kind of sociopath. *Here goes nothing.*

"THAT PERFUME YOU WERE WEARING THE OTHER NIGHT WAS SO PRETTY. I'D LIKE TO BUY SOME FOR CHARLOTTE FOR HER BIRTHDAY. WHAT'S IT CALLED?"

Was that a slight twitch at the corner of her mouth, did her blink rate increase, did she suddenly look pale, paler than usual? I had been reading a book on the subtle visual cues a person displays when telling a lie. Her voice remained perfectly relaxed.

"You liked it? It doesn't actually have a name. When I was on my honeymoon, my husband—my ex-husband—took me to a place that blended custom scents. It's my own private label French perfume. He was so romantic then." She closed her eyes and sighed. "I stopped wearing it when we got divorced. It reminded me of him, of everything that had happened, and I hated it. But the other day, I found it at the bottom of a drawer, and I just felt ready to wear it again."

Oh . . . my . . . gosh. Before Dr. O. could dismiss me, I was on my feet and out the door. "See you next month, Sasha," Dr. O. called after me as I ran to my car.

So much for not behaving suspiciously. I was a crap detective.

In the car, I texted Ben. **I did it. Asked her about perfume. Custom blend. Now what? Going home to check postmark cities with her travel schedule.**

Immediately he texted back. **I'll meet you at your house. Stay calm. Drive carefully.**

I was hyperventilating, but I managed to make it home without incident—although when I pulled into the driveway I couldn't remember how I'd gotten there. That was scary. Whatever happened, I needed to get a tighter rein on my emotions. If I was this distracted, I had no business driving.

So the perfume question had been answered. But what about the dozens of exotic destinations on Dr. O.'s passport? Plenty of people traveled all over the world, but when I took out the list that Mike Grant had given us that morning at Shakespeare's Flowers, every city she had named was there. So Dr. O. definitely had the opportunity to mail those blue envelopes, as the police detectives—or Jules—would say. Another piece of the puzzle was in place, at least in my mind. In Ben's, not so much.

"So she's well traveled and she wears a perfume you vaguely remember. It could just be a similar scent. It *has* been more than four years since you smelled it, and flowers kind of smell like flowers. Have you considered that?"

Why did Ben feel the need to play devil's advocate? He had picked me up at my house, and now we were walking along the beach. We were alone except for a few die-hard runners, as the wind was brisk, and it was cold even though the sun was shining brightly. Although it was spring on the calendar, Mother Nature hadn't yet turned the page. But the chilly air sharpened my thoughts, and I needed to talk this out with someone.

"The perfume is the same. I know it. And she's visited all those cities. That's huge. And she's a world-famous shrink who claims I can't be hypnotized, but your mother put me under like it was nothing. She told me I was her only failure—maybe she failed on purpose."

Everything I was saying made perfect sense. The evidence was piling up. Why didn't he get it?

"Gather the villagers, grab a rope, and light the torches," Ben shouted into the wind.

"Way to be supportive. I'm serious." I punched his arm playfully and he rubbed the spot, pretending I had actually hurt him.

"No hitting. All I'm saying is that what you're proposing is very serious business. Leaving the scene of an accident is a felony, isn't it, Counselor?" Not a particularly romantic statement, but it didn't take much. He bent down and kissed me, his body sheltering mine from the wind. After we came up for air, he said, "Why are we talking about this now? Your aunt and uncle won't be home for hours, will they? We should go back to your house and warm up. Your nose feels like an ice cube. And I can think of way better things to do this afternoon than play Agatha Christie."

"You can? Well, before I lose you completely, I looked it up, and the Statute of Limitations in Connecticut for leaving the scene of an accident is five years. In December, five years will have passed. We don't have much time before the clock runs out. It's already the middle of April."

I ran down the beach, and he chased me, easily catching me after about five steps. Not that I really wanted to get away. But I did want him to take me more seriously.

"You're not going anywhere, Sash, so just relax. On a completely different topic, and not to belittle your quest for justice, but don't you think your time would be better spent studying for the SAT? You never want to talk about school."

"I hate school."

"Very mature. Look, even if you solve every cold case in Connecticut, you have to go to college. And no matter how much sleuthing you do, you can't bring your family back."

Ben was right. Even if I unraveled my mystery, I couldn't retrieve all that I had lost. Mom and Dad and Liz would still be dead. Maybe it was time to start focusing on my future, especially if there was any possibility that Ben would be a part of it. Since the accident, I hadn't thought about school as a means to an end. I did my work, got good grades . . . but perhaps it was time to take control of my own destiny, even if that meant letting go of the past.

"Took it back in October, smartass. One of the few benefits of having no social life was that I got lots of studying done.

How about you? Aren't I keeping you from that big blue book of practice questions?"

It was obvious that Ben was really smart, but I had no idea where he wanted to go to college or what he wanted to be when he grew up. That was bad. Note to self: be more interested in boyfriend's hopes and dreams. Would it be weird if we went to the same school?

His smile was smug. "I already took it as well. At L'Istituto Americano in Florence. Now that we've established how disciplined and maybe a little bit obsessive we are, let's get back to where we are right now. What are you and the other Hardy Boy going to do next? It's clear you're not ready to pack it in."

"I don't know. Obviously you have a suggestion."

I waited politely for his mature, rational advice: let it go and move on with your life. Not that I was going to listen to him.

"First, stop. This is where I first kissed you that cold, windy day—I couldn't resist you in that hat. Remember?"

His hands were on my neck, cradling my head, just as they had that afternoon. My heart beat double-time again—it seemed so long ago, but it was only a few months.

I shook my head. "Not really. I think you need to refresh my memory."

"Just what I was hoping you'd say."

He pulled me close and leaned over, studying my face. In that second before his lips touched mine, I could feel how much he loved me, wanted me, even in my imperfect, perhaps unbalanced, state.

After three elderly joggers had trotted by, and each of them had whistled lasciviously, we finally let go of each other. I jumped up and down and then bent over and touched my toes. "You were going to give me some wise words, I think."

"What are you doing? You look possessed." Trying valiantly to hold back a laugh, but failing, Ben covered his mouth with his hand.

"I'm trying to get the blood back to my brain. I can't think straight." I rubbed my eyes and shook my head. "That's better. You don't get at all lightheaded when we kiss?"

"No, but trust me, it's all good. Maybe because I have a little more experience than you, I have better control over my body." Was he teasing? "You just need more practice."

"Exactly how much experience are we talking about?"

Until that moment, it had never occurred to me that Ben had done to other girls what he had done to me. Duh. As he'd just implied, you don't get so good without lots of practice.

"Exactly what *kind* of experience are you talking about?" he asked.

We sat down on a bench in a copse of trees, out of the wind. Without the stiff breeze, the sun was warm on my face. I leaned back and closed my eyes, breathing in the clean, slightly briny air.

"Where to begin?" Opening one eye, I peered sideways. Here goes nothing. "How many girls have you had sex with?"

"Cut to the chase, why don't you?"

"You're right. I'm sorry. It's none of my business."

"No, it's not a big deal. I don't mind telling you. Just one, but she wasn't really a girl. She was twenty-six, and I was sixteen."

Not at all what I'd expected to hear. My mouth fell open.

"Isn't that illegal? What would a grown woman want with a boy?"

Not that Ben wasn't totally edible, and more mature than most twenty-six-year-olds probably were, but still. Except for those middle-school teachers in Florida that I'd read about in the newspaper, I thought normal women in their twenties wanted full-fledged men, who shaved every day and had real jobs.

"She was a graduate student at the University of Florence. She was from Paris, and she was writing her dissertation on Italian Renaissance architecture. In Europe, things are different. That kind of age difference isn't a big deal. But my parents don't know, so please don't ever tell them. They would probably be as shocked as you are, and not too happy. But what guy would turn down a beautiful woman who made it very clear that she wanted more than a jogging partner?"

He ran his hands through his curls. At least he had the decency to look mildly abashed.

"Sounds like every teenage boy's fantasy."

How could I ever compete with that? Gorgeous, uninhibited, and obviously brilliant to boot.

"It was," he said matter-of-factly.

"So how beautiful was she?" It sounded like the almost-punch line of a bad joke, but I just kept going.

"Very. Something about you reminds me of her—tiny waist, great curves." He mimed an hourglass shape with his hands.

"So what you're saying is you have a type." But I already knew that. He had told me that statuesque, Amazonian Aubrey was not his taste.

"I never much thought about it, but I guess I do."

"So that makes me the less-exciting domestic version."

I was beginning to regret that I'd instigated this little voyage into his sexual history. Ignorance was definitely more blissful than a head filled with images of Ben losing his virginity to some French Mrs. Robinson in a grotto behind an eighteenth-century Italian villa.

"Don't be ridiculous. For one thing, except for your build, you don't look anything like her. She was blonde, tan, and ten years older than you. Your hair is nearly black, your skin is milky white, and you're still a sweet, innocent baby." He pinched my cheeks, puckering his lips like a grandmother and cooing nonsense.

"Ouch. So what you're saying is that I'm just a pale, unseasoned imitation of the real thing."

Rubbing my cheeks, I closed my eyes and saw Ben strolling arm in arm along the banks of the Arno with a dazzling girl who was a much better version of me.

"That's not at all what I mean. You're not going to let me off the hook, are you?"

"Nope. You dug yourself in deep when you started comparing me to your sex goddess." I was just teasing, but now that I knew a little bit, I had to know everything.

"Doesn't everybody have a type—freckles, curly hair, broad shoulders—some little thing that just hits us a certain way? Don't you prefer some physical traits over others?"

He had skillfully directed the conversation away from his delectable, sophisticated French pastry, but I wasn't finished.

"Whatever. So you're *my* type. But were you in love with her?"

He had told me more than once that he loved me. Was I the first recipient of those three precious words, or had my older, semi-doppelgänger, poacher of his innocence, gotten there first?

"Like I said before, it was pretty much all physical. We liked each other, had fun together, but it wasn't love. You're my first in that department. And that's what matters." Exactly what I wanted—needed—to hear.

"Good answer." We held hands and watched the shadows grow longer as the late afternoon sun dipped lower in the sky.

Truthfully, I was relieved that Ben had some experience. Otherwise it would be the blind leading the blind, and that wouldn't be nearly as much fun as what we had.

"But the most important thing Solange taught me was that if a man makes a woman happy—not just physically, but emotionally, spiritually—then he'll be happy. Stop making that face. You should be grateful to her. You're the beneficiary of her life lessons." He cleared his throat meaningfully.

"I'm not making a face. Do you have her address? I'd like to send her a fruit basket. You've been well schooled, and I'm very grateful. Her name was really Solange? Are you sure she wasn't a professional?" I asked, only half-joking.

"Catty much? A professional student, maybe, but nothing else. No money exchanged hands, although I spent a fortune on espresso. That woman never slept. It was exhausting."

Was he blushing at the memory, or was it just the sun that made his cheeks look pink?

"You win. I've had enough. What was it you were going to tell me? What sage advice were you about to offer before we got distracted by Solange?"

Ben tilted his head and thought for a second. "I have no idea what I was going to say. It couldn't have been that wise if I can't remember."

"I didn't want to know anyway. You were probably just going to tell me to let sleeping dogs lie or stop jumping to conclusions or think of this as the first day of the rest of my life. Some fortune cookie crap."

"That sounds about right. I just don't want you to be disappointed. Even if Dr. O. turns out to be the person you're looking for, unless she admits it, there's really no way for you to prove it. Your memory of some perfume isn't exactly hard evidence—definitely not enough to get a conviction. And then what? After reliving your nightmare in front of all kinds of strangers, you're still you. All your problems will still be there."

"Stop being so fucking rational. It's not helpful." I knew he was right, but I hated hearing it.

"Fine, if you don't want to listen to the voice of reason, you're going to have to find a way to shut me up," Ben murmured in my ear.

"Duct tape?" I offered.

"Not what I had in mind." He pulled me down into his lap and bent over me, his long eyelashes tickling my cheeks before he kissed me.

"I guess this is a little better than duct tape," I whispered back. But I wasn't quite ready to let go and move on.

Chapter 25

"Sasha, what are you doing here? I thought we agreed to meet next month. Did something happen since yesterday? Have you recovered a memory?" Dr. O. looked and sounded flustered to see me standing outside the door to her office.

I had already typed my question into my talk box, so I just pressed the play button. "I REMEMBERED A SMELL FROM THE ACCIDENT. PERFUME."

Now I had crossed the Rubicon—there was no going back. Beads of sweat ran down the back of my neck, but I felt a chill.

"Why don't you come in and sit down?" said the spider to the fly. I shivered. "My next appointment is not for another half hour. You're clearly upset. Let's talk." She took my arm and led me into her office.

Perching on the edge of the sofa, I jabbed at the keys.

"ON THE NIGHT OF THE ACCIDENT I SMELLED THE SAME PERFUME YOU WERE WEARING IN THE RESTAURANT. WERE YOU AT THE CRASH SITE? DID YOU LOOK INTO THE CAR WITH A FLASHLIGHT? DID YOU WRITE ALL THOSE POEMS? DID YOU KILL MY FAMILY?"

The last five words hung in the air like dense, black smoke. I was either bat-ass crazy, and Dr. O. would talk me down in her clear, rational shrink voice . . . or my family's killer was sitting three feet away from me, and now she knew that I knew. Uh-oh. It hadn't occurred to me until that moment that I could be in some kind of danger. Ben had almost but not quite convinced me that my nose was confused, and therefore I hadn't thought to tell anyone where I was going. If Dr. O. turned out to be a madwoman, I could be in big trouble.

She took a deep breath and squinted at me over her glasses. "That's quite an indictment, young lady. Are you intimating that I was in some way responsible for the accident that killed your family?"

I had expected her to launch into a lengthy tirade about sense memories and smells, and how the passage of time inevitably led to internal chaos and jumbled memories, but she didn't. We stared at each other without speaking for what felt like an hour, but according to the clock behind her head, was only a minute.

The initial shock at my own boldness began to wear off, and my curiosity overwhelmed me. "WELL?"

"Have you shared your outlandish allegations with anyone else?" she asked.

Taking out what looked like a metronome from the bookshelf behind her, she flipped a switch underneath and it began to tick. Shaped like a pyramid with a pointy top, it could have made a nasty weapon, and I gripped my talkie box tighter, wondering if I had the balls to defend myself. Now I knew I was crazy, thinking this world-renowned psychiatrist might hit me over the head with a metronome.

What did she ask me again? Oh, did anyone else know?
"NO. WHO WOULD BELIEVE ME?"

I didn't mention Ben or Jules. Why drag them into it if Dr. O. did turn out to be Jack the Ripper in a pleated skirt and pearls? *Tick, tick, tick.* The urgent need to know the truth was receding with every tick, like a tide going out. My eyelids felt unbearably heavy. Maybe we could continue this conversation after I took a little nap. Dr. O. said she didn't have another patient for half an hour. I only needed to close my eyes for a few minutes.

"Well, Sasha, that's a fascinating story. What a vivid imagination you have. I so enjoyed this unexpected visit, but my next patient is due any minute, so I'm afraid we'll have to continue our chat next time."

My eyelids flew open, and Dr. O. glanced pointedly at her watch. What story had I told her that was so fascinating? I barely remembered how I got there. Wasn't my appointment yesterday? My brain felt like a lava lamp, my thoughts moving sluggishly through the oil. Before I could begin to figure out what had just happened, Dr. O. was on her feet, opening the back door, ushering me out. Obediently I rose, a wave of dizziness almost forcing me back onto the couch, but I closed my eyes for a few seconds and when I opened them, the room had thankfully stopped spinning.

"Don't forget your talkie box," she said as she handed it to me and patted my back, almost pushing me out the door. "See you next month. And don't forget to take your medicine."

Before I could type in another word, she slammed the door and I was standing alone next to my car, feeling as if I'd just missed something, but I had no idea what it could be. In my car I rested my head against the steering wheel, listening to my own breathing, content not to move. What a peculiar sensation—it was almost as if I'd just had one too many wine coolers, or like I had drunk ten cups of Annie's dirt tea. Lethargy enveloped me, and all I wanted to do was go to bed, even though it was only four o'clock in the afternoon. Slapping my cheeks to keep myself awake, I opened all the car windows and started the engine. The wind in my face as I drove helped a little, although it was a struggle to keep my eyelids from falling down like a pair of Roman shades. Fortunately it was a short trip back home.

No one was there—Charlotte and Stuart wouldn't be home from work for hours—but Ben was supposed to come over, although I couldn't remember why or when. The way I was feeling it didn't matter. Dropping my backpack by the front door, I kicked off my shoes and staggered to my bedroom. When I fell onto my bed, I felt a lump. Inside my jacket pocket was a small brown plastic bottle filled with tiny white pills. There was no label, but this must have been the medicine Dr. O. was talking about. I pried off the lid and took all of them. Now I could go to sleep.

Chapter 26

My head throbbed, and when I opened my eyes I had gone back four years in time. Charlotte's sleeping head rested on the hospital blanket, her breathing slow and deep, and the smell of bleach and rubbing alcohol burned my nose.

Mom, Dad, and Liz were dead. Any second now that young doctor was going to walk through the door and start explaining my psychiatric condition, trying to paint a bright picture with his description of the flexible adolescent brain. But when the door opened, it was not a white-coated physician who came in: it was Ben. He hadn't been a dream.

"Are you okay? How do you feel?" He came around the side of the bed and kissed my forehead. "You had us really scared for a while."

I shook my head, trying to shake out the cobwebs. *What happened? How did I get here?*

"You took an overdose of sleeping pills. You don't remember?" he asked.

What are you talking about? But wait, there had been a tiny brown bottle, little white pills. I rubbed my temples, trying to recall. *I went to Dr. O.'s office. I asked her straight out if she killed them. She said something about taking my medicine and sent me home.*

"You went to see her, and you didn't tell me?" Ben sounded hurt.

What was it with guys? Somehow, no matter what happened, it was still all about them.

Sorry, I thought you'd laugh at me, or try to talk me out of it.

Ben swore under his breath. "I was the one who suggested it in the first place. What a terrible idea that turned out to be."

But nothing happened. She just said I had an active imagination and that she'd see me next month.

"You took an entire bottle of sleeping pills, Sasha. That's not nothing. Why would you do such a crazy thing?"

I don't know. I struggled to remember exactly what had happened. *Wait a second. Dr. O. had a metronome, and it was ticking, and I got so sleepy. I just wanted to go to bed, and I couldn't go to sleep until I took the pills.*

Ben said, "It's obvious, Sasha. She must have hypnotized you so you would take them."

All my thoughts were jumbled. My brain was a deck of cards, and someone had scattered them all over the floor. I could hardly follow Ben's words. *Hypnotized me?*

"Yes, Sasha. That's what the metronome was for. Sometimes my mother uses one to put people under. It's not uncommon."

But why would Dr. O. . . .

"Because it turns out you were right about everything." Ben took both my hands in his and squeezed hard. He looked like he was about to cry. "You've been right all this time. I didn't want to believe it, but it *was* Dr. O'Rourke who caused the crash." It felt like all the air had been sucked out of the room.

What? I tried to sit up, but the room began to go dark, as if something were moving across the sky, blocking out the sun. Standing inches away from me, Ben was lost in the shadows. I fell back against the pillows. *How do you know that?*

Putting his hands firmly on my shoulders, Ben said, "Sasha, you have to stay in bed. Don't you understand? You almost died."

My mental eclipse passed, and the room slowly brightened. *I need to talk to her. I need to know what happened.*

"The thing is, Sasha, you can't talk to her."

Why not? Did they arrest her? Why can't I go see her in jail?

Ben paused. "You can't talk to her because she's dead."

I had just seen her, just spoken to her. She couldn't be gone. The blackness threatened, but I gripped the bed rails, fighting to stay conscious. *How did she die?*

Ben hesitated again, as if he didn't know whether or not he should tell me the truth. "She shot herself when she found out that you were still alive."

She what? Like a crime scene photo, a picture of Dr. O. with blood spattered all over her pale blue cashmere sweater flashed through my mind. It didn't look real. It didn't feel real.

"You didn't answer the door when I came over Wednesday afternoon, and I couldn't feel you, so I let myself in with the key hidden under the rock in the flower bed. You were unconscious, and there was an empty bottle next to you. I called 911. The police took it from there." Ben was whispering, but Charlotte was sleeping so soundly, I doubt he could have woken her if he'd been shouting.

Thank you. You saved my life . . . again. I felt like a cat. How many lives did I have left?

"The doctors did all the heavy lifting. I just dialed the phone." Ben closed his eyes and said, "I thought I was going to lose you."

But how did you know where I got the pills?

"It didn't take ESP to figure that out. Where else would you get heavy-duty sedatives?" Ben paced back and forth next to my bed. "I told the police about your detective work, showed them the poems, and yesterday they went to talk to her."

Yesterday? What day is it? How long have I been here? I felt like Rip Van Winkle.

"Two days. It's Friday."

In one sense, it seemed like only a few hours had passed, but with all that had happened, months could have gone by since I stumbled out of Dr. O.'s office.

What did she say to the police?

"Not much," Ben said. "They told her you were in the hospital and they were investigating your overdose as well as the crash. She said something like, 'I can't do this anymore. Tell Sasha she was right,' and then she pulled a gun out of her desk drawer and shot herself in the head."

She said I was right? About which part? What does that even mean? I had been so close to finding out everything, and now I would never know.

"That's all she said. The police searched her office, but there was no evidence to explain how the crash happened."

Did you try to read their minds? Maybe the police weren't telling you everything.

Ben grinned. "They told me everything they knew. Besides Dr. O.'s crazy confession, the only strange thing was your chart. It was full of lies. She described you as seriously unstable, with suicidal tendencies, that she had caught you stealing meds from her office several times over the last few months. If you had died, it probably would have been ruled a suicide. No questions asked. She almost got away with it."

I don't know what to think.

"It's simple. Once she knew you knew the truth, she had to get rid of you."

But what is the truth?

"I don't know what happened four years ago, Sasha, but two days ago your psychiatrist tried to kill you. She was a very bad person. But she made one huge mistake. It didn't occur to her that you had already told me everything."

I told her that I hadn't told anyone. I didn't want to get you and Jules involved in my mess. At least I had done one thing right.

"She actually believed you wouldn't tell your boyfriend what was going on?"

My boyfriend. I like the way that sounds.

Even in the midst of all these shocking revelations, I was still easily distracted by the extraordinary fact that Ben loved me.

"That's all you have to say? I just told you that your psychiatrist tried to kill you, faked your medical records, and committed suicide in front of three policemen. What's wrong with you? You must still be kind of out of it," Ben said as he pressed his hand against my cheek.

Did you tell Jules what happened?

Ben nodded. "She was here this morning. I've never seen her so upset. She feels guilty, and she's kind of mad at me for being so skeptical before. You're lucky to have a friend like that. She's a pit bull."

She'll get over it. And it's not your fault. You were just being rational.

"I should have believed you. I'm so sorry."

Stop being sorry. Everything's okay. But there is one thing.

"Anything," Ben said.

I need you and Jules to figure out how to be friends. You're both so important to me.

"Don't worry. I'll make it work. I know you two come as a set. But forget about that. What about your voice? Try to talk. Now that it's over . . ."

It wasn't really over. Some of my questions had been answered, but the biggest one still remained, and the only person who could answer it for me was in the morgue. If my voice didn't work now, there was no place to go. I looked down at Charlotte, who was beginning to stir. One eye opened, then the other. She sat up and gently stroked my arm.

"Oh, Sasha, you're awake, thank goodness. It was almost like before, and we were so afraid you might not make it this time."

My heart banged against my rib cage as I opened my mouth. Maybe Ben was right. It was my time, my turn. Did I really need to have all the answers as long as my Prince Charming was standing next to me? But of course that would have been too simple. Nothing but air emerged from my parted lips. *Shit.* Tears pooled at the corners of my eyes, but I swallowed hard and they began to recede. It was far from perfect, but at least I was alive, and I wasn't alone, and no one in my family had died this time. On the table next to my bed was my talking box—I guess we were stuck with each other for a while longer.

"I'M FINE. DON'T WORRY. NOT LIKE BEFORE."

"You're right. It's not like before, but I can't believe what happened. Ben told me how you figured everything out. Why didn't you tell me what you were doing? I could have helped you . . . protected you." Charlotte plucked a tissue from her sleeve and dabbed at her eyes.

So this was where my procrastination had gotten me. I had quite a bit of explaining to do.

"YOU'RE RIGHT. I SHOULD HAVE TOLD YOU, BUT I FELT STUPID, AND I WAS GOING TO TELL YOU WHEN I WAS SURE ABOUT DR. O."

"Sasha, promise me you won't keep any more secrets from me. I promise not to judge or preach, but I need to know what's going on in your life."

Twisting the tissue around her fingers, Charlotte looked as if she were working hard at not being judgmental—either that, or she was already planning the lawsuit she was going to file against Dr. O'Rourke's estate. Ben had taken a seat in a chair in the corner, quietly observing the scene, pretending to be preoccupied with setting his watch.

I know, I need to come clean about your mother and the tea and spending time at your house.

Ben nodded.

But I'm not telling her about my selective mutism. She doesn't need to know about my talking until I can talk directly to her.

Ben nodded and shrugged. This was a very efficient means of communication. Now he was looking down, pretending to read a magazine as I was thinking at him. Then he lifted his head and our eyes locked.

I love you . . . so much.

He nodded, and nodded, and nodded. This was *way* different from last time.

"THERE'S SOMETHING ELSE I DIDN'T TELL YOU. I'VE BEEN SPENDING A LITTLE TIME AT SEASHELL LANE, AND BEN'S MOM HAS BEEN HYPNOTIZING ME, TRYING TO HELP ME FIND MY VOICE."

There. That wasn't so hard. I hoped that Charlotte would focus on my willingness to share my life with her now, instead of harping on how I had left her out of the loop for so long.

I don't think she needs to know about the tea.

Ben tipped his head dubiously, but he didn't have to live with Charlotte.

"Sasha, you've been living a secret life." Her voice was getting shrill, and I wished Stuart were there to throw a blanket over her indignation at being excluded from my inner circle.

"I JUST DIDN'T WANT YOU TO WORRY ABOUT ME ANY MORE THAN YOU ALREADY DO. I LOVE YOU AND STUART SO MUCH."

That did it. Her shoulders relaxed, and the creases in her forehead disappeared. All she needed was a little reaffirmation, a reminder that she meant the world to me. Something I needed to do more often.

"Oh darling, our job is to worry. Now tell me about Ben's mother," she said, smoothing the blankets. "I met Dr. and Mrs. Fisher the weekend they moved into the house—I had no idea she was a hypnotist."

"IT HASN'T WORKED, BUT I'M REMEMBERING MORE—STUFF FROM WHEN I WAS A KID, AND THE NIGHT OF THE ACCIDENT."

"How awful for you. You shouldn't have been going through that alone."

"NO, IT'S GOOD. I NEED TO DO IT. IT MAKES ME STRONGER. ASK BEN."

"It's been all good, Mrs. Thompson. I think whatever happens with Sasha's voice, she's going to be fine," Ben said. "And I'm sorry you were in the dark about everything. But Sasha really wanted to surprise you with her recovery. She meant well."

Charlotte went over to Ben and hugged him. This was a weird day. "You're such a sweet boy. Thank you for being so good to Sasha."

Quite the lovefest. Should I give you two some privacy?

Ben glared at me over Charlotte's shoulder. "You shouldn't thank me. I only wish I could do more."

Chapter 27

The next day I was released from the hospital, still feeling a little foggy, but grateful to be away from the fluorescent lights and that horrible smell, and to sleep in my own bed. It was hard to believe Dr. O'Rourke was actually dead. As crazy as it sounded, I kind of missed her, at least the Dr. O'Rourke that I knew before Jules and I started doing the detective thing.

"How can you miss her? She killed your family. She stonewalled your recovery for the past four years. And—just a minor detail—she tried to poison you." Ben flicked the side of my head as we cuddled on a chaise longue on the patio behind my house.

"I know, I'm an idiot. I guess I miss the idea of her. She made me feel safe after the accident, even if everything she said to me was bullshit."

When Ben and I were alone, my voice rang loud and clear. At least I hadn't lost that.

"Maybe the drugs aren't totally out of your system yet, or maybe you're just a head case. Talk about Stockholm Syndrome."

"Maybe she couldn't help it. She was clearly out of her mind." Why was I so intent on defending her? If Ben had come to pick me up an hour later that evening, I probably would have been dead. "I just wish I knew what really happened."

"I'm afraid you'll never know," Ben said.

"If I'd handled it better, maybe I would have gotten to the truth, and maybe Dr. O. wouldn't have splattered her brains all over her antique Chippendale desk."

Ben groaned. "Have you found another therapist yet? Besides coping with your old problem, I think you need someone to help you get over your old therapist. Sympathizing with your would-be killer isn't particularly normal."

My life was so far from being normal, I would probably need more than one psychiatrist to get me on track.

"Charlotte's working on it. She and Stuart are compiling dossiers on a few shrinks. They're being extra careful this time. They feel guilty, like they should have figured out who Dr. O. really was, like they could have protected me better," I said.

"They love you and don't want you to get hurt . . . just like me. And I'm the one with the sixth sense. I should have seen who she was immediately. But I totally missed it."

"Don't be ridiculous. Like you said, she had to be some kind of sociopath." I sighed. "You can't protect me from everything."

"But I can try. Maybe we should think about that. Do you have any idea where you might want to go to college? Some schools let guys and girls room together, you know."

"I read about that. But are we compatible? Are you an early riser? Are you messy or neat? Do you sleep with the window open or closed?"

He wanted to go to school with me, live with me? We could sleep in each other's arms every night? Charlotte would never go for it, but it was fun to dream.

"I'm easy. You choose. We might be able to convince Charlotte, if we spun it that I was more watchdog than sex fiend," he said.

"She's pretty clueless when it comes to stuff like that, but I think even she would see through that smokescreen." I imagined Ben with a studded leather collar around his neck, tied up in the corner of my bedroom.

"You're into that? I never thought of you as the dominatrix type. Now I know what to get you for your birthday." He cracked an imaginary whip.

"Ew. I was just imagining you as a dog. I haven't even gotten to the S&M chapter in Dr. Reuben's book yet. But I'll let you know."

"I look forward to it." Ben turned toward the house. "Your aunt and uncle are home. They're worried about you."

"They worry too much." I sat up, checking my buttons and zippers.

"That's what happens when people love you. And you look perfectly respectable. Not a hair out of place," he said as he tucked a lock behind my ear.

"I don't want them to think all we do is mess around. It's embarrassing," I said as I patted his untamable curls.

"Get used to it. I plan on embarrassing you for a very long time." Ben pinned me on the chaise and kissed me like no one was there, even as Charlotte and Stuart stood watching through the window.

Chapter 28

Early Sunday morning, just as the sun was pushing up over the horizon, I slipped out of the house. Dr. O. was gone, but I wasn't quite ready for it to be over. The roads were deserted, so I reached my destination in minutes, and as I pulled off the asphalt, I could already see it—a fresh bunch of white tulips propped against the tree trunk, the blue paper peeking out of the top. My psychiatrist even in death, she knew I needed the closure only she could provide.

Dear Sasha,

You have spent the last four years trying to remember. I have spent the last thirty trying to forget.

When I moved to Shoreland, I ran into your father—at church of all places—and all the memories I had managed to suppress for decades were reawakened. We reminisced about our days together at St. Matthew's Prep. I met your mother. It was all very civilized.

But there is so much more to the story. Your father and I were more than just friends. We loved each other. We made a baby together. (Are you shocked? Perhaps you don't really want to know, but as your therapist, I think you need to.) I was afraid he would leave me if he found out, so I never told anyone. I just took care of it. But he left

*me anyway. The summer after we graduated he met your
mother, and he never spoke to me again. For thirty years,
I buried that pain deep inside me, where it couldn't hurt
anyone. But seeing him again made me feel like it had just
happened. I killed my baby, our baby, because I loved him,
and he didn't love me back.*

*Revenge is so cliché, but that's all it was. He took a life,
and I took his. That's how karma works. The rest of you
were just victims of a tragedy that took place long before
you were born. When you survived the crash, I knew that
God was telling me to take care of you, to make you whole
again, to make up for my lost baby. You were my second
chance. But when you came to my office and asked me
about that night, I realized there are no second chances.
You and I could no longer go on. So this is how it ends.
After all these years, my secret no longer belongs to me. I
hope that by writing these words, I may help you speak
yours.*

Sincerely,

Dr. O.

So now I knew the truth. Ben had been right that day at
the beach. It didn't change anything. Mom and Dad and Liz
were still skeletons in a graveyard. But something was different.
My mind was clear, as if I'd finally gotten around to organizing
the closet inside my head. When I thought about my family,
I could remember the days at the beach, the vacations at
Silver Lake in New Hampshire, my mother's famous Friday
night dinner parties. And, like Jules said, I was still standing.
They were gone, but knowing that I could visit them in my
memories of the life we had shared was enough. It had to be.
After more than four years, I had found the path out of the

forest, and whether or not I ever spoke out loud to anyone but Ben for the rest of my life, I was going to be okay, as long as I didn't run out of batteries.

Leaving the bouquet of flowers at the base of the tree, I took the tear-stained paper and carefully folded it into a tiny blue rectangle. It seemed important to preserve this record of my tragedy, this final confession from the woman who had been a pivotal figure in my life for so long. Standing in front of the tree, running my finger along the gnarled ridge where the car had slammed into it, I rested my forehead against the rough trunk and closed my eyes. I saw the headlights, heard the din of annihilation, felt my world come to a screeching halt as the tree absorbed our momentum, and finally, I smelled the fragrance of spring mixed in with the stink of death. As I stepped away from the tree, I felt as if I'd somehow transferred the weight of those painful memories to the century-old oak, which, though scarred, continued to flourish. If I put my mind to it, that could be me.

It was time to go home. The sun was up and a few cars sped along, some slowing down as they passed by. I waved goodbye to my tree—it had given up all its secrets, and taken on a few of mine.

When I opened the front door, Charlotte and Stuart were already deep into their Sunday morning routine: coffee, bagels, and the *New York Times* crossword puzzle.

"We thought you were still asleep. Where have you been? Are you all right?" Charlotte asked, her worry wrinkles furrowing her brow.

I had left my Hawkie Talkie in my room, so I nodded and smiled. And then, I said, "I'm fine. Everything's great." I laughed out loud and walked into their arms.